D0684584

WITHDRAWN

GODAWFUL DREAMS

Two Tales of Academic Scandal

I: The Trials of Illyria

II: What Happened to Professor Elves?

Tom McBride

For Sarah:

Beloved, Admired, Life-Changing

Introduction

Beset with presidential narcissism, faculty chicanery and an obscene poem, will tiny Illyria College be forced to close its doors? And at tiny Belton College who may have murdered Professor Theodore Elves? –Anonymous, but often attributed to Tom McBride

Academies are apparently resistant to scandal. Places of civilized reason, or so it is said, they should be immune to the base emotions the cops encounter all the time, including jealousy, concealment, revenge, and greed. With all those long words one is obliged to pronounce on campus, who would have time to rump and pump? Yet academic scandals do occur, and they are often tasty when they do. Is this because they are not supposed to occur in the placid groves of academe, or because we are somehow pleased that that the vile side of human nature is so powerful?

These two novellas are about academic scandal. *The Trials of Illyria*, set in the 1950s, portrays a desperate small college, an obstreperous wealthy donor, a scheming young faculty—and a high-risk publishing decision by an idealistic editor. He prints an irreverent and unholy use of the term "wet dream," with shocks and after shocks he would never have imagined. *What Happened to Professor Elves* combines diary entries, letters, lecture notes, news stories, editorials, and wood carvings in order to tell an enigmatic story, set in the 1920s, of sudden death. This novel, too, ends in a godawful wet dream—this time one of actual blood.

The Trials of Illyria is wholly a work of fiction, with a purely coincidental similarity, if any, to actual persons, except for Crackle the Parakeet, who actually lived, once, in the author's household. *What Happened to Professor Elves* is based on an actual historic event, but the treatment is virtually all a matter of fiction and imagination--not to be confused with what few historical facts are extant about a long-ago and mysterious occurrence in southern Wisconsin, the trail of which is ice cold. –T.M.

The First Novella: The Trials of Illyria

Academic politics are the most vicious of all, because the stakes are so low. —Walter Sayre

It is a truth universally acknowledged that a small college with a fine mission is in desperate want of a rich patron. —Adapted from Jane Austen

Table of Contents

Dramatis Personae

Prologue

(The Present Day)

Chapter 1: The Alleged Inadequacies of Little Annie

(August 21, 1959)

Chapter 2: The Annoying Insufficiencies of Unrestricted Endowment

(July 14, 1959)

Chapter 3: The Remorseless Decisions of Editors

(August 22, 1959)

Chapter 4: The Absolute Necessity of Final Exam Periods

(Later That Same Day)

Chapter 5: The Gentle Decorum of Gardens

(August 23, 1959)

Chapter 6: The Subtle Omnipresence of Beards

(September 15, 1959)

Chapter 7: The Unavoidable Centrality of Machiavelli

(September 23, 1959)

Chapter 8: The Political Perils of Loose Fixtures

(October 1, 1959)

Chapter 9: The Ultimate Insignificance of Intent

(October 23, 1959)

Chapter 10: The Awful Evanescence of Striving

(October 23, 1959—Later in the Day)

Chapter 11: The Ghastly Dread of a Dean's Terminology
(November 16, 1959)

Chapter 12: The Accursed Spittle of Everything
(November 19, 1959)

Chapter 13: The Determined Non-Contingency of Going On
To the End of the Term
December 6, 1959

Chapter 14: The Glorious Opportunities of Beckoning
Former Spouses
(December 7, 1959)

Chapter 15: The Regrettable Unavoidability of
Strategic Distance
(December 9, 1959)

Chapter 16: The Mandatory Enforcement of Periods
(December 10, 1959)

Chapter 17: The General Utility of Emissaries
(December 20, 1959)

Chapter 18: The Relentless Power of Wetness
December 28, 1959)

Chapter 19: The Menacing Habits of Telephones
(December 30, 1959)

Chapter 20: The Likely Shrewdness of Pre-emptions
(January 2, 1960)

Chapter 21: The Irritating Surprises of Unexpected Visitors
(January 14, 1960)

Chapter 22: The Edifying Tale of Tigers and Lambs

(January 15, 1960)

Chapter 23: The Stupidity of Questions About the Devil

(January 15, 1960)

Chapter 24: The Turgid Confusions of Registrars

(January 17, 1960)

Chapter 25: The Uncanny Events of Committee Rooms

(January 25, 1960)

Chapter 26: The Unpleasant Shocks of Trash Cans

(January 26, 1960)

Chapter 27: The Tragic Poignancy of Collective Closure

(February 10, 1960-May 25, 1981)

Epilogue

(November 14, 1989)

Dramatis Personae

Winston Adams: Stentorian president of Illyria College, long on rhetoric, short on funds.

Eve Wilberforce, formerly Mrs. Winston Adams: The president's ex-wife: trenchant and acidulous, and of whom Winston is somewhat fearful.

Ann Kemler Adams: Winston's current, second wife, of whom great things were expected.

Faye Roberts: Unofficial but rather beloved president of the Illyria College grapevine: annoying to some, scary to most, incisive to all.

Michael Moggs: Assistant professor of English: with an inordinate love of poetic word play, especially round and about the word "wet."

Henry Taylor: Assistant professor of German: with a tendency to ingratiate himself with solid senior faculty.

Elise Morgan: Precocious Illyrian student: possessed of superb logic and valuable visual information alike. She knows what she thinks, and knows what she has seen.

10

Charles Burdette: Eighty-something wealthy donor: he feels the country is on the verge of betrayal by Catholics and Communists alike.

Michael Mole: Fussy, somewhat ineffectual head of the Illyria College Board of Trustees.

Paul Hamlin: Snarky member of the Board, who has never forgiven Winston Adams for once having given him a B because he did know the precise locale of some islands or other.

Mamie Rogers: Professor Moggs's on-again, off-again Platonic girlfriend—and an Illyrian College student.

Royce Rex Jamison: Congregational minister and acquaintance of Charles Burdette; Pastor Jamison reads widely and narrowly.

Eloise McCrory (Mrs.): A singular night crawler, also the secretary to President Adams. She mourns her late parakeet Crackle and her late husband, the former more so.

Lester Cole: Professor of History, Illyria College—officious and martial.

Harry Finch: Professor of Economics, Illyria College—puffer of pipes and puffery alike

Horace Fuller: Professor of Classics, Illyria College; known for years as "Hortatory Horace" for his long-winded, polysyllabic, and soporific lectures.

Ronald Richards: Dean of Illyria College, plump with flesh and decanal" jargon alike, "decanal" meaning "pertaining to deans" and just the sort of argot Ronald loved.

Waldo Vole: Addled but rather lovable Registrar of Illyria College; once in possession of a secret, eager to share it with anyone important enough

William Montague: Amiable if sexless Professor of History and dedicated friend of Faye Roberts, who inverted his specialty on the Bill of Rights by calling him "The Bill of Wrongs."

Jonathan Upton: Minor trustee, walrus-like of visage, former roommate of Hortatory Horace, and gossip addict.

Dr. Edwin Poynter: an inquisitive oncologist in Ohio.

The Illyrian: The most famous feature of the Illyria College campus, this modernist sculpture blends a space ship and a praying mantis. A Boston *Globe* writer said that it was a "must see and a must retch at once. Only a blind person could laugh at it."

Prologue

(The Present Day)

Illyria College was founded in the early 1800s, south of Burlington, Vermont. In order to get to many colleges one must go "over" or "up." With Illyria one always had to go "down," not only because of its southward position relative to Vermont's largest city but also because Illyria, and the town of Illyria, too, was situated in a valley. Whether or not its downward destination forecast its later tribulations is an unanswerable question, but throughout its history walkers and wagons and cars alike have had to traverse an unmistakable downhill route in order to reach it.

Once there, however, few were disappointed in what they found. Although many colleges are built after a wilderness has been cleared, Illyria, because of the happy accident of being unable to afford enough foresters, removed only as many trees as necessary for a building to be placed in a small clearing. The result was, and is, that one can see the campus as a whole better in winter, when leaves have fled; while in spring, summer, and early fall one can see the folly of buildings—neoclassical, Romanesque, Palladian—only one at a time. Every building is surrounded by lavishly remaining ash and oak, maple and elm, chestnut and willow. Those who taught and studied and administered at Illyria, then, were dwelling in what was, in effect, a nature trail. One went from class to class, and from building to building, as though one were hiking in a forest.

The minimal clearing of arbors, once an economic necessity, in time became a tradition at Illyria. Its unofficial motto was "Enlightenment in a Darkened Wood."

On occasion a new student might get lost. He or she was told to listen to the Illyrian Chapel bell for orientation. The bell was not especially loud or majestic but soft and timid, as though registering perhaps a mild complaint against a profusion of woods that kept its own natural and unpredictable time. It was nonetheless an aural landmark.

If we imagine hard, we can all hear it. Let us, then, go down to Illyria College—for that is the place—in the one hundred fifty seventh year of its life.

Chapter 1: The Alleged Inadequacies of Little Annie
(August 21, 1959)

"*She's* coming back? No!"

William knew Faye wasn't kidding, though. Faye wasn't the sort to kid, especially about something like this.

"Yes, yes, yes. She *is* coming back. I've got this on good authority, Mr. History Prof," said Faye. "But I don't know exactly when."

Faye Roberts was a professional redhead, though at her age you got the idea it may have come from a bottle. She had an acid tongue that seemed to go well with a splotchy face, as though the carbolic sarcasm in her mouth had risen, like sap in a tree. Her late husband had taught chemistry, and she had done much for Illyria College, from teaching a seminar on Emily Dickinson to helping out in accounting to taking the lead during her younger years in the student production of *Medea*, all sans pay. As Media she had murdered her children; in life she had none. Her somewhat lamented spouse had had excellent life insurance. Faye was a fixture, a well-informed one.

"But why? Why," asked William Montague, 46, and ten years younger than Faye.

"Because little Annie can't cut it, Darling. And this school is in trouble."

"Is it really as bad as I've heard?"

"Worse," said Faye "We could go under at any time."

Her low and guttural voice tolled like the coming of doom, putting the innocuous ringing of the chapel bell to shame. But inside the bell tower of her own consciousness she had to admit that she was just guessing about *her* return. It was based on surmise.

***

Little Annie was the Illyria College president's second wife. She'd also been his student, years ago, when he deigned to teach geography at Illyria. That was before he'd risen, somewhat like the acid on Faye's tongue, to the rank of dean and then president. Annie had been one of his prize students, adept in maps and climate; a rich girl and hence a world-traveler every summer. Professor Winston Adams—now president Adams—had never gotten over her--though, as the faculty wives said back then, there was assumedly no "penetration" between them during her student days.

After all, Professor Adams was married. His wife Eve was what was known a "handsome" woman, not beautiful but "striking." She was of only average height and even walked with a slightly side ways gait, as though someone had set her moderately wrong years before, like a thermostat instructed to stay at 63 on a bitterly cold Illyria day. She hardly picked up her feet, which gave her a sliding motion as she made her approach. But she had something else: command. No one could gainsay Eve's sense that she and she alone was in charge. Her ever-present wine-colored velvet dresses, always to the floor, came to seem nearly militaristic. She didn't "take" the faculty men's coats at the annual Presidential Christmas Party. She told them how to take them off (left sleeve first) and where to hang them (one floor up, take the first left, do *not* lay it on the bed).

As the faculty wives, what was left of them, had long said: The professors weren't working for Winston. They were working for Eve. Once she had sprained a leg and sat on a stool for the Christmas receiving line. A bumbling and anxious assistant professor of geology had accidently bumped into her with his elbow. Her "Watch it, buster!" brought him to near urination. That night his wife threatened to leave him because, she said, Eve would surely forbid his tenure. The next day he made an appointment with an officious and frazzled Dean Richards, who assured him he had nothing to worry about. Richards loved to pretend his every answer was exhaustive. The young man then asked Faye—everyone thought she was the campus Sibyl—and she told him he had plenty to worry about. He resigned the following week.

So of course Annie Kemler, who had been only Winston's star student of years past, had no chance against Eve, who could run the U.S.S. Missouri out of town. Ah, but that was before Annie Kemler's father gave five million to Illyria on the condition that his daughter become a member of the Board. It was hard for even Eve to compete with five million for a school that needed every sou. The faculty wives used to say, "Send money. Keep Illyria green." Kemler had sent money, and he sent Annie, too. For a while she wore exclusively green skirts.

Just as the fabled butterfly flaps its wings in Seattle and causes in time a tornado in Texas, Winston and Annie began working together—did they not both have Illyria's interests at heart. Soon enough it seemed they had their own interests in both their hearts. Illyria was but the pretense of the pheromones between them.

Only the high regard that Winston enjoyed with the faculty and board saved him. He had been one of theirs for so long that he had become, at only fifty-two, an institution. On campus was a modernist statue of "The Illyria," a mix of praying mantis and space ship done by a famed sculptor. It was the prize and pride of the grounds. Tourists from Japan and Bolivia alike came to see it. Winston was the human counterpart to The Illyria. It wasn't that he looked like a space ship morphing into a praying mantis. It was that he was a tall man, granite faced, of utmost rectitude in demeanor and cunningly declamatory in style. His rather ponderous speech disguised the fact that he had little to say. But gravity seemed to drip from his every syllable.

Illyria could not possibly see how it could get along without Winston, who had been president for fifteen years. So when he told them that, "with mutual respect, Eve and I are separating," the community, while aghast, could not envision how this would mean the end of his presidency. It was as if The Illyrian only needed a new bolt here and there and then would be as always. In time, though, Winston also revealed that he required not only a new bolt. He also needed a new wife: Annie Kemler. And this too Illyrians around the globe accepted as though separation, divorce, and remarriage to a much younger woman were no more to be objected to than bear tracks in an autumnal wood.

Winston was safe, if not quite as good as new.

***

But he was not safe from Eve. He had to tell her, too, of course, and well before he could tell anyone else. Eve was canny. However much she was bossy, she was realistic. She knew that her power base was really Winston and that no faculty vote or trustee resolution could save her marriage. She even realized that the faculty and board had grown tired of her tyranny. For a dictator she was uncannily pragmatic.

She did enjoy her grapefruit juice cocktails, however, and poor Winston, hovering over her like Jefferson on Mount Rushmore, regrettably picked cocktail hour to break the news. She threw the juice into his petrified visage—bulls-eye—and prompted him to wear dark glasses next day in order to conceal his stinging pupils. He said the doctor had told him to rest his eyes lest a sty return, but no one was fooled, especially not the always well-connected Faye and the remnants of faculty wives. Besides, it was winter in Vermont, a succession of cloudy days.

But to keep up appearances Winston wore the shades for a month. This was also about a month after Eve had moved out. One morning in early February the campus awoke to an Allied van in the presidential circular driveway. Five hours later a black Lincoln came for Eve, who boarded it with a dignity that denied the mere existence of any and all the gapers, as though she were Queen Elizabeth on her way to command the battle against the Spanish Armada and expected to win.

In fact, however, she was moving to the Philadelphia apartment, Main Line, which Winston had guaranteed her. The question was whether she would become a queen in exile, a pretender of sorts, while the younger Little Annie tried to make all and one happy back in the Green Mountains.

But now, according to Faye and the faculty wives news service, the question was answerable, and affirmative. It was likely that Eve would become, in time, a returning empress, her majestic train and august entourage perhaps visible from a distance if one climbed the campus' highest silver maple.

For whom would this recurrence of Eve be negative? Hamlet, had he taught Shakespeare at Illyria College, would have said that that was the question and then perhaps asked for a raise, which penurious Illyria would be ill-suited to award.

Chapter 2: The Annoying Insufficiencies of Unrestricted Endowment

(July 14, 1959)

"Well, there you have it," said Malcolm Mole, "it looks pretty ghastly, doesn't it?"

This was six weeks *before* Faye Roberts had told History Professor William Montague that Illyria College was in deep trouble.

Mole was the chairman of the Board's finance committee. In Boston he always wore charcoal gray suits, but when he descended upon Illyria, Vermont, he managed a corduroy jacket with leather elbow patches. He'd made a mild fortune in debentures, but he'd really wanted to be an academic. So when he came back to the old sod of Illyria he dressed like one, or rather as he thought one dressed, or should do.

"I simply cannot believe things are this bad," protested President Winston Adams, resplendent as always in his pin striped Hart/Schaffner/Marx.

There was a low growling from the other men in the room, as though Winston had said something almost minatory and they were dogs to warn him off. "After all, we don't expect a bad admissions year."

"Yes, but the budget hasn't been balanced in six years," inserted Paul Hamlin, the budgetary vice-chair. "We've gone into endowment to the tune of several million every one of those years. And we didn't have much endowment to start with. I have to say, Winston, that's a bit on you."

Winston Adams said nothing. He might be a failed fund-raiser—he was too dignified to engage in such begging—but he would not take the execrably sour bait of Paul Hamilin, whom he'd once taught when he was a student and given him a B because he could never keep the Greek isles straight. He probably still couldn't.

Instead, Winston offered that after all, there was always the loan from the Second National Bank of Burlington. "We've always kept that aside for emergencies—a sort of rainy day, if you will, and now I sense a few clouds forming." Winston said this slowly and gravely, as though to add to the direness of the situation while suggesting that a man of his basso mettle could always head it off.

"But Winston," asked Malcolm Mote, "could we even pay that loan back?"

"Why, of course, we could, Malcolm. Of course we could." Winston applied his most monumental sense of being offended.

Paul Hamlin sprung out of his chair, all sixty-five inches of him. It irritated Winston that a small man with a baby face could get the better of his own seventy-five inches of solid, stolid, and earnest mountain.

"Where are you off to, Paul," asked Harry Davenport, a prominent dentist from Manchester and new to the board.

"To find a telephone."

"Oh, but is that for college business?"

"It is. I plan to call the Second National Bank of Burlington. Don't worry. I'll be discrete. I'll just say I'm an officer of Illyria College, which in my way I am. I know them there. As a small furniture manufacturer I've borrowed from there a few times— always, I might add, paying back on time. I want to see what the collateral is on that bank loan Winston's so assured about. I think it's a three million dollar note."

If a baby face could glower, Paul's did, targeting Winston, as though to say that he might not know the isle of Lesbos on pop quizzes but he knew the difference between a sound loan and desperate plight. He left the room and headed to President Adams' outer office where he was assured that Mrs. Eloise McCrory, the sugary secretary he'd known since his student days and flattered for years, would let him use the telephone.

The rest of them sat stunned. Winston's stone face seemed unusually impassive. Finally, Malcolm averred that at least they would know all the facts and added, with forced cheer, that that was half the battle. Privately he considered how large a figure 50 percent was, however, in the context of saving Illyria College.

In seven minutes Paul returned with something between a grimace and a smirk. "Well, I have the answer. Our *four* million dollar loan from the august Second National Bank of Burlingon, Vermont, is the unrestricted endowment of Illyria College. And the unrestricted endowment of Illyria College is…what?"

Malcolm answered so that Winston wouldn't have to. Winston Adams had served Illyria long and well. Well, he'd served it long, anyhow. His sense of self-worth and status must be preserved. Well, he wasn't sure about "must." Malcolm was rather put out with Winston these days and had been, rather, since that business with Ann and Eve.

"There is no unrestricted endowment at this college," said Malcolm. "It's all restricted, every penny."

Thus, said Paul, "Winston's rainy day fund is not just a leaky roof. It's no roof at all. I think, gentlemen, we are likely to get wet, perhaps drenched, and perhaps flooded away. I for one do not wish my degree to come from a defunct college. Pardon me for wanting too much. I've always been greedy that way."

The sarcasm seemed at odds with the cherubic face, but also made it seem more dreadful, as though a one-year old had just voiced out the most savage lacerations of irony. It was like something out of one of a monster movie, starring a deadly living male doll—a sort of menacing male version of Barbie, some cross between Ken Doll and the Creature from the Black Lagoon.

"But surely there's something we can do," said Jonathan Upton through his walrus mustache. Upton was a budget committee veteran but never elected chair. His remark didn't improve he mood. A quivering aquatic mammal was unbecoming and only made things worse.

"There is," said Winston. "We can un-restrict the endowment." As he said it, Winston was instantly proud of himself. He wasn't just a Mount Rushmore man. He could be nimble too—not just a statue but a bit of Fred Astaire thrown in.

"But how?" they all asked at once, not quite in unison.

"We can get Charles Burdette to let us lease his building for meetings. In fact, we could even ask him to permit us to sell it to some large convention organizer or impresario. You see, Illyria is a perfect spot for meetings and concerts, especially in the summers, which are mild here, as you must surely know. People will drive many miles to enjoy the mountains, the verdant lawns, and the cool air. And our campus is a genuine hiker's paradise if one doesn't mind passing the same trees three times an hour. They will want to see 'The Illyrian' and the gardens where it dwells, with its alternations of moon daisies or narcissi. And the Burdette building, with its acoustics in the auditorium and its meeting rooms upstairs, would be the perfect venue: lectures, concerts, meetings of professional and charitable organizations."

Winston realized he'd just made a speech in his most deep and deliberative majesty. That was all right. It was what he was good at. He thought the measured accumulation of this one especially good, and went even better with pin stripes. He realized how much more competent and potent he had been feeling since the very day the Stalinesque Eve had gone away.

"But Charles gave that building for Illyria College, for our most sacred events. The many rooms upstairs are to be reserved for group discussions of these events—what Charles called Aftermath Gatherings." This objection came, predictably, Winston thought, from Baby Face Hamlin.

"Oh, when Charles realizes our situation, when he considers it properly and in context, I am confident he'll agree to let us use the building—it's a neo-neo-classical gem and quite vast—as an asset. We could put into the sales or lease contract a provision that gives the college usage for two or three occasions a year— hardly the ten Charles envisaged, I grant you."

Malcolm said, "But Winston—and here I speak with kindness but candor—Charles doesn't much like you. He's a rather strait- laced sort of fellow. He hated that Ann-Eve business. He'd been married to Matilda—one wife—since God was a tadpole, or so it seems. He'll never go for this idea."

Winston had to admit it was true. The meeting was on the verge of fragmenting into despair. It did not end happily. They were stuck. Yet somewhere beneath all his grand circumspection, Winston had a dim idea.

Charles Burdette had always liked *Eve*; adored her, in fact.

Of course he was no longer married to Eve. He had felt so much more in charge since divorcing her, until now.

Chapter 3: The Remorseless Decisions of Editors
(August 22, 1959)

Michael Moggs always prided himself on having his own filing system. His office was what Othello—his favorite character—called "chaos come again." Othello used that line when he considered that Desdemona might be faithless to him. Michael wasn't worried about Mamie's being unfaithful to *him*. It just wasn't in Mamie's repertoire. He well knew this: he'd been dating her on the sly since the previous March.

Now he was a professor of modern English and American poetry at Illyria, emperor of his messy official rooms in creaky Calaboose Hall—which used to be the science building back before anyone knew there were even germs or so Michael thought. Calaboose was a Romanesque castle, still not renovated after all these years of promises because Illyria didn't have the money. Michael wasn't alone in thinking that the third stair to the second floor might give way at any time. Meanwhile, the bricks of Calaboose had surrendered to endless soot from local manufacturing plants. It now sported the color of Faye Roberts' hair had she decided to dye it henna instead of red.

This was an important day for Michael as days in the life of an academic go. His two senior colleagues, normally the editors of the *Illyria Iamb*, had decided to take a term off to do research in

Venice (on the American literati who had settled there). They had left him to make the final selections for the upcoming issue.

In a way this annoyed Michael, a professorial looking man with horn-rimmed glasses who knew that, if and when he removed them, he was a raven-haired and attractive man of eminently regular features. Michael sensed that the contrasts between the bespectacled and non-bespectacled versions of himself played to his advantage—not that he was drop-dead handsome with glasses off, but compared to Professor Michael Moggs with glasses on....

Michael thought it careless of his colleagues to leave him in charge of the *Iamb*. But it also flattered him. They trusted an assistant professor. Besides, it gave him power. It would look good on the upcoming tenure vita. And wasn't he qualified? After all, he had written his doctoral thesis at Indiana on the middle poems of Hart Crane.

Still, it was an undertaking something short of easy. He'd had to go the post office every day to pick up the submissions. He'd practically needed a wheelbarrow. Who knew that so many Americans wanted to be poets? He thought of an essay by Randall Jarrell, who noted that some poets, though wonderful people, wrote verse so inappropriate they might as well be doing somersaults at their own funerals.

The menu of options seemed impossible for a while: verse, or what claimed to be verse, about the deaths of horses and gerbils, hopelessly abstract and cryptic stuff about everything from the so-called fractals of beauty to the vagaries of quantum theory— why did some physicist in Montana think he could write a poem? One poem began as follows:

The vase of entropy
Is full of emptiness
Among the cruelest of stars
In the lilies of the valley.

This one, like ninety-nine percent of them, was fated for the round file. But then rejection letters had to go out. Fortunately, even penurious Illyria College had managed to get him a poetry journal secretary, even if she did only come three days a week.

There was one poem he wasn't sure about, but Michael was nearly certain nevertheless that he would accept it. It was called "Wet" and was, in Michael's considered expert view, a wonderful exegesis on the different uses of the word. Michael had become imbued with Ludwig Wittgenstein's very fashionable view that the meanings of words lay in their uses. It seemed that the author of "Wet," Philip Rayster, had been inspired with the same idea. All right. That settled it. "Wet" would be published in just over a month. He would write Mr. Rayster in Philadelphia a personal note of congratulations. If you couldn't go wrong selling I.B.M. you also couldn't err in following Wittgenstein. Besides, Michael thought, Rayster's semi-sestina format was brilliant.

And so, he thought, was Mamie in her way. Michael thought the faculty underestimated Mamie, still a junior, who was at best a B student. To be sure, she was an average psychology major, but Michael was equally of the conviction that she could apply psychological concepts better than anyone else on campus could. She certainly applied them when she dealt with *him*, ministering with skill to his mélange of annoyances and pride, insecurities and self-congratulations.

Of course, once the term began, Michael shouldn't be seeing Mamie so much away from classes. She had hours after all, which meant that she had to be in and accounted for by no later than 10 PM. To think that they would have sex was out of the question. But they weren't having sex, not yet. They could sneak off to Burlington, though, for a milkshake. They could smooch and pet in Michael's old Impala. No one need know.

And someday they would be wed. Mamie would be his helpmate. She would give parties until he became department chairman. The cup, or was it a cocktail glass, of his self-satisfaction runneth over. The ten-year age gap was nothing. Michael assessed the risks of the present engagement as compared to the payoff of years of contentment. He began to sweat with both social anxiety and sexual excitement. Sweat, he thought, rhymes with "wet" and sweat *is* wet. Yet another point, Michael thought, for Poet Philip Rayster. The more he thought about "Wet" the better he liked it. He was sure it would be a sensation when published.

Who knows? It might make Michael famous, too. Mamie, a future wife surely, would be proud of him. His very breath inhaled an air of gargantuan self-satisfaction. It felt good, as though his soul had migrated to his lungs. Come to think of it, he thought, that too would be a brilliant line of verse. He inhaled again.

Chapter 4: The Absolute Necessity of Final Exam Periods
(Later That Same Day)

As he sat in the committee room among his senior colleagues, Henry Taylor knew he had an ordinary name, but he thought this was actually a good thing because it would keep everybody underestimating him. Besides, he thought usual sorts of names, easily pronounced, were precisely the kind that could become famous, partly because they were so easy to remember and say. "John Adams" was hardly an exotic name after all. Of course he wondered what sort of president John Adams had been—a good one, Henry assumed, yet presumably not one of the greats. Although Henry's discipline was German, he had a spattering of knowledge about other things and thought he knew enough to know that Adams was a respectable, if not truly sterling, president, rather like Illyria's own president Adams.

Oh, well, Henry thought. What difference does that make? He really shouldn't let his thoughts wander. After all, he had been elected to Illyria's powerful Curriculum Committee, the youngest member of the group and the only assistant professor so honored in many years. He had done it, he thought, because he was precisely the sort of tactful and courteous young man the older faculty could look at and be reassured about the future of Illyria. Though it was thought on campus to be an august committee, it sat in the basement of a building so non-descriptive as to be called, simply, West Hall, merely because it was in the west end of campus. In the winter it was said to be the warmest spot on campus, snuggled as it was behind a grove of leafless elms and heated by a furnace far too big for the building, which whirred so loudly that committee members had to shout—which they often did anyhow, for academic politics is famously fiendish due to the irrelevance and insignificance of its issues.

Henry thought—why oh why could he not focus on the meeting—that the way of Michael Moggs, his chief rival among the younger set, was *not* a sound methodology for enduring respectability. Moggs, to be sure, had managed to look both academic and handsome at once, while one of Henry's old girlfriends, furious at him for refusing to take a stand about a dispute between her and her stepfather, said that he looked passably like a salamander. As for the good-looking Moggs, his teaching a group of poets called, for whatever reason, "The Modernists," had students in what must be in the intellectual counterpart to smelling salts. But Henry thought these Modernists were only a fad. Michael would be sorry he'd invested so much in a mere fashion. Goethe, on the other hand, would last. "Sell thy Hart Crane; buy thy Goethe." This was an excellent motto. Henry could not help thinking how clever he was.

But back to the meeting: Professor Lester Cole had just explained why the current system of final exams was no longer sustainable. "We have no consistency in the policy. Some professors can give them while others elect not to. Some professors can load up: make a term paper due on the next-to-last class and give a final on the last one. Others of us let students off without making them do anything. The only way around this is to have a separate final exam period *with strict regulations about how it is to be used.* Enough of this 'let's just end the semester' business: it's failed, I tell you, failed and failed utterly."

Cole had been in World War II. He sported an erect and marching posture and a trim military cut, though if one looked with care one could see that he didn't let his hair grow long only because it would accentuate an emerging bald spot. He was a man of certain views, adhered to with all the stubbornness of well-driven industrial strength nails. Sometimes Henry thought Lester was addressing the troops, the way the unlamented Eve Adams (no relationship to John) had bossed the campus of Illyria College. But Eve was much more imperious than Lester, a poor man's dictator.

"I don't agree, Lester," said Harry Finch. Cole was a historian, while Finch taught math, and yet it was Finch, master of the more exacting field, who always seemed to be the flexible one. Listening to them debate, one would have thought that history was an unalterable equation while a real equation could be solved in multiple, contradictory ways. Perhaps the two of them should have traded fields. "We can put in a dogmatic policy, but the faculty will just get around it. Most of us have tenure. We can't be fired or shot at sunrise. We're always putting in rules at Illyria and always seeing them flouted. That's because our colleagues are independent operators who solve different problems in different ways. Besides, without a final exam period we all get out of here earlier for Christmas and can hold commencement in late May rather than early June."

The committee seemed rather split 2-2 and, although no one would say so, it expected Henry Taylor, young Henry Taylor, polite Henry Taylor, skillfully flattering Henry Taylor, to break the tie. No wonder, Henry thought, he had been thinking about John Adams and Michael Moggs—what a pair—instead of attending to the discussion. He was the whippersnapper of the group, and yet it was he who was meant to spell the difference on one of Illyria's most contentious issues.

But he had to say *something*. What would Machiavelli do? Or Bismarck—who was at least German and thus in Henry's "field."

"I'm thinking we should hold this over until the next meeting and wait for some further thought and study. I am attracted to what both Lester and Harry have said. Well, perhaps we could do this: We could have a final exam period for two years and see how it goes. Nothing needs to be forever." His voice had begun in the register of a boyish piccolo but soon enough devolved in to a pseudo-gravitas that, despite or because of its fakery, made him seem possessed of a sound judgment beyond his years.

Henry thought he had done a masterful job of splitting the difference between two of the major senior grumps of the faculty, though it must be said that the boyish but gray and leonine Harry seemed more dignified than sour, and more pragmatic than rule-bound. Could it be, Henry thought, that Harry really believed rules should be made for people rather than the other way around? Henry thought that such wisdom was probably beyond the comprehension of the average citizen, even on a college campus, for which he had a wee but developing sense of contempt.

Am I becoming an operator, Henry asked, neither a true believer like Lester nor a mellow wise man like Harry?

But being an operator had its advantages, Henry thought, especially as even Harry Finch spoke up and said that perhaps Henry's idea was a good one. "After all, Lester, I could be wrong. Yes, I can see young Henry's point. We can try the exam period and monitor it. I'm in favor of that not, obviously, because I'm sure it won't work but because I'm *not sure* it won't work. Skepticism but tolerance has always been my mantra. I see no reason to stop now. Good work, Henry!"

Henry thought that Harry's speech was definitely on the self-important side and that being proud of one's tolerance was a rather intolerant thing in and of itself. But that was beside the point. Henry thought the most important thing was what worked—for Henry Taylor. He wanted to get ahead. He'd not come from a wealthy family, not born to the academic manor, not brought into this world with an Oxford High Table spoon in his mouth. If Lester and Harry, who came from academic backgrounds, wanted to play their roles as high-minded judge and self-congratulatory skeptic, that was fine by Henry. Unlike them, with their inherited privileges, Henry was a Faustian striver, however much he had to conceal the intensity of his endeavors.

For Henry, the really capital thing was making something of himself. He was clever. What was it Goethe said? "Character develops itself in the stream of life." Henry took the Master to mean that one must adapt one's character to the moment. All right, so it's a bit of a perverse reading. So what? Besides, old-timers like Lester and Harry would respect someone who studied Goethe. They'd have a different idea—probably did already—about someone who concentrated on Hart Crane, who couldn't finish his poems and was probably homosexual as well. Take that, Moggs!

After agreeing to recommend a trial of two years for a mandatory final exam period, the committee adjourned. Henry had been a hit, a smash one. And he knew it.

Chapter 5: The Gentle Decorum of Gardens
(August 23, 1959)

Even when he was a professor and she a student, Winston and Ann had sat together in the Illyria Gardens, often near the praying missile known as "The Illyrian." How wonderful it had been, back in the late 40s, when the Illyrian president of that era, Carey Compton, had managed to get a well-known Henry Moore acolyte to create the sculpture. It was just bizarre enough to qualify as modern, and yet its curious blend of rocket and insect was just representational enough to become popular to viewers, who drove or even flew many miles in order to see it. Well, it wasn't the only thing most of them planned to see, but it was nicely on the way to the Green Mountains or Montreal.

The Gardens were impressive in their own way—not every garden has an exact alternation of moon daisies and narcissi, with neither flower erroneously appearing twice in succession. Winston mused that the exactness of the flora put the mess of the college endowment to shame. But the Gardens were more setting for The Illyrian than anything else. Winston thought back on this mild August day—a touch of cool autumn weaseling past his granite face—how he and Ann would gather in the garden fifteen years before and discuss such arcane subjects as the deserts and barter economy of Mongolia. Even then, the ostensible dry subject could barely disguise a liquidity of passion on both sides.

If only Illyria College could bottle that original liquidity and convert passions into dollars! Its tribulations would be done.

Now Winston could call her, openly, "My passion," as he did now, when he said to her, "So, my passion, how was your trip to Boston?"

Ann had been an elegantly wiry young woman of twenty when Winston first met her and towered over her, as a rock seventy-five inches high will tend to do over most other mortals. Now she was a women of nearly forty, fifteen years Winston's junior, of svelte gaiety, slightly receding visage (the bloom of youth now in its early September phase), and turquoise silk or velvet dresses, the latter her personal favorite. No one would call her perky, as she was too restrained for that, and yet she had that enthusiasm oft linked to the pert. Only her excellent breeding kept me from being a New England version of Debbie Reynolds, which could have been an embarrassment.

"My trip to Boston, yes. Well, I enjoyed myself: Ritz-Carleton, and so on. Before you ask, I did chat up Daddy's friend Maurice Reaper—Uncle Mo, we used to call him—and he's going to get back in touch with me."

"Grand, simply grand, my passion!"

"It is grand, Winston. However, we mustn't get ahead of ourselves. You know, I hate to say this, but ever since Daddy died there's been less attention paid to him every year. I can't really gauge this, Winston. Years ago, you taught me in your courses to face the facts on the ground whatever they might be. Remember when you said that geography, not economics, was the dismal science?"

"I do, my passion—one of my more amusing and penetrating remarks if I say it myself."

"Yes, well, there are two unpleasant social facts here. One is 'out of sight, out of mind.' Daddy died three years ago, and the survivors in his cohort are simply starting to forget about him."

"And the other unpleasant fact, my passion?" Winston momentarily decided to forget what she was saying and focus instead on the loveliness of the speaker, whose fresh fields and pastures still somewhat new delighted him still.

"Yes, well, the other one is that now that Daddy's dead, others are taking a more realistic inventory of his character. Daddy was often conniving, sometimes cruel, always self-centered."

"And?"

"And so people like Uncle Mo are simply less interested than they might have been in making a gift to us in Daddy's memory."

"But, darling, didn't you tell him how it would help our endowment?"

"Well, sweet Winston, I think that may be the problem. You see, 'helping the endowment' seems a bit abstract for Maurice. But despite this—and despite what I think may be going on as he remembers Daddy—there is some hope."

"Hope? Thank God. How so?"

"He did say he might be interested in donating a memorial, on campus, to Daddy's memory."

"What sort of memorial?" Energy drained at once from Winston's lengthy frame. It sometimes seemed as though Annie had more pep in her pinky that Winston in his entire ponderous body. Observers on campus had especially been noting this phenomenon of late.

"Well—and now I ask you to be patient and hear me out—some sort of marble mound."

"A marble *mound*?"

"Yes, well, you see Uncle Mo has gotten into mounds as a sort of art form. If I may be discrete but candid, Winston, we've long known he's light on his feet. And a young sculptor 'friend' of his has sold him on what's called 'Mound Art.' The basic idea is that mounds are part of nature, so if one 'sculpts' a mound, one is respecting one of nature's most recurring forms."

"But what, what, what would this mound consist of?"

"Uncle Mo wasn't overly specific. But I think it would be a marble mound that comes out of the campus earth to a height of about, oh, ten feet, and across it, in elegantly carved italic letters, would be Daddy's name, a reference to him as 'arch-patron' or something like that, and his dates."

"And you say he wasn't *specific*? Not that I wish to chastise *you*, my passion, but this seems quite specific to me. Must it be ten feet high at the top? Why, that's taller than I am...not that I'm the measure of all things, but might not this play havoc with, with the sight lines on campus?"

"Well, dear, it might. It just might."

"Anything else?"

"Ah, yes, yes, yes. He wants to place it at the entrance to the gardens here, in the same sight line as the most prominent one leading up to The Illyrian. He also wants a large sign, all granite, celebrating the fact that it was *he* who gave the mound."

For a moment Winston mused about how he knew many on campus called *him* "Old Granite Face." He thought it a compliment, whatever the scoffers behind his back might think. Winston wondered if there were room on the Illyria College campus for more than one great granite monument.

"But, my passion, won't a ten foot marble mound at the top ruin the view of The Illyrian?"

"It might, Winston, but let's not become upset just yet. Uncle Mo has made no firm offer. He just said this is something he's thinking over for the moment. You know, I wish I had better news for you. I hate to question Uncle Mo, but there were times when I thought he almost relished blocking out The Illyrian as a way of saying something nasty about Daddy. I really think it's just that he wants something with his name attached to it. As I say, just buttressing the endowment isn't so appealing to him. You know: men and their vanity about the tangible."

As she said it, she had a faint sense that it might apply to her husband as well.

"I cannot say I'm not disappointed, Annie [no 'my passion' this time], but these are early days with Maurice, I suppose. After all he didn't attend Illyria. He's not even from New England. What was the name of that little school in Wisconsin he went to? Belton? I can't recall. Anyhow, let's not fret overmuch now."

He gave her a hug, his short-sleeved blue dress shirt (tie tied) against her yellow silk skirt, ballooned with legions of petticoats, careful to restrain his own strength, as the locale of the stone bench gave them an especially inspiring view of The Illyrian—they neither had to crane their necks to see its top nor were they so close as to miss its ultimate, if peculiar, majesty. Meanwhile, the garden was still intact in all its flourishing, gloriously insensate to the fact that chills were on their way.

"I recall, Winston, once during my student days when we sat in this garden to discuss the Gobi. It was all so intellectual back then, early spring as I recall. No one cared that we were sitting here. You were but a professor, and professors and students often visited here for after-class discussions. The Gobi was a safely dehydrated subject—no pun intended—and spring was unstoppable that day, even if not fully blown. You were the source of all founding wisdom and I, if I may say it, the fount of all eager youth. It was heaven. I felt both free and secure at once—later, I learned, alas, that freedom and protection are often foes. But not that day: I felt safe with you, enchanted by your knowledge, swept by your good looks—hardly faded, I might add."

"That's quite a speech, my passion. I see we taught you well here at Illyria! Yes, it was heaven for me as well. May heavenly days not be done!"

"And you aren't overly disappointed that Maurice won't help with the endowment? Have I failed you, the college? It's not as though we have no endowment now, Winston. And Maurice might come through yet."

Winston decided not to tell her about the recent meeting of the Finance Committee, nor would he, today, offer a gentle reproof to her declaration about the security and size of the endowment. That could wait, It would only disturb her. Besides, he didn't like the idea that His Passion would think him a failure. Granite and feet of clay were to have nothing to do with each other, Winston thought, firmly.

"OK, you two! Break it up!"

It was Faye Roberts. The two of them looked at one another with the same thought: Of course they would not have enduring privacy in Illyria Gardens, not on a mild summer's day in the late afternoon, even if classes had yet to resume for the autumn term.

"Why, hello, Faye. Out for a stroll?"

"No, Winston, not out for a stroll. I'm out specifically to stalk you!"

Winston laughed, almost a squirmy giggle. He vaguely thought of Faye as the Fates in pursuit of his lack of endowment building.

"Surely not, Faye! It would be far too unbecoming of you!"

"Almost nothing becomes me, Winston: too old and wrinkled for that. I hear you've been in Boston, Annie."

"Yes, yes, Faye. Just got back. How did you know?" Annie thought this shorthaired female baritone was a tad on the minatory side. She resented it somehow.

"The praying mantis rocket over there told me!"

"I wish it would tell *me* more, Faye!"

"Well, you have only to ask, Winston. Any old how, I must get back to my lair, or my cage, or whatever it is that I foul each day. See you two lovebirds later!"

Off Faye went, or did she stalk? It gave Winston and Ann an eerie sense that she'd been spying on them the whole time. Annie didn't want the world (translation: the campus) to know about her difficulties in Boston.

And Winston didn't want the world to know about his arduous meeting with the Finance Committee. Why did it seem that the world knew already? He always felt that way about discrete matters after chatting with Faye Roberts, who, it seemed, had been here since the beginning of time and had watched the college grow up around her.

When, Winston wondered, would he and Annie get their heaven back? Suddenly the Gobi Desert seemed rather welcoming. Winston wondered if there were any direct flights from Burlington to Ulaanbaatr, the largest city in Mongolia if he recalled correctly. He doubted that there were, but he could always check with ubiquitous and menacing Faye Roberts.

She'd know the answer. She seemed to know everything.

Chapter 6: The Subtle Omnipresence of Beards
September 15, 1959

Assistant Professor Michael Moggs was a contented man as he sat at a marble round table in Burlington. He was in the Currie Pharmacy, complete with soda fountain, a welcome variation on an old theme, for it had not only a marble counter but also marble side tables. Nothing excelled their cool curlicues. Michael was waiting for Mamie. He had driven over, while she would be taking the bus. It seemed unwise and precarious for them to drive together, she as student and he as prof. People would not understand, Michael thought, or perhaps they would understand all too well. Either way was risky in this new term, not yet out of its diapers.

He'd already been told the bus would be late in a temporary downpour, so he turned to the new and submitted poems he'd brought with him to while away the minutes. Philip Rayling's "Wet," Michael continued to believe, was a gem. He read it over again with wonder. The die was cast. He had written Mr. Rayling a veritably fawning acceptance letter. Well, Michael wondered if it were fawning. He feared it might have been: too late now. But how can a letter about a masterpiece be called fawning?

Michael also reflected, almost giddily, about Illyria and his own place in it. Founded in 1802 by Mr. Wallace Dermott Stout, a wealthy attorney with a fascination for Shakespeare, it had been called Illyria from the outset. Stout's favorite Shakespearean play was *Twelfth Night* with its imaginary land of Illyria. From the beginning Illyria was to remain tiny, devoted to the liberal arts in no practical or utilitarian way. Stout and every prominent Illyrian since had thought that one could always become "professional" after college—emerge as a doctor or lawyer or teacher or minister—but only after "exposure" to the likes of Homer and Chaucer, Racine and Aristotle. "Exposure" suddenly gave Michael the willies. It sounded a bit like catching a cold. Why was he so anxious on this fine day?

At Illyria there was a bias in favor of credentialed "classics." Even Ibsen and especially stormy Strindberg were subjects of suspicion. After all, they hadn't been dead for a hundred years even. As for Hart Crane and the "modernists," Michael's promotion of them might yet produce a stir. He had to take care. There it was again: this nerve business.

But, Michael thought, his ardent pursuit of traditional literature, especially those sentimental favorites Tennyson, Browning, and Arnold, had so far thrown any censorious hounds off their scent. In effect, Tennyson, Browning, and Arnold were his "beard," his cover-up and camouflage for his love of Hart Crane, just as this drug store, in Burlington, thirty miles from campus, was his beard for his love of prettily bovine Mamie Rogers.

Michael was confident. Illyria had been founded in a love of literature. He loved literature. Ergo, he and Illyria were a perfect assemblage. Suddenly he worried about the strict logic of this syllogism, just as he had fretted about a fawning letter to a masterful young poet. Why couldn't he stop being anxious? How could he go from self-assurance to precipitous fear in a matter of seconds?

As he cooled his hands on the marvelous marble of Currie's Drug, he was little aware of other things happening about him, such as the uselessness of other contemplated marble (Mo Stapleton's) for the survival of Illyria College. He knew nothing of pressures on the populations of golden-winged warblers or brown thrashers or cottontail rabbits. He had never heard that all the wild turkeys in Vermont had been killed off and that deer and moose were being dangerously thinned out. He knew that Illyria was near a fine Vermont forest, but Michael was not aware of the constant struggle between the stern maples and the parasitical honeysuckle. For Michael it was all one and all fine. He knew his Victorian poets, his beards, but he had not bothered to read Darwin's words about how the loveliness of nature is itself a beard, behind which lurks incessant battle. Michael thought Arnold's words about "ignorant armies clashing by night" was a brilliant linguistic stroke, not an apt description of the world.

So benighted about other beards—arguably more important than his own (Victorian poets, Currie's Drug)—Michael turned once more to Rayling's poem:

The rain is, always;
Sometimes even fire
is wet; and pimpled boys
that cannot fox trot are
all
wet.
Most of the globe
is wet, and even God
must have wet dreams,
mustn't
He?

For a second or two Michael wondered if the poem were a bit gimmicky before soon circling back to his earlier view that it was a classic already, at once witty and magisterial, an innovative verse about Important Things. He did wonder, though, why he'd once thought it was semi-sestina when it was obviously free verse entirely? Was he mixing it up with another entry—yes, maybe that was the glitch? The poem "Not," which he'd turned down, *was* in that form.

Again, why all this back-and-forth? Why couldn't he settle, secure behind his many beards? Besides, the students loved him. In fact, here came one now. She had stayed in Illyria all summer to conduct campus tours, the real reason being that she could see Michael. It was another beard.

"Mamie! My, the bus *was* late!"

"The driver—and we—could barely see five feet ahead. The rain didn't come down in sheets, but in walls."

Michael was delighted with Mamie's wit. He'd known her for two years, when she'd written such a piercing analysis of "My Last Duchess" that he'd given her an A+ with the comment, "Keep it up and dedicate a book to me." She was totally taken. So was he. She was the daughter of a pharmaceutical salesman and a housewife from West Roxbury. Raven-haired, round of face, a tad sallow in skin tone, a bit too large in the hips—but her relatively trim waist in contrast gave her a curvaceous if circumscribed outline of flesh that made her, Michael thought, exceptional. He had no intentions of focusing solely on hips. There was the silvery laugh, as though her every giggle opened a fresh bottle of Pepsi; and the precocious expertise with metaphor that could turn rainfall into drops and then to sheets and walls. He thought she would love "Wet." She was halfway there already in her comment about the bus driver and the storm. She wore a plaid skirt, ballooning outward of course, perhaps a bit too snug for late summer. The black and white saddle shoes, he decided, were conventional but intentionally misleading. She was obviously posing as a regular girl when in fact she was his Secret One, advanced beyond her years, a prodigy faculty spouse to be.

The shoes: that was just another beard behind which they both could stay concealed.

"If you are 'of a mind of rain,' as Wallace Stevens might put it, then just listen to this," and he read her the passage from "Wet." And after his reading he asked:

"Isn't that just the best?"

"Well, Michael, it certainly is striking, yes."

"Just striking? I think it's damned brilliant, shimmering really in the endeavor of word jousting." He wondered if he should have said "damned" but thought she would probably think him daring and even grander. He didn't want her to think of him as effete; a little rough would be a nice balancing act.

"Well, by 'striking' I mean that business about God's wet dream."

"Oh, but that's the finest of all. He's saying, you see—his name is Rayling—that water and wet are so omnipresent that even God is elemental, even God has wet dreams. I think it's both archetypal in the Jungian sense and a poem about the weather in the Wallace Stevens mode. Just brilliant!" He decided to stop: no use in lecturing his once and true bride.

"Yes, well, Darling Prof Mike. You know best. I wouldn't want Illyria College to hear about God's wet dream, though."

"What do you mean?"

"I mean that it would be too risqué for Illyria. I always apply a Mom-and-Pop test. Would my parents be shocked? If so, then Illyria probably would be. They aren't so far apart. And let me say that my parents would be shocked to learn that a poet thinks God has sexual fantasies and, well, you know…."

"Emissions?"

"Yes."

"Oh, Mamie, I think you're overreacting."

"If you say so, Prof," and she planted a lightning smooch beneath the left stem of his glasses, just before they ordered the blameless milkshakes.

Michael was a lucky man. He knew it. Her comment about "Wet" had unnerved him, though. And that girl asking the druggist where he sold his Pepto-Bismol: she looked slightly familiar.

Michael swallowed. Mamie was going to be his wife, but she *was* just a young student. Her scary response to "Wet" was easily dismissible. Besides, no one on campus much read the *Illyria Iamb* anyhow. And he was certainly not going to recall the acceptance—not after his fulsome letter to Philip Rayling. He decided to screw his courage to the sticking place—or, in other words, to relax.

Who *was* that girl by the Pepto?

Chapter 7: The Unavoidable Centrality of Machiavelli
(September 23, 1959)

William Montague was such a beloved professor of American constitutional history at Illyria that students called him the *"Bill of Rights."* He was mid-40s, asexual, unmarried of course, but in firm possession of a fine absurdist sense and an addiction to gossip. The last time he'd talked to Faye Roberts, the campus know-it-all who generally knew it all, she'd said Eve Adams, the president's ex-, was returning to campus.

Now, an hour after the latest Faculty Senate meeting—they'd started having them in the mornings in hopes that everyone's humor would be better—he was sitting down to tea and coffee cake in Faye's spacious mansard house. He wondered why it shouldn't have been *coffee* and coffee cake, but Faye was known for the fierce habit of being uncanny. That, and information, was her trademark. She was also an actress, never off stage.

"So, Faye, I've not spoken with you in about a month. Do you still say Eve—*she*--is returning to campus?"

"All right, Bill Darling, I must make a confession. I'm not certain she is. But I think she might. And you know me: dramatic effect must rule and petty facts must drool. I *had* to say that she *was* coming back when I saw you last month. Otherwise, you'd not have listened."

"Of course I'd have listened, either way. But you admit that you don't know for sure."

"I don't know for sure. I'll go further, Mr. Bill of Rights, I don't even have a shred of evidence. I'm basing all this on my own speculations—and of course on my special brand of Faye logic. Call it Faye-mous Logic, if you must."

"Ha! But what is this Logic?"

"That Winston is folding like a tent in a typhoon; that the college is in big money trouble; that only Eve has the authority to straighten us up. She's the only one around here that everyone is scared of, or once was."

"Even the bankers?"

"When the bankers have met Eve, they will be scared of her."

"But there was the nasty divorce. Annie's First Lady now."

"Yes, and Annie has some financial contacts…friends of her wealthy father, may he rest in saintly memory, the old bastard. But Annie can't take charge."

"Shouldn't Winston be taking charge?"

"Don't make me laugh, Bill. How long have you been around here? I'd think you just parachuted in. Winston has always been what on the luxury liners was called the 'show captain.' He looked good in his uniform, the show captain did, and he'd show up to dine with the top passengers and dance with their wives. But he wasn't the captain. He didn't know the difference between the pilot's wheel and the boiler room."

"You mean Winston just has that granite face of what a president should look like."

"Precisely. You've broken the code! Winston isn't an empty suit. He's an empty boulder."

"But how did he manage in the early days of his presidency? Forgive me, Faye, I've spent too much time with Madison and Hamilton and the Federalist Papers to notice. Or maybe I noticed but have forgotten. Scholarship will do that to a man."

Faye inwardly snorted at Bill's calling himself a man. She thought his asexuality made him a walking amoeba. But this was no matter. She liked him. She continued:

"Don't you remember that when Winston became president he had four things going for him besides his own stentorian looks? He had the economy, which was excellent. He had Eve, who kept him from stumbling in his vanity and picked him when he did; he had George Brown, his provost; and he had David Berger, his dean. We used to call Winston Stone Face; George, Prune Face; and Berger, Clown Face. But they were both able men: diplomatic, efficient, cunning. They all went on to better places. And they protected Winston. It wasn't so much, check that, that they protected him as made him look good. No one really noticed, other than I, the mistress of Faye-mous Logic, that Winston was the façade of a ship that others piloted and for which others shoveled coal."

"And now?"

"And now Prune Face is president of Hamilton and Clown Face provost at Haverford. Eve has been sent packing because The Great Stone Face Winston went into his mid-life crisis and had an ache for an old student he couldn't slough off. The national economy is suspect. Winston is too proud to ask for money, and too tongue-tied, when he gets away from his script, to articulate the college's real needs. Annie's rich father is dead and dissed. There are cracks in Winston's rocky visage. The worry lines are gathering like savages in a John Ford Western."

"But, sweet, dear Faye, this *doesn't* mean Eve is coming back!"

"It's not out of the question either. We're in trouble, Bill of Rights. I think your Mr. Alexander Hamilton, he of the national bank, if he could see the books, would agree. Maybe you'd believe it if it came from him."

Faye's face disappeared from Bill's view. Only her red hair could be seen. She was bending with slight servility to pour his tea. Even then, there seemed less humility than an implicit order that he should drink it and like it.

"By the way, Faye, what did you think of today's Senate meeting—the vote about a reserved Final Exam period? I thought Senate meetings in the morning were supposed to be better humored than the ones we used to have in late afternoon, when all were tired and grumpy and the nights were drawing in already. What happened?"

"I never went along with that 'we'll all be happier in the morning' stuff. But this morning's meeting would have been cheerful if the Young and the Restless hadn't opposed the new policy. They should watch themselves. They're clever, yes, but the mossbacks always win in the end. That young Michael Moggs is a bit too struck, I think, with his own intelligence. And now, Bill of Rights, let's toast with our Earl Gray the new Final Exam Period! Worse things have been praised. We could be drinking to Winston."

***

(Afternoon, The Same Day)

Unusual for him, Henry Taylor noted the season. Nights came on faster. Leaves had left their luster back in July. Squirrels seemed frantic for nuts. What was happening to him—was he journeying into some sort of mellow mood? Would he retire to a tower in order to meditate? Was he browning out in autumn?

Fat chance, Henry thought. Perhaps some of the older Illyria professors, the ones born with trust funds, could retire early and watch the snow fall and write the memoirs no one but their grandchildren would read—and even they would do so only upon threat of withdrawn inheritance. Not Henry. He had ambitions. Poor men must have them if they wish to rise.

Henry thought of this morning's Senate Meeting. Of course he had voted with the great majority, the law-and-order crowd of established professors. They had tired of anything goes where finals were concerned. They wanted rules: ye must give a final exam—even if it's just a quiz in drawing or sculpting—and ye must do so at a pre-scheduled time. One size was to fit all. The people were made for the laws. Henry thought young colleagues who had voted against had been unwise. They had been improvident about their power. They were careless. They seemed to be in favor of chaos. The old heavies on the faculty just might remember, come tenure-time.

But, Henry thought, they would remember *him* with favor. "We have to think about this place once we're gone, and this young Henry Taylor makes me think our labors won't have been in vain...." He could just imagine the old fossils' encomium of him. He couldn't help but smile at the old joke, "Suppose I were an academic, and suppose I were an ancient artifact. But I repeat myself."

What would be the sky for him at Illyria? *Dean* Henry Taylor? *Provost*? Even *President*? Of course he first needed to be elected Chairman of the Curriculum Committee. Above all, he had to distinguish himself from the Young Turks and identify himself as Young and Responsible. How might this be done?

He must think on this later. It was time for his comparative literature seminar. Henry was not overly fond of teaching. But today's topic was one he adored. It almost made him wish he'd done Italian instead of German for his doctorate.

***

(Later That Same Day in Comparative Literature 213)

"Today we take up Machiavelli, whom we'll compare to his approximate contemporary Montaigne in the sixteenth century. The latter was rich and retreated to his tower in early modern France. He was rich and could afford to, wasn't he? Machiavelli was also wealthy, but while Montaigne represents the skeptical side of the Renaissance, Machiavelli represents its ambitious side, its will to power. We'll focus on Machiavelli this week."

A hand went up, The young man with hair cut like a well-manicured lawn asked in earnest, "But isn't Machiavelli thought to have written a manual for gangsters, Professor Taylor?"

"No. Machiavelli is central. His insights might be useful for gangsters, yes, but they really travel everywhere, and lots of non-gangsters have depended on them, including many political leaders. It's said that politicians, kings and cardinals and dukes, in the Renaissance always condemned *The Prince* while secretly reading it for wisdom. You see, while I've said that Montaigne was a skeptic—and he was, for he even wondered if we were the same persons minute to minute—so was Machiavelli. Most of us are naïve enough to think there's only one morality system, of honesty and kindness. Machiavelli said there were two: one for our friends and family and another for our, say, work lives. Among close friends and relatives we can afford to be nice and tell the truth always. But in the political world—in any world where we can't count on others to help or trust us—we must change our ethics. If a city-state is depending on its leader for protection, then that leader *must* double-cross the leaders or rival city-states. It would be unethical not to."

Henry was sometimes astonished at how animated he became when discussing Machiavelli. In fact, if these students read Machiavelli's *Discourses on Livy* they would find a lot of contradiction with *The Prince*. But undergraduates never read the former, and Henry had no intention of assigning it. He wanted them to know that Machiavelli had been right in *The Prince* about such things as managing impressions and betraying others. This *was* ethical in its way.

It was even ethical in academic politics. As he surveyed the students in front of him, the irony-free youngster who'd asked the question and the girls in their petticoats out to the wall, he almost felt sorry about how naïve they were.

But then so were his fellow faculty members.

Henry was proud of how eloquent he was about Machiavelli. He so passionately believed it. Sometimes he thought his cynicism was so sincere, inwardly, that it was almost moral.

Chapter 8: The Political Perils of Loose Fixtures
(October 1, 1959)

Nothing was more boring to Winston than the monthly meeting of the academic staff, a group of which he was an ex officio member and to whom he had little if anything to say. But Dean Ronald Richards had insisted that he come, and so once monthly Winston sat around a table in decaying Bolt Hall where Ronald and his registrar's staff and the student advisor staff whiled away a couple of hours discussing the arcane topics of student records policies and new psychological techniques to bring aid and comfort to troubled students, especially the ones with wealthy parents. Only with regard to this latter topic did Winston sometimes pay attention. Money was on his mind these days, too much so, he thought. He'd always believed himself to transcend the soiled lucre. He was a gentleman, after all, and of joyous necessity a scholar.

He was also displeased with himself because he could not get Eve off his mind. It wasn't fair to Annie, and after all it had been his decision to break with Eve. Sometimes he was beside himself with how persistent were memories of her cleverness. One incident especially recurred, so often one would think it was the Nile revisiting the flood plain, not once a year but once a day. Winston would think of this analogy. He was, after all, not only a gentleman but also, once anyhow, a geographer.

It had all begun, three years before, when Harriet Smithson, one of Illyria's rare women faculty members, had taken the lead in opposing one of Winston's prize projects. He'd read an article about Buckminster Fuller's geodesic dome and simply decided, at once, that Illyria College must have one. Winston had to admit he'd fallen in love, not only with the odd blend of triangles and circles in the design but also with the publicity for Illyria he was sure would be in hottest pursuit. It hadn't been lost on Winston, Winston now confessed, while keeping one ear open to the discussion about raising fees for transcript release, that it would be he, Winston, who would get the credit. He fancied himself on the cover of a 1956 *Life*, with Illyria's dome in the background of course.

There could be worse things than being known as "The President from Geodesia College." Winston admired himself for the wit of the neologism.

"Don't you agree, Winston?" asked Dean Ronald Richards.

"Agree? Oh, certainly, I do. About raising the transcript fees two dollars, you mean?"

"Only one dollar, Winston. But I'm glad you concur."

Winston had announced his Fuller idea to the faculty, only to find the prim and conservative Harriett—the campus Spenserian—in immediate opposition. She rose in Faculty Senate:

"I don't see the relevance of this idea to our needs, Winston. Faculty salaries lag. Facilities become more rickety with every passing month. How would you finance such a scheme? Aren't you going in for science fiction in place of bricks and mortar and funds?"

Harriet always wore chained glasses around what Winston had come to regard, unkindly, as a gobbler's neck. When she put them on and peered over them, she reminded him somehow of General Patton looking through binoculars just before ordering a hundred tanks to commence firing in the Argonne Forest.

"Oh, now, Harriett! What was it Spenser said, 'reason not the need?' This is about vision, not about dollars and cents."

"It was Shakespeare—Lear actually—and Lear's visions hardly did him or ancient England any good."

"Point taken, Harriet. But perhaps Lear should have thought more about Geodesic Domes instead of his daughters. [Here Winston tried to chuckle, but there is nothing more solitary than he who chuckles alone.] At any rate, if we could raise the money to construct one, we could have Mr. Fuller here to dedicate it and lecture about it. It needn't be large. And it would be functional. It could be used for small classes. I say to you, my colleagues and friends, that the dome's design—the geodesics—of triangles and circles will have an almost mystical effect on the learning of Illyria students. You see, the shapes, the circled triangles or if you will the triangular circles, are a constant reminder that what seems hopelessly opposite might be creatively synthesizable. Think of how this insight, constantly being expressed visually, could enhance the study of every Illyrian discipline. To be in the dome is to be inspired to, to greater cognitive heights!"

Winston had been proud of this speech. Of course he had carefully rehearsed it. He still thought it his best rhetoric in the year 1956, barely exceeded since.

"And, Winston, do we have your permission to send Gloria Hawkins to this conference in Baltimore on new advising techniques? It's sponsored by Hopkins, you know."

Winston heard what the dean had asked him, but he accessed it late.

"Of course, Ronald. Whatever you think is fine."

Why did they bother him with such picayune matters? What was a new advising technique in 1959 to the magnificence of a Geodesic Dome, even a small one, in 1956? It had been his best idea yet. But then Harriet Smithson had to fight him.

"But Winston," she said on that drab November day, "you've been taken in by mystical mumbo-jumbo. Our students don't need to see triangular circles in order to grasp how opposites can be united. They have only to read my man, Spenser, and learn how the Red Cross Knight's rescue of the damsel Una was the perfect analogue to Queen Elizabeth's union of Protestant and Catholic. Not only that, Winston, but I'm already here, on the faculty, to teach our students this sort of thing. I won't cost you a penny extra. The same goes for all my colleagues, already here, and already teaching our students how to harmonize contrasts. Expensive circular triangles will be nothing but supererogatory."

Winston was still bitter about this speech. For one thing, she had likely not practiced it in advance, which made him wonder if her articulate skills were better than his. And her dry *Faerie Queen, Book I,* was but persiflage compared to his vision—well, it was really Fuller's vision—of triangular circles. And she'd used that word "supererogatory," which sent everyone after the meeting to the dictionary and made everyone think Harriett was brilliant.

He was off the back foot, Winston was. He felt that day like a Yale quarterback being rushed by every lineman on the earth. Ah, but then Eve—blessed, cursed Eve—came to his rescue.

Eve and Faye Roberts attended every Faculty Senate meeting. Faye was no longer on the faculty—she was in accounting now—but she always came and sat where her late husband Lewis had resided in sternest bliss. In fact, by tradition no one else sat in that chair, towards the back and on the left. It was the Roberts Seat, and Faye sat in it. She never tried to vote and never said anything. But she listened with precise care and coughed with exact timing, especially when someone said something arguably quite stupid. Winston noted two or three coughs during the Great Dome Debate (as later it was called), and none of them during Harriet's part of the discussion.

Eve also came to every Faculty Senate meeting. She sat wherever she wished. She too did not vote. She was not a member of the faculty.

But she did talk from time to time. And now, just as Harriett was finishing off her supererogatory remarks, she raised with delicacy a mauve gloved hand. Winston would never call on her by name—that wouldn't do—but he did acknowledge her right to speak. It was a right that several faculty members questioned, but never openly. If assistant professor Henry Taylor had profound affection for Machiavelli by temperament and scholarship, Eve's approach to the great Florentine was more basic, virtually physical. She did not need to read *The Prince* to know that fear was more potent than love. The joke on campus was that Eve was nursed not because her parents loved her but because they were terrified of her.

Yet Eve's secret was that while people feared her, it took a while before they realized it. Before that, they thought they liked her because of her charm, not because they had no choice.

"Professor Smithson—Harriet if I may—is surely right to say that amid visions we must also think of solid objects. Does that not include the solid object above my head [Eve stuck her gloved palm upward as though beseeching something above]—a light fixture about to become detached, *whereupon it will impale someone sitting beneath it in this very august meeting?*"

At this point Eve graciously left her seat to move to a safer one. Those on her right and on her left did the same, smiles of relief upon their learned visages.

Ah, Winston reflected, poor Harriet Smithson. All that erudition, and yet a woman headed for Spinsterville *will* marry beneath herself! And so Harriett had wed Jim Smithson, the college's maintenance director, who was responsible for that self-same precarious light fixture, dangling now like a dagger ready to strike.

Eve's move had been nothing short of brilliant, and Winston— even sometimes slow-to-reason Winston—had seen it immediately. Eve had changed the subject just when her husband was scrambling. She had sent a message to Jim Smithson about how well he wasn't doing his job, and an indirect ding at Harriet, his wife, as well. Being someone's—anyone's--wife was important to Harriett, and scattered Jim was not all that lucrative on the market of building administration should he lose his way at Illyria. Harriett said nothing more in opposition to Winston's sugar plum faeries of geodesics at Illyria. Other faculty members might have been tempted to join in protest once Harriett had changed the momentum. Now they stayed shut up.

Winston was free to pursue the dome. The Great Dome Debate had died in childbirth. Winston could chase what some faculty members called his "Bucky Full-Of-Himself" idea.

Winston, however, though free to follow up, found that no one wanted to follow *him*. Bucky Fuller never replied to Winston's letter. Donors found the idea eccentric. The faculty, though silenced by Eve—and Harriet Smithson refused to discuss the matter, even at the most discrete of dinner parties—had all the enthusiasm of the file cabinets that lined their offices.

Nonetheless, Winston persisted. He even hired an architect to discuss the idea with, but this particular designer, for whatever reason, told Winston that there could be no door as such in the dome. Anything that swung on a hinge would destroy the integrity of the whole. Winston finally settled for a trap door at the bottom, through which faculty and students could climb on their way into the dome for those inspiring classes about which Winston had been so eloquent.

Alas, this bit of dirt got out—Faye Roberts had, per ever, her sources. Many a jest went about campus on Winston's idea not of entering a classroom but *climbing up to it off the Vermont ice and snow.*

Eve said nothing to Winston about any of this. She had apparently decided to let him wallow in his own mini-disaster, unless of course it all went too far, in which event she would step in, which might well have meant stepping *on* Winston.

"Winston, do you have anything to add," asked Dean Richards.

"Nothing," said Winston. "Nothing whatever." The academic staff meeting was over, thank God, for another month. But Winston's gratitude was mixed with an odd longing for Eve. If only she hadn't steered him around so, thought Winston. But then it occurred to him that such was a venial sin only if he could steer himself.

The only detail that Winston had really absorbed from the academic staff meeting was that with the new Final Exam Period the doors would be staying open almost a whole extra week. Heating bills would go up.

It was the only practical information Winston had picked up on this otherwise cheery October day. All the rest had been reminiscence about Eve and the Great Dome Debate. He wondered if there were any link between higher heating bills, the money to pay them, and the tactical cleverness of his former wife.

Winston wanted so desperately to think there wasn't.

Chapter 9: The Ultimate Insignificance of Intent
(October 23, 1959)

Elise Morgan was a pale young woman—or girl, as Michael would call her—with stringy brown hair that drooped down an elongated face. Everything about her seemed vertical, and a little sad. He was not surprised to see her walk into his clutter of an office.

"Yes, Elise. Good to see you. I suspect you're here to discuss the paper."

"I am, Professor Moggs. I was disappointed with a C+."

"Well, it does seem to be lower than your general work, Elise. But wait! This can be a great teachable moment for us both!"

"I hope so, Professor Moggs. You see: I want to improve. The thing is, though, I'm not sure I *can* improve if I'm only going to be graded on small details."

"Small details? I must say, Elise, you're getting to the point rather quickly. By this time in a student-professor conference we should still be discussing the weather."

"The weather outside is stormy. Black clouds promise early snow."

"Ah. It is getting dark. Are you speaking literally or metaphorically?"

"Both, Professor Moggs."

"Ah, I see. But what, now, of these 'small details?'" Michael felt unease. Elise had not smiled. This was not entirely unusual. She was a serious girl. Yet when she did smile it was so rare that Old Sol, as the poets would insist on calling the sun, emerged from the most implacable vapors. Michael always thought Elise Morgan demonstrated the contrast principle in aesthetics better than anyone else he currently knew, just as he did when he removed his specs to manifest his young Greg Peck look. He thought of using the idea to write a new paper on Crane's "Bridge." This consoled him, as he knew he must plough ahead with this conference.

"I refer, Professor Moggs, to this 'serious misuse of the semicolon' business."

"Let's see. Oh, yes. Well, it is a serious misuse of the semicolon. 'Tennyson has his Ulysses speak not of the strivings of the young man but of the wit and pluck of the old one; where a man must battle not just enemies without but despair within.' Yes, Elise. You should have used a comma or (even better) a dash where you employed a semicolon."

"A comma, I think, would be too weak. A dash would be too sudden—the graded distinction I made doesn't call for such a dramatic shift. I believe the semicolon is appropriate there. In any event, Professor Moggs, surely it's a matter of opinion, not strict grammatical law. And how much did you deduct from my final grade with his semicolon business?"

"Uh, well, I'd say about ten points. I'm a stickler for grammar, I fear, Elise. Of course I don't agree with your analysis of the punctuation involved. But your C+ entailed more than just the semicolon error, if that's what it was." Michael didn't like that last concession. It had seemingly come unbidden. He wanted done with this Elise Morgan.

"Well, what else, then, Professor?"

"Well, there was your term for 'seek to strive and not to yield'— that passage. You called it alliteration, but really it's consonance. Those aren't vowel but consonant repetitions, you see."

"But, Professor Moggs, you must know that alliteration is the general term. I wasn't wrong to say 'alliteration.'"

"No, no, no. Not wrong—but imprecise."

"This seems a sort of overkill. I've always gotten A's in literature. If this were sociology I'd be less upset. I do want to improve—please believe that—and I like your course. You're a vital lecturer. But I feel you have graded me here on whim. How can I improve if it depends on anticipating your whims?"

Michael was unsettled. He felt like an engine with a corroded cylinder. He started to sputter. "These aren't whims, Elise. These are solid principles of grammar and usage." There! He'd said that clearly enough. Yet it seemed to come out in a sort of bad jazz riff. Michael liked good jazz. He thought it an important taste for a modernist to acquire.

"I must confess, Professor Moggs, with all due respect, to believing that you are a whimsical grader. Of course I've not seen it come out before. Perhaps this is a single, unique event."

Michael liked this remark even less. It was though she was giving *him* a pass—"we'll let it go this time."

"Well, Elise. I'm sure you intended well on both these points. But you see, I can't grade on intent. I must grade on outcome." Michael thought this remark would redress the balance and move the dial back to law-and-order, something juridical, where *he* would have the advantage.

"Do you like the milkshakes at Currie's Drug?"

What was *this*?

"I'm sorry, Elise. Are we done with the paper? I presume so, since I fail to see the link between the milkshakes and semicolons or consonance." Michael thought this comment had also been a nice enough pushback. But that was before he began to recall the girl looking for the Pepto-Bismol.

"Oh, I'm not sure there's no link, Professor. But do you like Currie's milkshakes?"

"Have I had one?" He felt himself gulping, as though he just *finished* one of Currie's milkshakes.

"You have. Back in August, I saw you there, in Burlington."

"Are you sure it was I, Elise?"

"Very, Professor. You weren't alone. You were having one of their divine milkshakes with Mamie Rogers. Isn't she lovely? A very sweet girl, too, I might add."

Michael suddenly realized why he had given Elise Morgan a C+. He wanted to teach her a lesson. She should realize that her fabulous intelligence would not always be rewarded. He now realized that she was precocious in sarcasm as well. Would *it* be rewarded?

"Oh, yes, yes. You're right. Mamie and I happened to run into each other there and decided to chat over a couple of malted milks."

"Milkshakes, actually. There's a difference. Don't forget errors of usage. And while I'm sure your intent was just to chat, Professor Moggs, as you just said about the paper, it's the outcome that counts. We can't grade on intentions. Well, I should tell you why I happened to be there. My father owns the antiques shop across the street—Boutique Antiques. It's very exclusive. I had indigestion and was looking for a remedy at Currie's. Did you and Mamie have indigestion after those rich milkshakes?"

"Oh, er, I don't know. It's not the sort of thing a professor and student discuss of course!"

"Of course not. I'm sure you were discussing Browning or perhaps Beatniks. Anyhow, you should stop in sometime to

Boutique Antiques. Perhaps the next time you and Mamie happen to find each other in Burlington. My father specializes in Ming Dynasty Vases and Vermont Spinning Wheels. I call it the high-class junk shop. Well, I should be going, I suppose. I don't think we've gotten far about this C+."

"Uh, yes, well, look, Elise. In future bring your essay into me in advance. I can go over it, and we can get any bugs out before you turn it for real."

"Very generous of you, Professor Moggs."

"Oh, well, now thank you, Elise."

"I'll be going. But, oh, one other thing, Professor: There are antiques in Burlington but also here in Illyria."

"You mean an antique shop. Here?"

"No, on campus. There are lots of old antiques, human ones, set in their ways. Sometimes they must have difficulty understanding the ways of young professors like you. Well, off I go to learn the difference between assonance and consonance. See you in class, Professor."

Michael sat back in his swivel chair, batting the air in fury and in the process colliding with his desk copy of Matthew Arnold's verse, which happened to be open at the time to the poem "The Scholar Gypsy," about a roving intellectual with no fixed abode. Michael picked it up. He was disconsolate. He looked at the poem. He took in its title.

Michael badly wished to believe it was just a coincidence. He and Winston, in their different ways, both resisted the very idea of unhappy coincidence, but neither knew much about the other, not yet.

Chapter 10: The Awful Evanescence of Striving

(October 23, 1959—Later in the Day)

"Do you mind if an ugly old hag joins you?"

Oh. My. God. It was Faye Roberts. He did mind, but of course he couldn't say anything. She was a campus institution. He would sooner be discourteous to The Illyrian, cut off one of its praying mantis limbs or torch its rocket ship on the pad.

"Oh, Faye! Why, of course not. I'd be delighted, I'm sure."

"I doubt that, Henry. But William, the Bill of Rights or Bill of Wrongs, usually joins me for 3 PM coffee. He's down in the back—when is he not? So I thought I'd latch on to you instead."

"Well, of course."

"So tell me about this comparative lit seminar. Since I'm as old as the walls around here, and since the walls have ears, I know you gave a passionate talk on Machiavelli a while back. I used to teach political theory around here you know—most have forgotten I have an M.A. in the stuff from Boston University to go with my Smith B.A. in English. I loved teaching old Mach. He offended the virtues of Illyria students. I like that."

"Oh, that's not my emphasis at all, Faye. I'm not trying to shock anyone. I just think Machiavelli is a realist, and realism is the way to go. We shouldn't get too caught up in our own wishes and pieties."

"Well, that sounds like a shocker to me! Speaking of realities, I trust you younger faculty know that Illyria's in the Valley of Despond."

"What do you mean?"

"I mean we've got what might politely be called a liquidity problem. The school's on fire; only a hose of money water can put it out; and the hydrant seems clogged."

"Oh, I've heard something like that, yes. I try not to pay it much mind. Nothing I can do; besides, it's not really my area."

"I know most people around here wish Old Faye would stop going on about it. And I've got to confess: I don't know whether I just love gossip or if I just love this old place (there: I've used the L word) so much I can't stop worrying about it. It's probably a bit of both."

"Again, Faye. My theory of realism tells me there's nothing I can do." Henry thought himself clever to bring matters back to his original thesis.

"Well, I'm not sure about that, but I don't want to pry."

"Pry? What does prying have to do with it?" Henry so wished she'd not found him. He looked around this cubbyhole of a snack bar—so small the joke was that you'd not call it a cubbyhole because that insults cubbies. He glanced at the little round tables and the pathetically miniscule order counter; he recalled the stupid insistence of the loudmouthed manager that all orders had to be written down with a pencil constantly broken. He saw no escape. He felt he was a tiny little man, the snack bar a vice, Faye the squeezer. He could have sworn she had biceps.

For just a moment Henry hated his life.

"Oh, my dear young Henry. I think prying has everything to do with it."

"It does?" Henry was desperate. "But why?"

"Because of who I think you are: young, ambitious, anxious to get along by going along; determined to be the FHBOTOF!"

"FHBOTOF?" She had pronounced it f-h-botof."

"Yes, the Fair Haired Boy of the Old Farts. It's a term my late friend Kiffin Stillwater and I concocted years ago. I miss Kiffin. He was a cynical Virginian, a classicist who sensed the dreary comedy of just about everything. I'll have to admit that F. H. Botof was really more his idea than mine."

"Should I feel insulted?"

"Not at all. It's a nasty job, but someone has to do it. *The Old Farts must be comforted!* They must feel that they aren't old and outmoded—yet—and so they glom on to some young faculty member all the time to assure themselves. I'd say, Henry, that you're performing a great public service—except of course that Illyria is a private school."

Very funny—not—Henry thought. "But, well, I do like some of the older faculty—it's true. Sometimes I just don't feel as comfortable with those my own generation. I think they like rebellion for its own sake and novelty for its own sake. They're like teenagers, some of them. These older faculty members— they've been around here for a while, they know what they're doing; they have some wisdom. Well, in my opinion they do anyhow."

"Oh, of course. There's a lot in what you say. But that takes us back to your realism."

"How?" Henry thought this talk was a sort of doped-up merry-go-round. Perhaps this homely old hag, as she correctly called herself, was just torturing him. She had a rep for being carbolic acid with nary a drop of water added.

"Because you're planning, you're flattering, you're bonding—all because you think moving up the ladder is important. And it is important, in a way, but you've got to see how ridiculous it is, too. You've got to be serious, Henry, my friend, but not too serious. You've got to see yourself as this striving, absurd fellow. That's realism for you."

"It is? How's that realistic?"

"Because otherwise you'll come a cropper. You're not the first clever young man who's strode the hallowed halls of dear Illyria C. I've seen plenty of them. And it never works out. They always fail to see something coming, or their allies turn on them, or they end up becoming Old Farts themselves, looking for consolation as their hair thins along with their enrollments. There's only one exception I can think of."

"Who?" Henry asked this hopefully. Maybe Faye was about to offer him a role model.

"Winston Adams. He was the Henry Taylor of his day."

"But Winston Adams has done very well." Suddenly Henry felt as though ancient Faye had thrown an unbidden encomium his way.

"Has he? Now he's got an ex-wife he wishes he still had, a new wife he's losing faith in, and so many fiscal troubles he might as well be trying to shave a rock—a big one, like his own pretty face—with a razor blade. And there's another reason for realism, Henry."

"What is?"

"Just remember. In five years you might not be be scheming about Illyria because there might not be an Illyria to scheme about. You can't have two hundred grand in your pocket if you don't have a pocket."

At this point Henry finished his coffee with a gulp and left the table. He said goodbye. He was also borderline rude. He thought Faye's last statement was stupid and dismissible: If you don't have a pocket for your two hundred thousand dollars—Henry wouldn't be so vulgar as to say "two hundred grand"—you could just put it in a bank.

Still, he was a bit short with her. Henry hoped she didn't have any powerful allies among the older professors.

Chapter 11: The Ghastly Dread of a Dean's Terminology
(November 16, 1959)

"Hello, Ronald. Sit down. Coffee? I can have Eloise get you some. Sugar? You wanted to see me."

Actually Dean Richards, however normally afflicted with incisors that craved sweets, didn't want any coffee or sugar at all. He declined. But Winston sensed that it might be in his interest to put off the discussion as long as he could.

"How's Donna, Ronald? Still doing her research on campaign theme songs?" Donna Richards was known in two counties for collecting campaign theme songs, especially sheet music, and then singing them at local women's clubs. Of late she'd made a rare find for New England: a pamphlet with the words to "James G. Blaine: Liar, Liar from the State of Maine." Donna had no idea what the tune was and so set it to "My Darling Clementine." It was a clumsy rendering, and Donna sang through her nose: not a contralto, as Faye Roberts said, but a nosaltro. Yet the discovery itself had put Donna Richards on a map, albeit a very small one.

"Oh, yes, Winston. Of course! At the moment she's searching for an original recording of 'Happy Days Are Here Again.' Did you know that the words of that song as used by Roosevelt's campaign included 'Let's give a cheer for three-two beer'?"

"I did not, Ronald. Of course FDR didn't carry Vermont, as you know." Winston was divided. He thought this palaver tedious, yet it pleased him. It delayed whatever Richards wanted to talk about. Winston was on edge these days. Ronald was a plump, lethargic man, who could deliver the worst sort of news out of breath, but it wasn't that he was panicky about it. He was just fat. Sometimes Winston missed his old dean, the one he knew they called Prune Face. Well, he might have been a crooked character out of Dick Tracy, Prune Face was, but he served Winston well and moved upward and onward—far better than the well-padded Ronald, who had come from Psychology, though some thought he had actually come from the kitchen and cared more for canapés than he did for Chapel, which was required and over which he presided three days a week.

"I do know that, Winston, though I have to confess for having voted for the old socialist in '36. Oh, well. Anyhow, Winston, I'll arrive at last at my point. We have a retention problem."

"A what?" One of the most annoying things about Ronald was that he went off to the dean's conferences, especially the ones held in cities with fine eateries, and came back not only five pounds heavier of flesh but ten pounds heavier with the latest argot.

"A retention problem, Winston, and I fear it's a serious one."

"Are you referring to that little saline problem we had with the campus water a while back?"

"What? Oh, no, nothing to do with the water."

Winston wanted to believe that Ronald had stuffed himself so that he had driven his gut to the runs. A retention problem! But Winston knew the problem wasn't Ronald's personally, and even he, Winston, was appalled at how lame his secret humor had been. Quite precipitously, he began to regard existence as a thing to be despised.

"What then, Ronald? What?"

"The registrar has just given me the number of students signing up for Spring Term. I can't believe it. We're down a little over 75 students. If we had 1500 students all told, this wouldn't be a problem. But we now have fewer than 800. This is almost a ten percent drop—an alarming diminution in revenue going forward."

Winston didn't know why Ronald insisted on such pompous language. Perhaps it was to pad the impact. Ronald was good at padding. Winston was bitter.

"But how would we deal with this? And why has this happened, Ronald?"

"I'll answer the second if I can, Winston. But I'm just guessing. The scuttlebutt is that it's the new final exam policy."

"Good grief! Why?"

"Well, not to put too fine a point on it, Winston, but we've had to compromise about our admissions standards—not that we just take warm bodies. And, well, it seems that we've got a critical mass of students who don't like required finals and just want to go home early for Christmas or summer parties. Illyria isn't the school for them—not any more, they think—and so they're transferring or, more likely, just taking next term off before they do transfer."

"But I paid scant attention to this whole final exam debate, this whole imbroglio." Winston quickly thought that anything he didn't attend to in life shouldn't matter. He saw at once the illogic of this thought. For some odd reason he wondered if James G. Blaine had ever been tempted by the same idea.

"Yes, Winston. I myself stayed quite neutral in the whole affair. The older faculty wanted more order. I didn't see it as having any real impact."

"But what do we do?"

"Ah, that's a toughie. I suppose we cancel classes and lay off faculty, but that will be difficult, as even the non-tenured have one-year contracts. We can probably cancel some contracts, but then we cancel courses, and the word gets out that we're doing so, and the more the outside world thinks we're reeling, the fewer parents will send students here. It snowballs."

Winston looked outside: no snow yet, but only a fool would deny that it was coming, sooner not later. Every person he saw walking wore a heavy coat. Knit caps abounded. The air seemed to be waiting for ice as a Boston junkie yearned for dope. Winston was astonished at the louche fancy of this comparison. What was happening to him?

What was happening to everything?

"And then—I must put this gingerly, Winston—this couldn't have come at a worse time in terms of the entire context." "The entire context": more dean argot, Winston thought with a burgeoning inner typhoon. He swore one day he would call Richards "Dean Jargon" to his chunky face. He would address the unflattering sobriquet to all three chins. But then suddenly Winston was brought up short. He had never had such catty thoughts before and had always fancied himself not a naughty housecat but a leonine, dignified Great Dane. Winston wondered once again about a certain slippage in his life.

"You mean the overall financial picture?"

"I do, Winston. I've not been made privy to the books, as you know. You and the Finance Committee keep that bottled up. Even the treasurer doesn't know, or so Jack tells me: that even he doesn't know. But I've heard things."

"Ronald, pay no mind to what you hear. If rumors were popcorn we'd be at the movies all the time." Winston thought this clever, as though he still had some wit, and if he had that, somehow all would be well. It wasn't just any wit. It was Winston's Wit after all.

"All right, Winston. That's all I have. Oh, one other thing: I asked about giving these students a special tuition arrangement to hold them but was told that most of them are rich and need no deal and that we'd have to give it to everybody. So that won't work."

"Yes, all right, Ronald. I see. I'll be in touch with you. I need to find out more. Thank you for telling me."

Ronald waddled out, but not before asking Eloise McCrory for a large coffee, sugar *and* cream.

Winston issued immediate instructions to Louise.

A few moments later, she appeared at his door: "Your call to Mr. Burdette in Connecticut has gone through. He's waiting on line 2."

"Charles! How are you?"

"Winston, it's good to hear from you. I've been thinking about giving you a ring."

"Ah, well, it's good I called *you* then."

"Yes, I was thinking about you the other day when I read an article by a prominent theologian on the subject, can God be taught? He said not; it was all a matter of faith. I disagree. You know I've always been a man for the liberal arts. Learning enhances anything, even belief in God. So I think God can be taught. And so I said to myself, 'I'll call Winston, offer a donation to require studies in God for every Illyria student, and prove the theologian wrong.'"

"Studies…in God?"

"Yes, why not?"

"Well, Charles, I think we could make that happen." Winston couldn't believe he'd said what he just said. He wondered if Charles Burdette could donate enough to a dictionary-publisher in order to banish "retention" from the English language.

"Wonderful, Winston. Just wonderful! There's only one catch."

"What? But what?"

"I'm just *kidding*. You see, I'm worth a mint, maybe two. But I've not got much more money for dear old Illyria. I wish I *could* make it happen, though."

"Oh, I see, Charles." Winston imagined himself hovering five thousand feet over The Illyrian, headed straight for a moon daisy (or maybe narcissus), finding his parachute failing to open, praying to God and then learning that He was no longer studied at Illyria College and becoming quite sore about it.

"But that's not my only trouble, Winston. In fact, my lack of further funds for Illyria is only a small part of my difficulty."

"What else?"

"Oh, just about everything. You know how widely I read now that I'm retired. There's this fellow Brown who writes about something corrupt called 'polymorphous perversity' and this author, Mailer, who writes of these sinister unshaven types he calls 'hipsters.' *Look* Magazine published a poll confirming that a majority of Americans thinks that anything goes as long as the neighbors approve of it. I don't like this Castro who's taking over Cuba. He seems to be one of Mailer's hipsters. And it's clear we're losing to Russia in outer space. I worry about the decline of this great land, Winston. You should as well. We're the last moral redoubt on earth, and if we go down, well, then...."

"Oh, I quite agree, Charles."

"Good. But look, Winston, you didn't call me to hear me carry on about God and Castro. What's on your mind? But oh, wait a minute, Winston. I do want to insist on one thing."

"Which is, Charles?"

"That of next academic year's ten Great Events and After Meetings at the Burdette Center, we devote at least eight to the question, 'Is America In Moral Decline?' All right? Do I have your word?"

Winston blanched. "Oh, that sounds good, Charles." But Winston did have the fortitude to add, "Of course we'll have to discuss the details, in which God resides." Winston thought Charles would like both the humor and reference to the deity, for Mr. Burdette thought of himself as witty and godly in equal measure.

"Good, good, good, Winston. Now what did you wish to speak to *me* about? I trust you aren't thinking of taking a third wife. I'd be disappointed sorely. You know my views on that. You should have stuck with the first one. She's worth more than rubies and gold combined."

Winston wished Eve *had* been worth more than rubies and gold combined. If she were, at this leaden fork in Illyria's path, he'd re-wed her at once.

"Oh, I just wanted to check in, Charles. Nothing in particular other than that...."

"It isn't every day that someone calls just to check up on dear old Charles, Winston. I can't say I'm ungrateful, or at least I shouldn't say it."

"Wonderful, Charles. It's been a swell chat." Winston wondered if this sort of undergraduate bonhomie still worked with Illyria's greatest donor in history, who was himself a freshman once at old Illyria. It was hard to think of Burdette as a freshman, though, Winston thought. Of course, in 1890 New England there was such a thing as morally earnest pubescence. It was all the rage back then.

After a few more idle words, which Winston later compared to idle tears (his), they hung up.

Winston moved to his couch. He shut his eyes. He reclined. He breathed with the approximate difficulty, or so it appeared, of Dean Richards trying to sprint between The Illyrian and Bolt Hall. Presently he sat up.

"Eloise! I need you to get someone else on the line for me...now! Absolutely confidential!"

Chapter 12: The Accursed Spittle of Everything
(November 19, 1959)

"And this long wake of phosphor,

iridescent

Furrow of all our travel—trailed derision!

Eyes crumble at its kiss. Its long-drawn spell

Incites a yell. Slid on that backward vision

The mind is churned to spittle, whispering hell."

Michael had just quoted a central passage from Hart Crane's *Bridge*. It was his favorite poem of all. He read the passage, but he could have quoted it by heart, and when Michael used the word *heart* about Crane, Michael meant it. About Crane, Michael was all in. One of his graduate professors at Indiana had once told him, "Michael, you are lifted by a Crane from the muck on up." It was a small pun, and not an altogether nice one, but Michael appreciated the attention.

"Now you have all read this passage in preparation for today's class, and your first response was to say that it is obscure. This is always an issue with Hart Crane: he appears to be opaque, and even more educated readers than you have been tempted to give up on it. 'If I can't get the sense,' they say, 'what's the point?' I'm here in English 295 today to say that there is a point because you can get the sense. But you'll only get it if you surrender. Yes, Elise?"

"Surrender what, Dr. Moggs?" Her pale face was super sensate with impish inquisition.

"Surrender your love of ordinary logic and language, Elise. You see, Crane's logic is *felt*. You must feel what he is saying. Then the logic will follow. OK, Elise?"

"But isn't feeling the opposite of logic?"

"Well, yes, in ordinary terms it is. But, Elise, please, and you others, stay with me. Take this passage, the one I just read. What's its mood? The answer: despair; self-destruction; being rendered small and insignificant. But what is the image? Answer: Phosphor; iridescence; the sort of wonder that 'incites a yell' — of what, of excitement, astonishment, or pain? What? You see, here Crane gives us this contradiction. The iridescent phosphorus should make us yell with joy or thrills, yet it's associated with this terrible reduction in the human spirit, where we once joyful humans are being reduced to 'spittle.' So you get this strange mixture of amazement and humiliation, a yelp at once of ecstasy and misery. Yes, Elise."

"So ecstasy and misery are the logic, then? Is that what you're saying?"

"Yes, Elise, and the rest of you: Elise has said it well. *'Ecstasy and misery are the logic of the passage.'* But you see, you have to feel your way into it. You have to surrender your head and give way to your heart. That's what makes Crane's verse so challenging and difficult, and yet so thrilling."

He thought he had parried Elise's queries well. He sensed enmity, not curiosity. He wondered what would happen if he tripped up. Would there only be a little scar on the brickwork of his intellect? Or would the whole tower fall into a heap? He had some time ago concluded, bitterly, that if he himself were to write a poem about Elise it would be called "The Paleface Who Saw the Milkshakes." He wondered what Hart Crane, who'd slept with sailors, would make of a title like that. He had no intention of ever telling Illyrian students about Hart Crane's maritime endeavors.

But of course this same Elise didn't wait to raise her hand. She said, "But Dr. Moggs, if misery and ecstasy are just the same, then words don't mean anything. Isn't that like saying that black and white, pain and pleasure, A+ and C+ are just the same? Can human beings live in a world like that? We couldn't even talk to one another. Don't get me wrong. I think what you say about Mr.

Crane is interesting, but it's of no practical use after all the trouble one goes to in order to grasp it."

Michael felt the tiny origins of an inner keening, one that would need strictest regulation, at least until class was done.

The A+/C+ reference was not lost on him. But instead of cowering he became peevish. Hart Crane meant all to him, even more than Mamie and milkshakes did.

"I disagree, Elise. Paradox is a key poetic practice, and it's good for us practically because it forces us to think about the usual things in a new way. If I say, 'God has wet dreams,' (that's in a new poem coming out in the *Iamb*) then I'm not literally saying that God has nocturnal emissions, but I am suggesting that God is a human invention in a way. And it's good for us to hypothesize about such things. The more fresh thinking we bring to the so-called 'real world' the better off we are."

The bell rang.

Michael thought his last answer was packed with humanistic fortitude. Why did he also feel it reeked of sheer impotence?

As she filed out, Elise stopped briefly by Michael's lectern. "I have a love-hate relationship with Crane's poetry, I guess. It's ingenious, but I don't want to live in a world where God has wet dreams because it's pretty obvious that someone who does isn't God, and the whole meaning of the word is lost."

"But wait, Elise! The thing about God's having wet dreams doesn't come from Crane."

"Oh!" said Elise and kept walking out, as though the only distinction that mattered was the difference between this class and the next, which happened to be Henry Taylor's seminar on Schiller.

Chapter 13: The Determined Non-Contingency of Going On To the End of the Term

December 6, 1959

"Unacceptable. Absolutely, utterly, totally unacceptable: it will mean a mess beyond human understanding, not to mention human control. This I shall not have. You shall not have it. *We* shall not have it!"

Lester Cole's buzz cut seemed shorter than ever, and yet Henry might have sworn he saw broadswords emerging from every semi-invisible follicle. Lester seemed to speaking to the Curriculum Committee as though he were an eight-star general dressing down the junior officers.

"Now, be calm, Les. We've not arrived at chaos yet. I'm just reporting what I've picked up from what I think is a good source."

"I'm not doubting your source, Harry, but I am doubting the contents. May I speak plainly? I believe this is another one of Winston's devious moves."

When Lester asked if he could speak plainly, Henry thought he had left his generalship for an appointment to become a fussy, and rather unoriginal, academic, as though the war had been over for too long and now Professor Cole was just another hysterical intellectual. The broadswords had vanished. Dull gray hair stubs had replaced them. The glory thinned along with General Cole's hair.

"Oh, I don't know that it has anything to do with Winston," rejoined Harry. "Besides, Winston's not all that devious. If he were more cunning, you and I and young Henry here might be making more money."

"Point taken, Harry."

The scuttlebutt was that Illyria was losing students at an alarming rate and that the new Final Exam Period was to blame.

"What I don't like about your report, Harry, and this is no disrespect to you, is its underlying assumption," said Horace Fuller of Classics, a.k.a. Hortatory Horace to three generations of irreverent Illyria students who'd regrettably chosen Latin as one of their required general courses. "The idea seems to be this: These punctilious Illyria faculty thought they could raise standards, little realizing, little being in touch with the fact, little comprehending, that Illyria students are now too shoddy, too irresponsible, too ill-prepared, to accept strict, logical, and demanding rigor." Henry thought Horace could have said it with at least twenty fewer words, but he wasn't called HH for nothing.

"You mean, Horace," asked Lester, "that we should known that Illyria had gotten too sloppy for three hour-finals?"

"Yes, Lester: precisely, exactly, undeviatingly, that is what I mean, what I meant, and what I say even now." Only ten words over this time, thought Henry, who was becoming disgusted and not a little fearful. What sort of group was this that he had been so eager to join once, and what had it wrought? What would happen to *him*? Would Faye Roberts be standing over his political grave and rasping that she had told him so—or, as HH might put it, that she had told, uttered, proclaimed, and declared it to be true?

"Well," said Lester, "I say we cannot possibly back down now. Harry, you're right to this extent: Winston has not *asked* us to back off the Final Exam Period. The plans and schedule have been published. Illyrian students will have to take finals, and some of them will have to spend three hours doing so, and some will have to stay nearly a week longer in order to finish them all. For Illyria College, at this moment in its century and a half of history, to cancel the final exam schedule in a reckless attempt to keep its students from leaving, would be to open us to every form of academic opprobrium, and I should not even exempt us from exposure by prominent New England newspapers."

"Henry," continued Lester, "we've heard that the younger faculty, your cohort in a way, have been running covert interference against these final exams. Can't you speak to them, slow them down, chastise them, or something? What can you do for our cause?"

Henry hated this question. He despised having to discern the wind's direction without benefit of pinky wetting. Bright and calculating young men such as he should not have to gamble. On the other hand, hadn't Machiavelli himself said that Fortuna, Lady Luck, is fickle and unreadable?

"Oh, yes, Lester, of course I'll do what I can. I quite agree that we can't back down now."

"Right you are, young man," contributed Harry Finch. "But in the larger sense this is all really down to Winston. Why is the loss of fifty or more students such a blow? It's because Winston has not raised enough money so that we have better facilities, a better admissions office, and more scholarships. But tell us more precisely, Henry, what *will* you do for us in the short run?"

"Well, sir, I sort of think at this point we must, at a minimum, make sure the Final Exam Period works well, by which I mean that it goes off as planned and every professor participates as ordered, I mean required. So I shall do what I can to make that happen."

"But what?"

"Well, I shall pass the word to everyone: 'We must make this work well. We've passed it and now must be men of our word.' I'll stress of course that this is only an experiment and that we will be visiting it again later. I'll emphasize that it is not irrevocable, but that there is no alternative to rendering it functional this month."

Henry thought it was an anodyne enough answer. He had no intentions of doing any of these things unless he could find out which side he needed to join. He knew that passions at this stage would do him no good, unless they belonged to others.

Henry's response seemed to be enough to please the martial drama queen Lester, the pusillanimous and proudly skeptical Harry, and the volubly pompous Horace. Henry thought that his declaration was spirited and yet said very little. Henry was happy with himself. The meeting soon adjourned, though not without a minor matter, the appeal of a mid-term grade by a student in Theater, which was immediately decided in favor of the student and against the professor, a hemming and hawing twerp that no one much liked. No committee member said anything, but this was not the time to be losing yet another paying customer.

Snow had fallen, but a warm front was melting it away, leaving in its wake a premature riff on March Mud Time. The cold slush, Henry thought, exuded a sort of human misery as he made his way to his office in Calaboose Hall, the last building Illyria had been able to afford on its own, without the indispensable ministrations of Charles Burdette. It had gone up just before the Depression, when the country seemed awash in cash. Even so, it was but a wooden structure, looking more like a miniature mansion than handsome hall. It suffered from what Faye Roberts called "premature creakery." Perhaps it was what the humanities at Illyria deserved, or maybe it was a welcome sign that the pursuit of languages and literature could rise above the lure of imposing facades.

He veered through a maze of corners and turns to reach his office, there to write a letter of recommendation for one of his best among recent students, who had decided to study the quasi-forgotten Stefan Zweig at the University of Connecticut. Henry was still perplexed over what he should do about his future: become linked with a group to be blamed for losing students or sticking with the hitherto dominant senior faculty. He looked downward as though a careful perusal of the linoleum would guide him, its various squares some key to the hieroglyphics of current Illyrian politics. He measured each step rapidly. His purview narrowed. He glared at the problem in the abstract. He did not look ahead. What was the incidental external world compared to the vagaries of his own prospects? He stumbled over a wastebasket, knocking it off its bottom and wincing in pain as he stumbled along with it.

But he did not fall. He cursed mutely, bent to gather the mélange of spilled papers and milk cartons—wasn't drinking milk in the building against the rules—and found a piece of paper headed *EXAM*.

Henry knew at once: It was a sign. Now he knew what to do. But he would wait for the maximally opportune time to strike. Besides, it would do no harm to mull the matter over. If mulling were heat, he could wait until his new discovery was thoroughly well done.

Chapter 14: The Glorious Opportunities of Beckoning Former Spouses
(December 7, 1959)

A phone rang in Philadelphia. Someone picked up and said hello.

"Eve? Eve! Where have you been?"

"Winston, it must be you. May I say that I'm shocked, as the man said in *Casablanca*, to be hearing from you, of all people?"

"But where on earth have you been?"

"I've been in Florence for over a month. I should have stayed. It's wintering rapidly here in Philadelphia, but I couldn't afford Italy any longer. Your settlement, Daddy's money, and the little stipend sent by your current wife's late father only go so far...not that I'm uncomfortable."

"Oh, my goodness. I had become worried about you. I've had my secretary calling you every day."

"Really? Well, I continue to be amazed, Winston. First, I don't know why your secretary—is she still luscious Ella McCrory-- should be instructed to call *me*. Are you thinking that we'll bond over nail polish? Second, I have no idea why you of all people would fret over *me*."

When Winston heard this reply he knew at once why he had loved Eve (liveliness). He knew at once why he had hated her (putdowns).

"Oh, uh, well, Eve. I do hope we can let bygones be, well, whatever bygones are." (Winston prided himself on his resistance to hackneyed phrases; he thought it one of his cleverest attributes.) "It's that every now and then I do become slightly panicky about you, living on Chestnut Street by yourself all year."

"I don't see why, Winston. It's a very safe neighborhood. No ruffians will dare invade a bastion of American history. For one thing, they'd be too bored. They want to get away from what made them sleep in class on their way to become high school dropouts and burglars. Now, Winston, why don't you get to the point?"

"The point? Ah, yes, well, the point. The point is that I am asking a favor of you, Eve."

"Winston! Surely you don't want me to send baking soda for your grapefruit-juice soused eyes after all this time. We've been split after all for nearly five years."

"Ha, ha: very funny, Eve. No, I don't want you to do that. I deserved that little splash of acid. After all, I'd not been candid with you about my feelings for Annie."

"Candid? Do you mean honest, Winston? The utility of 'candid' tells me that you've not lost your gift for euphemistic pomposity."

Winston thought perhaps he'd never loved Eve after all. Perchance he'd only despised her, and it was precisely his gift for "euphemistic pomposity" alone that had convinced him that he loved her. This musing was like a little stone in Winston's tea, which he decided at once to drink around.

"All right, Eve. You win. But really, I'm now at your humble service. I so desperately need your help. I'll not blame you for declining. But I feel I must ask."

"Is this when I'm supposed, cattily, to say that you should ask little Annie for assistance instead?"

"Oh, that. Well, Annie is of course doing her part, you understand. But we all of us have divers talents, and this particular favor falls within the ambit of your perfected devices."

"My God, Winston, You've been president of Illyria for so long that you're starting to talk like that old classics teacher. What was his name?"

"You mean Horace?"

"Yes, Horace: Hortatory Horace. Shall we all soon be discussing Windy Winston?"

"Really, Eve. You *are* a caution. May I at least mention the favor?"

"What else have I to do other than unpack? Don't answer that Winston. If you do, I'll hang up."

"Oh, no, no. I won't answer it" (Winston was so nervous he had lost even his very finite ability to take a joke.) "I want you, in a word, to have a word with Charles Burdette."

"Charles? But what would I have to say to that old Biblical Buzzard?"

Winston thought the whole point was being lost in witty alliterations. But he persevered.

"Eve, the truth is that Illyria's in trouble. May I speak frankly?"

"Don't you mean honestly, Winston?"

"Yes, honestly. We're fast running out of endowment, both of the disposable and non-disposable kind. We're having a seventy-five student short fall next term. I can envision one, and one only, way out: to rent out Charles's building for conventions. In fact, I think the best solution, in theory of course, is to sell the building to a large organization that books meetings. It could raise a fortune for Illyria and save the great institution that we've all worked for so long."

"The great institution we've all worked for....really, Winston, you're not at the podium, and I'm not a member of an audience. You don't need to *declaim*."

"Right. Sorry, Eve. Well, anyhow, I have no real influence with Charles. But he's always had a soft spot for you. I don't think his attitude towards me or Illyria has quite been the same ever since we, ah, separated. Sometimes I think he's just having me on. For example, he thinks of calling me to complain about the decline of the West, mostly, I believe, just to irritate me with the sound of his voice. You know I think he's a dear man. None of us is likely to forget what he's done for Illyria. The Burdette Building—the Burdette Auditorium, I should say--is one of our jewels and our sole recent one. But now we need to think of it as more than a diamond or a ruby. We must think of it as an asset. The problem is: Charles himself may not wish to think of it that way. This is where you could be doing a favor, Eve: not a favor to me but a favor to old Illyria. Could you try to convince Charles?"

"But Winston, a favor to old Illyria, as you call it, can hardly be separated from a favor for *you*!"

"Oh, if you wish to say so, Eve." Winston was unsure whether Eve's words were a compliment or an insult.

"Well, I'm glad you agree, Winston, and hence it must follow as the night the day, as old Polonius might put it, that I must consider whether or not to do a favor for *you*. I'm rather inclined to say that I should not. And—don't interrupt, Winston—there are fairly obvious reasons why. You left me for another woman, younger, and a former student. You created a scandal that would have been much greater had I not left with a statement that the separation was cordial and unbridgeable. You couldn't stand that I was cleverer than you, quicker than you, and that I was also more feared than you. In short, Winston, behind that august stone visage of yours—was that you or David I saw in Florence at the

Academy—there lurks a mouse, and you were more comfy marrying another mouse. Mickey and Minnie have nothing on Winnie and Annie. And before you say 'ouch,' Winston, let me say that nevertheless I shall think about your request. It's true that Charles has always had a weakness for me. I think he likes my frankness, and once he liked my legs. And I don't want Illyria to collapse. In fact, Winston, it's because I think you and Illyria College are *not* the same that I'm at least willing to consider your petition."

She put down the phone.

Winston veered between gratitude and fury, thankfulness and chagrin, until he gulped out that he certainly appreciated it, by which time the connection had vanished. He should have raised more money. Then he wouldn't be in this fix, having to go hat in hand to an ex-wife who blended equal parts of Mussolini and Vlad the Impaler. Now he had to wonder what she would do, and admit, privately, that no amount of bluster could conceal his supine position. He was an ex-rock, now reduced to sand, and (to mix metaphors) the winds of fiduciary ruin could blow his house down, and himself, to the earth's round corners. He was dependent upon the grudging forgiveness of an ex-wife once known for her capacity to scatter a regiment by her mere appearance.

Why couldn't donors have just given money to Illyria, Winston asked, based on his own impressive if silent demeanor? The comparisons with Michelangelo's David were, Eve's sarcasm notwithstanding, not so far-fetched after all. And people paid good money to see David.

Why couldn't rich men have paid good money—to Illyria of course (Winston was not personally greedy)—just to see Winston?

Chapter 15: The Regrettable Unavoidability of Strategic Distance

(December 9, 1959)

Michael liked the Burlington Free Library. He always had. It was snug with books, punctuated by sleepy leather chairs, circumscribed by oaken doors. Here, it seemed to say, knowledge has nothing to do with anything unpleasant. It was as though all the wars, the blood, the rapine, the refugees, the failed experiments, the heartache, and the balance (or imbalance) of human perfidy, through which knowledge had been hard gained, was distilled into tranquil volumes, silent as the tomb until opened, at which point emerged an order, in prudent grandeur, that belied the human misery from which it had come. It was as though every human disappointment and loss had occurred only so that they might be written of in books.

Michael knew that this transformation of human unhappiness into the purity of hard binders was an illusion, but it was one he needed about now, for he was not seated across from the ancient history shelves but from the perilously contemporary and labile Mamie Rogers, his semi- or quasi-inamorata, his forbidden fruit that, while as yet not tasted, was still against the rules, even to look at or contemplate. In truth, Elise Morgan had unnerved Michael. Her voyeurism at the drug store, even if accidental, and her protestations about the poetic illogic of saintly Hart Crane, had taken Michael off his game. He had become tetchy. Just yesterday he had exploded in a class when another student, a frat boy, had asked, after Michael had dissected the poetics of Arnold's "Buried Life," if the analysis would be on the final exam. The inane indecorum of the question was out of line, but Michael's shouting imprecations at a defective brain, at a sensate warm body whose tuition was vitally needed, was equally misplaced.

Michael knew he had to act, and act soon. Mamie's pretty but overly rounded face, her healthy but slightly bulging calves, had made him wonder what he had been thinking. She was a dear, and an industrious and faithful one, for whom any sort of treachery was not in her moralistic lexicon. Yet Elise had seen the two of them. She was an obviously brilliant girl, uncanny in what she might do or say. Michael could have handled, perhaps, an overt blackmail, but Elise's very studied ambiguity forced him to think he was dealing with something for which he was unprepared. Who knew that Illyria College, sunk in the foothills of the Green Mountains, long known for its melding of learning and rectitude, of forest and attainment, might spew forth, after a century and a half, a female sociopath in possession of verbal stilettos?

Michael decided to afford no chances.

But Curry's Drug for a rendezvous was deemed too dangerous; Elise might be lurking about. Meanwhile, his conversation with Mamie had progressed far enough that her alarm was about to go off. He could hear it already.

"It's not that we won't see each other again, Mamie. It's just that I think we should maintain greater distance for a while, you see. I'm thinking that it would help us, uh, clarify our feelings."

"This has come out of the blue, Michael. I know I've barely left New England, but I wasn't born just last week. What's really going on?"

"Why must something be going on? You know, Mamie, that I've long advocated that in the intellectual life, a '*mental* event' is the important thing. Nothing has 'happened,' other than a turn in my own ruminations."

"Yes, Michael, but what has caused this turn? You see, I know something or other has happened. People don't just live in their heads, not even you."

"Well, you really want to know my logic. That's what you're asking. And here it is then. I wonder if you're not too young to be so serious about someone several years older; if you shouldn't, well, not date anyone else, but just take some time away from me to see how you feel about me. Think of this as a sort of test."

"You mean examination? Ah, ha: perhaps you've been inspired by the new Final Examination Period."

Michael thought this play on "examination" would have been beyond Mamie. It was the sort of wickedness he'd have associated with Elise. He was momentarily perplexed.

"That's witty, Mamie. I like that. But no: nothing to do with the new exam period. I mean this in the Socratic sense: the unexamined life is not worth living for man, including woman of course. I think you just need time to think, to make sure. That's why I'd like this distance—perhaps a sort of tactical distance— nothing strategic."

But Michael knew it was strategic. He had decided he shouldn't lay intimate eyes on Mamie Rogers again until she had graduated in two years, and probably not then because forty-eight months later their feelings would have become modified beyond prior recognizance. He no longer believed in unending love. He believed in professional survival.

"Michael, you know I respect your ideas about the intellectual life. But I know something outside your head has happened. Is it a new girl? Am I too young for you, too dull, too…whatever? I'd rather know than wonder."

Michael was quite sure that Mamie would be better off wondering. He remembered Keats: "to *know* is to sorrow." But of course Keats was thinking about TB. Michael didn't have TB. Neither did Mamie, as far as he knew. She didn't look as though she had TB. She seemed in eminently good health.

"Well, Mamie. I don't *want* you to wonder. I want you to *know*. I want you to *know* that I'm just musing about our need for distance. But obviously you want an operational definition. That's understandable, and I owe you this much. I suggest that we not see one another again until the summer. I can drive to your hometown, and we can visit in a local park or something."

"Next *summer*! That's five or six months away. Michael: This is a break-up. You are rejecting me, and that really hurts." Michael noted the mists about Mamie's eyes. He thought of Wordsworth and the pearly air droplets of the Lake District. He sneaked a brief look at the books and hoped this episode might someday be written up in one of them, preferably in rhymed couplets in order to add a cerebral dimension to what were now, undeniably, Mamie's choked words of longing, betrayal, and injury, as well as her gasping exit from the wainscoted walls of the Burlington Free Library.

Michael felt a brief harrowing pain gallop onto his temples, like some outrageous violation of his cranial sanctum sanctorum. He had dared wish for a more reasonable reaction. He gulped with second thoughts about the wisdom of his act. He felt ashamed, though perhaps not so much about his covert self-removal from Mamie as about so much mayhem having breached the pulped disposition of knowledge otherwise known as the reference room. He would miss Mamie, too. He might have even loved her. But a firing would do neither of them good.

He felt better.

He looked out the immaculate windows. None of them failed to reveal the same wind-driven sleet. Mamie would have a heartbroken walk to the bus station. He wondered if she would draw any comfort from the weather. Wallace Stevens might say that the elements have a mind of their own (speaking figuratively of course), so Mamie might infer that the world, and not only she, is suffering.

But he doubted it. Elise Morgan would have the necessary cleverness to make such a connection. Mamie would not. Mamie would never think it, would never have the capacity to do so. Elise would think it, and instantly dismiss it as sentimental verbiage, and then, no doubt, continue devising ways to bedevil Michael's very existence.

He hated to dismiss Mamie, though he must admit that she had taken his non-dismissal dismissal just as he had hoped she would. Now he could never be blamed fro breaking up with her, for it was she, in a way, who had left him. Mamie was too tender to complain to the dean about him.

He had denied Elise Morgan new material. He had begun to starve the Grendel Girl of his life (sometimes he was amazed at the smart range of his literary allusions). Now he could concentrate on the final printing of the *Illyria Iamb*, and especially the radically delicious "Wet."

He would amount to something important yet. A temporary ache in the temples was minimal overhead for an endeavor so free of meanness and ignobility.

Chapter 16: The Mandatory Enforcement of Periods
(December 10, 1959)

"I must say, Henry, that I'm unsure that all this is as self-evident as you say it is." Harry Finch was being at his absolute worst. Added to his fussy doubts about everything from the color of the sky to the precedence of essence over existence was his pipe, which he brought along occasionally, there to assault the nostrils of his colleagues and to give him an added advantage in argument, since he could puff and pause while thinking of what next to say.

"This document (puff, puff) I wonder if there isn't (puff, puff) well, some sort of larger context. It may prove (puff, puff) something else entirely," at which point he removed the vile instrument from his mouth and began to clean it for the eighth time in twenty minutes, the dark and slimy spittle oozing onto yet another repository of tissue.

Henry was repelled. He had showed the Curriculum Committee the depleted mimeograph master, headed EXAM and quite self-evidently issued by Professor Michael Moggs as a written interrogation about the verse of that dipsomaniacal Welsh poet Dylan Thomas. "Trace two color patterns in 'Fern Hill'" and (worst of all) "Defend Thomas on seminal paradox in 'The Force

That Through the Green Fuse.'" Henry was certain that the senior members of the Curriculum Committee would find something disgusting and precarious about that use of "seminal," especially because Thomas, before his death six years earlier, had made a drunken fool of himself in New York City, posing as a soused Lord Byron only much uglier to look at and devoid of any heroics on behalf of Greek liberation.

Instead, most of the meeting had been composed of something even more off-putting: the poignant deliberations of Harry Finch and auburn spittle of his Meerschaum-infested saliva. Henry was aghast.

Of course Henry had not exactly been forthright with the committee. He had, not to put too fine a point on it, been rather less than fully forthcoming in implying that he had found the document only the day before. Not that he'd said he'd found it then. But he hadn't said he'd found it a month before. If he had, he'd have given the game away: This was no Final Exam but a short quiz labeled, if somewhat misleadingly and carelessly, EXAM. Well, that was what Moggs got for using the language without care—and him an English professor, or was that just a rumor. Besides, Moggs had been guilty of other things. One of them was actively opposing Henry himself in faculty meetings. It had been Moggs above all who had protested the need for a Final Examination Period.

Now, alas, Moggs was looking good. The news that the Period (as it was mischievously labeled) had caused a bleeding of student bodies had spread like the microbes of the common cold in a Vermont January. That hag Faye Roberts had been caterwauling about it from The Illyrian to Bolt Hall. Henry and the Curriculum Committee were looking awful. But Henry also knew that since every faculty member had acquired the bad faith to go along with the Period—"everyone has a Period now, "the joke had gone—his colleagues would resent anyone, including the fair-hired Michael Moggs, who tried to get around it. If Henry had bet on the wrong nag, the Curriculum Committee, at least he could discredit Moggs, who would rightly deny the charge but be dogged by suspicions for the balance of his Illyrian days. And sooner or later the Period would be forgotten, and Henry would have one fewer rival with which to reckon.

Such were the Machiavellian musings of Henry Taylor, academic, who fancied he thought like a Florentine of the sixteenth century.

"Well, Harry, although what you say may be true, it seems clear to me that young Moggs is trying to get around regulations. He's obviously planning to give a short quiz and call it an EXAMINATION." This was Lester Cole, sounding as if Michael

Moggs were a buck private in severe need of being court-martialed.

"Thus, gentlemen," continued Lester, "regardless of what you want to do I shall undertake to refer this matter to the Registrar, who can then if he wishes take it up with the dean and possibly Winston. We'll let young Moggs explain himself. I don't think we need to take a vote on this. I'm the chairman of the Curriculum Committee and have the proper standing, I think, to act. It need not be in your name. But someone flouting these important new rules must be brought to justice."

Henry couldn't decide whether Lester sounded more like General Pershing or the High Sheriff of Illyria County. It mattered not. Everyone on the Curriculum Committee concurred. Not even Harried Harry or Hortatory Horace had ever dreamed that they could conceal what Henry had found. Les could act for them and assure them of germ-free hands.

It was exactly the sort of thing that confirmed Henry's mordant view of the motives of humankind, and the type of hard fact that justified his machinations. He'd not told them about stumbling over the wastebasket in chilly November. Instead, he related a tale of having had the eagle eye to see the word EXAM having been tossed away just the day before, in frozen December, as though to hide incriminating evidence. If Lester Cole were High

Sheriff of Illyria County, Henry could pose as the leading enforcement agent of Calaboose Hall.

He smiled as the meeting adjourned, but not before complimenting Hortatory Horace on having recently conducted a fine class of Tacitus about which Henry said he had heard, though in fact no such encomium had ever reached his highly politicized ears.

Chapter 17: The General Utility of Emissaries
(December 20, 1959)

Before he entered the boardroom Winston took out Eve's letter once more as a source of fortitude.

Dear Winston: In 1927 Calvin Coolidge said he chose not to run for president in 1928. I wanted to write you, after your phone call, to say that I choose not to butter up old buzzards named Burdette in 1960. And I still don't. However, he and I have made a "date" of sorts in Boston between Christmas and New Year's. I shall explain the need of the college to sell the Burdette Building to some organization that will turn it into flea circuses. You may wish to ask why, after all the suffering I have endured due to your raging insecurities and roving vision, I am doing this. Don't. I cannot say. Of course I expect to be compensated (to be discussed later), but that's not the reason. Eve

How could Eve's handwriting be so whorled and yet still so controlled? It was though her hand was like some stunt man cavorting on a tightrope above the Charles River. It would not do to ask how Eve did such things. It must be, Winston thought, like not asking why Eve was going to try to convince Charles Burdette to do something that only Eve could convince Charles Burdette to do.

Winston was dreading this meeting, and yet he almost looked forward to it. The conversation with Annie that morning had been a sticky wicket.

"Let me understand this, Winston. You are asking your ex-wife to intervene with Charles Burdette, in effect, to snatch Illyria from the jaws of death."

"Not so melodramatic, dearest one. I'm merely asking her to speak to Charles about a matter of some fiduciary urgency."

"Why, Winston? Why? How do you think this makes me feel?"

"It should not affect you one way or the other. Eve has a way with Charles that none of us has. You should not put yourself down because you have not mastered the route to Charles's heart. I haven't any idea of what road to take either."

"But Winston. Winston. Our special thing—our indissoluble bond--was that we would always work together. We would share our love for each other. We would share our love for Illyria. We would be joined in affection and coordination, mutual admiration and concerted endeavor...my God, Winston. I'm starting to sound like you. I've got to say, Winston: damn you! You should have talked this over with me. You've gone behind my back. The whole campus will say that Eve should have remained the hostess and keeper of this house. I'm not 'Little Annie' any more, Winston. I'm no longer your prized miniature scholar. I'm your wife. I'm your wife, and you have disgraced me."

"Annie. That rather misses the mark. No one will know of Eve's role. We'll only know the result, which will be that Charles will come through for us, and then you can, very publicly if you wish, go to Maurice Reaper about the memorial to your father, and you will be presiding over the ceremony and everyone will be asking 'Eve who,' if they mention her name at all."

"That's what this is about, Winston. I couldn't 'cut' it with Uncle Mo. So you turned to your former wife. You see, Winston, this is what I'm talking about. This is what I'm trying to say to you!"

It had gone on like that for an hour, Winston saying Annie was making a Federal case out of jaywalking and she saying that Winston was the most traitorous college president since Benedict Arnold, if Arnold had *been* a college president. They both wore themselves out. Their rapprochement was a matter of fatigue. Winston thought they had decided to make up only because they were tired of thinking about anything at all. *Of course* if Annie had managed to secure funds from Uncle Mo the whole Burdette gambit wouldn't have been needed. She was right about that. But he had convinced her, or maybe he had, that the problem was with Uncle Mo, not with her. He'd even hinted that the real problem was that her father had been a rapscallion, but he knew better than to go too far with that one. Otherwise, Annie might think *he* was a rapscallion.

Well, he knew this discussion was going to be rough. Annie's whole thing was to be his helpmate. She'd signed on to be the kinder, gentler Eve. Now, Winston feared, she was *becoming* Eve, though without the glass-breaking wit and indispensable entrée to Charles. Winston thought this a baleful eventuality.

But he and Annie rarely quarreled. The civil broil was over for now. Winston walked into the meeting room. He had chosen the more modest room of the two. It included only a wooden table of slightly embarrassing thinness, next to which were lined, of all things, folding chairs. But Winston thought the subject of the meeting called for somewhat humbled circumstances. He even thought he might bring this up if necessary. He knew some thought him far too practiced in spurious majesty and believed the more primitive demeanor of the room would argue against that. He would give it to them with the bark off. They would not be able to accuse him of gilding lilies, or moon daisies.

The first thing he noted was that Malcolm Mole was not trying to dress like a faculty member. Though back on his beloved Illyrian grounds, he seemed, this time, to be coming as a businessman. His gray pinstripes seemed ominous. Other than that, the usual suspects seemed usual as ever. Paul Hamlin had the smirk on his cherubic visage that was his wont. Jonathan Upton looked as much as ever like a walrus from some sea world. Franklin Grammer, who, like Malcolm, had made a fortune in debentures, seemed to be a color symphony of white: between the shine of his baldness and the sheen of the deep snow easily visible through the spacious transom windowpanes. Added to that was that every one of his teeth were capped. Winston mused an inward joke about debentures and dentures dining together but quickly pivoted off it. This was no time for humor, most especially Winston's somewhat disabled attempts at it. Even Winston saw that

Malcolm Mole said, "I must say, Winston. I'm wondering why you're calling us here just five days before Christmas. It's inconvenient, especially because the full board is due to meet in early February."

"I realize that, Malcolm. But you see, I wanted to give you some startling news. Let me say at once that it's both good and bad, or, more properly, bad but good. I don't want you to think that I'm concealing anything. Of course I could have called each of you, but I wanted this face-to-face. Sometimes I think that's more candid—I mean honest." Winston was annoyed at himself for remembering Eve's earlier correction of candid with honest.

"Of what do you speak, Winston? I know our last meeting was discouraging, to say the least. Do you have an update? And why are you settling us into these folding chairs? Do you think we should be practicing for a tent revival meeting?"

"On the contrary, Malcolm. You are not souls to be saved. You are my key Board members. You are my right hand, and my left hand, too. I suppose if we were at a revival meeting I could say you are my rock and my salvation!"

This joke made an impression approximately equal to that made by a rusty hatrack. Winston knew this but decided not to be deterred.

"And yes, Malcolm, the hardships of the room are intentional. I want you to have the unvarnished facts."

"Well, all right, Winston. Before you came in, we all agreed that we had families to attend to, travel to do, presents to buy. What are these, these unpainted shack facts?"

Malcolm's humor also had no talent for travel. If anything, it irritated everyone even more, including Winston. It perished in the womb.

"All right, Malcolm. Here they are. We're running out of endowment—you already knew this—and are very near the point where we can't really dip into it, for there's little into which to dip." Winston liked the fact that he'd avoided the ending preposition, but he sensed it wouldn't raise any dollars. "And on top of all that, seventy-five students have informed us that they will not become paying guests of Illyria College this coming winter term. That's almost one hundred thousand dollars in lost incoming revenue. In short, gentlemen, we are perilously near to writing a bad check. We have few options for laying anyone off this next term unless we want to breach contracts. The difficulty is, how can we pay them?"

Paul Hamlin sniffed violently, as though a skunk had just climbed upon the folding chair next to him. Paul wasn't popular, even with those who agreed with him. His self-righteous visage, strangely like that of an angry young child, and self-important low alto, annoyed his fellow rich men, who knew he'd long had it out for Winston. There were even rumors that he'd once dated the present Ann Adams.

But Paul said nothing, as though to indicate that now that Winston was drowning the best thing was to remain silent and watch it happen.

"The only possibility left, Winston—and you know this—is to find a loan. Who will lend to us?" Jonathan Upton's tone answered his own question—"nobody"—while his walrus brush might have hinted that one would sooner weave the Shroud of Turin with his mustache than get anyone to lend money to hapless little Illyria. Every fiber of his three-pieced suited being expressed skepticism.

"This is really your fault, Winston. I say this in sorrow, not anger," said Franklin Grammer, though Winston thought that if his face had been on Mount Rushmore, Franklin might have tried to climb that part of the rock with a chisel in hand.

"Well, Franklin, Perhaps it is. Perhaps it isn't. I won't gainsay either way. It's apparent, though, that we must try to salvage the situation. Before you ask, our seventy-five traitors may be leaving us because we've installed a Final Examination Period. At least we shall go down with our standards intact, our academically rigorous heads held high, our famed Illyrian sculpture proud, in effect, to have been part of such an old and noble enterprise as this, self-confident in…."

"For the Lord's sake, Winston. Don't, please, make another one of your speeches. You said you had good news. What is it? And, by the way, don't ask us for any more money. We've all agreed.

We're tapped out, and none of us has the sort of funds that can keep a college going month to month."

"I was carried away, Malcolm"—Winston was getting semi-sharp all of a sudden—"but I was about to say 'self-confident in our capacity to carry on.' Do you want to hear more of *that* part of the speech?"

Winston thought that he would look best in surprising them after all had thought him down for the long count.

"I do have better news. I think Charles Burdette will agree, per my remarks last time, to let us sell his building to a convention organizer. It will bring in well over a million. The building's features and location are excellent for all sorts of meetings. It will give us a chance to regroup. If you want a new president for that, so be it. But I shall at least go down as the one who snatched us from final defeat."

At this point Paul Hamlin could no longer discipline himself. "Leaving aside your histrionics and self-proclaimed heroism, Winston, why is there any earthly reason to believe Charles would agree to such a thing. May I speak frankly? Charles gave this auditorium plus seminar rooms to the college in order to promote his principles of plain living and high thinking. The events are to be organized around these themes. They are to be

Illyria College events, sponsored by us, and on subjects that will promote Illyria's educational goals of purity and learning. Charles is *not* going to agree to turn his jewel over to the Shriners or the annual meeting of the American Taxidermy Association."

Winston could not help himself. "That's where you're quite wrong, Paul. May *I* say, very, very, very, very, very wrong!"

Voice rising, Paul asked, "*Why* am I wrong, Winston? Why? Why are *you* very, very, very, very, very, very *right*?"

"Because I've sent an emissary who will persuade Charles. That's why, Paul."

"Emissary? What emissary? Do you care to reveal the name of this emissary, Winston? You mean you're not going to approach Charles yourself?"

"Well, Paul, you may think it ignoble of me not to do it myself. But you see this is where you and I differ: I am willing to admit when someone else can do the job better."

"Really, Winston. Are you prepared to extend that argument to the presidency of Illyria College?"

"All right, gentlemen, that's quite enough," said Malcolm. "This is getting precisely nowhere. Tell us, Winston, who is your diplomat? Let's not get into personalities. We are just trying to get facts here about an institution we all love but which is in trouble."

"I knew you'd ask, Malcolm, and it was never my intention to keep the identity a secret. It's Eve Wilberforce, the former Eve Adams."

"Eve?" There was a quasi-unison of late middle-aged voices, except for Paul's boyish high tenor.

"Eve. I know what you're thinking, but Eve and I, ahem, have kept up a cordial friendship over the years. She loves Illyria, as do you and I. She will meet with Charles and make the case. And as you know, she has almost mesmeric credibility with him— much more so than I."

"Yes, so we've heard, Winston. What is the basis for it?"

"Oh, if you must know what I think, Malcolm, it's that they're both rather Type A personalities. Each respects the other's sheer will. There may even be something erotic, but if so, it's quite subtle and certainly not appropriate to speculate about. Anyhow, I predict she'll get the job done. And I've thrown in a important sweetener for Mr. Burdette. I'm asking Charles, through Eve, to let us lease the building to a convention organizer for a million dollars over the next twelve years. After that, we'll take it back, out of the red and ready to flourish again as New England's premier site for the purest acquisition of enduring knowledge. None of us may be here to see that. It's hardly significant whether we are or not. What is vital is that we are going to save Old Illyria from the trenchant evil of insolvency."

At this point Winston knew he was speechifying again. He thought he deserved it. After all, he'd amazed them all, including the scheming and scabrous Hamlin, with a creative plan to rescue Illyria, and using an agent they'd all forgotten about. How many of them could talk *their* ex-wives into doing such a thing? Then he realized they'd all been married but once. This was mildly depressing.

"Even so, Winston. I've known Eve since my student days, when you and she would invite me and other prominent Illyrians over for tea. Eve is not mercenary—we all appreciate her efforts both then and now—but she never strikes me as one who would undertake something like this, as a former wife to boot, without some compensation? What is it?"

Winston hadn't been prepared for this. Paul Hamlin's eyes, he thought, should be damned. (Perhaps his own should have been when they strayed towards Annie, but that was hardly the point now.)

"We've not talked about any such thing, Paul—Eve and I." This was technically true.

"Yes, but what will you do if and when she asks for something?"

"I cannot in fairness fail to give her something, in exchange for doing this crucial deed, Paul."

"Yes, Winston. But she is your ex-wife. This is like a boost in alimony payments. Shouldn't you give her such a boost as recompense out of your own pocket? We don't want college funds—scarce as they are, Winston—co-mingling with your marital settlement. Now do we?"

Hamlin was gloating. Winston knew it. Everyone else knew it. Paul knew it and loved it.

"I shall *of course* make any monetary settlement with Eve totally private and out of my own personal funds, Paul. I must say that this strikes me as a bit silly. If Eve is doing something for the college, she should be *paid* by the college. But we shan't have any appearance of impropriety, so I will handle her compensation privately. You will never know about it. And of course I shan't be asking for any raises in my own salary."

Winston had not expected the meeting to end on such a note. He had planned to end in victory. He rather thought of himself taking his last driver's lesson and, upon being asked to show what he had learned by his teacher, promptly steered the car into a ditch.

"All right, Winston," said Malcolm. "I think we all need to get back to our homes now. Merry Christmas, and may Eve's mission succeed. I know none of us has any sway with Charles, and frankly, I know I speak for all of us when I say that we don't want the jollity of our own seasons ruined by any of us having to move him along on this matter, especially with so much at stake. I'll close, try to have the last word, by saying, Winston, that we've underestimated you before, but in the past you've been able to make an inspiring speech, at least, that cheered us and kept us in the Illyria marathon. This time, though, it will have to be your choice of messenger, and not your stentorian skills, that see you, us, and Illyria through."

They filed out in solemnity, except for Paul's rather prissy swagger. There was a dearth of Christmas cheer. Winston still thought it had gone well. Whether it had or hadn't, all depended upon the ministrations of the former Eve Adams. He wondered how much she would insist upon if she succeeded. He inquired unto himself whether or not it would be possible to get her to reduce the amount. He was not an affluent man, however rich in rhetoric.

Of course that too was beside the point, for, Winston knew, this was not a question of Eve's returning to the Garden of Eden but of Eve's helping determine whether there would be even *be* a Garden, of Illyria.

Chapter 18: The Relentless Power of Wetness

(December 28, 1959)

"I've got to tell you, Eve, formerly Adams, that my admiration for you has known very few outer limits. I can't explain it. I think it's your forthright wit and, well, compared to me, your relative youth. I'd have felt the same once about Faye Roberts if she had been a bit younger and single. Both of you are no-nonsense gals who can make a punch sound like a punch-line. All right, I'll admit it: I rehearsed this little speech."

"Charles, you cunning old bastard. Rehearsing at your age!"

"You know my weakness for you, Eve. Did I ever tell you that in my younger days I was actually a Prohibitionist? I remember the old Will Rogers joke about people stumbling drunk to the polls in order to vote Dry. Though I've not changed my duty to high moral standards, I've grown more sophisticated, I hope. Today I'm a mild Wet—I have a dry gulch martini once a week—and I must say I'm a wild Wet over you!"

What a bag of wind! Phew! Charles, Eve thought, was as homely as he'd ever been. It was incredible that his face hadn't landed him in penury. Of course it was his shrewdness and industry that had told the difference. Odd, though, that most of his money had been made manufacturing candy kisses—the old Candy Kisses King—since he himself was a mostly sour man. Eve used to tell Winston that Charles should have made massive amounts of lemon drops, not chocolate kisses. Charles, destined for permanent bachelorhood, had wed his secretary Matilda, a fated Old Maid, to save them both from what Eve with understated mischief had called "formal solitude." Sans his wealth, even Matilda wouldn't have married him. Eve thought he had married her partly for her Victorian name.

As Eve gazed upon Charles this sleety Boston day she also thought there was a certain kind of originality about his face, a strangely pleasing form of long swooping. Charles had always had an interminably vertical face—when he had been thirty he must have looked already like the Iowa farmer in Wood's *American Gothic*—and now that his face drooped with aging it hardly showed. The sag was just an extension of what was already a natural, thus shameless, spectacle of the protracted. He'd added trailing sideburns to enhance the effect. So while Charles's face was ugly and bitter, it was redeemed by a pleasing uniformity of accumulated gravity. And when he smiled—his teeth had had lots of costly work—it was an especially joyful moment, because he rarely did it and so even a semi-grin seemed to be a miracle.

He was smiling now. But he withdrew it immediately, as though guilty of self-indulgence.

"Nonetheless, Eve, though my ardor for you remains and while I'm aware of my approaching death and the increasing dementia of Matilda—did I tell you that she's not withdrawn into silence but into a occasional chatter that no one comprehends—I still believe in my principles."

Eve thought that "the dementia of Matilda" had a catchiness about it. "Your principles? My goodness, Charles: no one should ever tamper with those. I do not come here today, on behalf of our beloved Illyria and supercilious ex-husband (Charles smiled again) to challenge your principles. To me—and you must remember that I once had philosophy at Radcliffe with a student of George Santayana—it's only a matter of how best to apply them. I would call it 'principled pragmatism.' I think your idea is capital. Lease your building to a booking agency but only on the proviso that it not schedule any events of which you personally disapprove. I agree: these events should be morally uplifting and not contribute to the decay that we all around us see."

Eve thought the reversed order of "all around" and "see" was a nice touch—just the sort of elevated eloquence that the decaying Charles associated with manning the barricades against all sorts of imagined minatory change. If Charles had been a violin, she was his Heifetz. But she didn't like to think of Charles as a violin but more of a snare drum in excruciating need of being hit.

"Well, is Winston all right with this condition? Or should we even care what Winston is all right with? He's failed, you know, Eve. He should never have driven you off for that little tart, the offspring of a man whose lucre was always, if you ask me, rather unsanitary."

"Don't you worry about Winston, Charles, or that little tart, birthed of dirty hands."

"You are a delight!"

"Thank you, Charles. So are you. May you live well into the 1970s! I should think a personal centenary celebration at Illyria would not be out of order. But flattery aside, Charles—and I know it will get me *everywhere* with you—Winston will have no choice but to agree. And if we cannot get an *agency* that will agree to these clauses, then there will be no lease of the Burdette Building at all. Illyria will simply have to fend for itself. But I must say, Charles, that this agreement by you, governed wisely by your moral principles, may well mean that there will *be* an Illyria College next year, when otherwise there might not be."

Charles clapped his hands in a feeble ecstasy, the energy residing more in the intention than in the act itself. Eve wondered if he were applauding her, himself, the informal agreement, or old Illyria. Later she decided that he was clapping for the idea of continued existence—his own, Illyria's. No matter how much money Charles had, or how much he trumpeted his ridiculously abstract precepts, he was, in the end, a sucker for the idea that something bright might glow a few seconds longer. This was also why he adored her. He fell for the frankness that seemed at one with his own style. He was helpless before the teasing flattery that made him imagine he was even more special than his vast funds would suggest. Eve had the formula. Eve had Charles's number, and it was not a low one.

Lofty, sententious Winston, who would be giving her an extra thousand a month, did not.

As she endured Charles's drooling farewell peck, Eve preferred to think of her boost in alimony as 120 one hundred dollar bills a year. Such a pile made the last ninety minutes seem much less onerous. And the oysters he'd had his chef prepare at least had been the stuff of divinity, however roughhewn by the blather of the crotchety, the vainglorious, the easily played Charles Burdette.

***

The Very Reverend Royce Rex Jamison had been pastor of the Burlington First Congregational Church for nearly twenty years. His beloved Mary had passed on nearly fifteen years ago, or about six after he received his appointment, not without prestige, as pastor of First Con. Royce knew people used the term "First Con"—his parishioners even did it in front of him—but he disliked it as scoffing, not to mention the objectionable implied pun. Royce was no confidence man, nor was the Church an institution of trickery. That seemed self-evident.

He had never remarried, possibly because he missed Mary something awful but also just maybe because she was a perfect trope for his sermons. He mentioned her at least once a month and occasionally wondered if worshippers tired of it. If so, that was just too bad, for he been devoted to little Mary and besides, she was the perfect test for the substance of those invisible bonds that were the essential promise of Christ.

Royce never tired of saying that God cannot be seen so that God can be everywhere. Were he corporeal we should have to drive somewhere to consult with "Him." This seemed to Royce a profound observation, though it probably wasn't original with him, and it put paid to those who wanted some tangible proof of God's existence and Christ's divinity. God was Spirit and beyond understanding. His bonds are to be intuited, not viewed; felt but not touched. It was God, he told his congregation (or "con" as some of the irreverent would insist upon putting it) *that* (not Who) guaranteed for him the enduring love of Mary and of his for her. God was no Who.

Someday, he assured his flock, they would meet again, he and Mary, but Royce was too sensitive to the time and place to get into specifics. This was a church in the starchy New England North, not a holy roller in the swampy tropics of the Old (and rightly defeated) Confederacy. So he kept his and Mary's reunion vague, rather like God, whom he never called God *Himself* (nor God Herself, as that would be too radical, or God Itself, as that would be too uninspiring). Royce prided himself on sticking with "God" as some holy entity, mystical, that eluded what some of the fancy new theologians called "personhood." Royce liked where he kept God: abstract and restrained, reserved and impalpable. He thought this pleased his church members and would have pleased Mary, about whom he intended to speak this very coming Sunday.

But this was a Saturday morning, a time of regular relaxation for Royce. The Burlington Free Library had a tidy, if not overly generous, collection of mainstream journals, along with the occasional more esoteric one, such as the *Illyria Iamb*. Royce thumbed the new issue. He noted the titles this issue were blander than usual—"Cottage by the Lane" and "Bronze Memento" among the drearier ones. Then he spied, in the Table of Contents, "Wet" and though the title alluring—perhaps even a thoughtful disquisition of baptism. He turned to the poem.

Royce was also a 1922 graduate of Illyria College, an active alumnus. He had been the very first Burdette Scholar, financial aid offered by one Charles Burdette, also an alumnus and thirty years Royce's senior.

***

"This is wet," said Faye. "What's going on?"

Henry, returning from urinary relief in the faculty restroom, had not expected to see Faye Roberts in Calaboose Hall during the intersession. He had not expected to see much of anyone. Winter was deadening more with each passing hour, and classes were not due to resume for ten days. Henry had only come to his office to pick up a recommendation form he'd promised to fill out. The campus was a snowy ghost, and a dense sleet storm had been predicted for Boston to the south. The last time Henry had seen one of those, visibility was limited to about a block. It was a plague of frozen locusts. There was, Henry barely thought, a sense of Biblical doom in the air.

"Faye! What are you doing in Calaboose Hall on such a bad and deserted day?"

"I dropped in to leave Bill Montague a note. I'm having a tea party if you must know, and every drop of Earl Gray will be 90 proof."

"Why not just send him an invitation in the post?"

"At my age a four cent stamp is worth saving. Besides, I thought the walk would do me good. The party isn't until mid-January, so the Bill of Wrongs will have plenty of time to find the invite. He's not got much else going on anyhow. Speaking of which, why don't you come, too?"

"I could, yes."

"Not only that, you should. We can all gossip about the GWC—great fun?"

"Thanks. The GWC?"

"You've not heard? The Great Wastebasket Caper! Young Michael Moggs was accused anonymously of having tried to cheat the magnificent Final Examination Period that seems to have robbed us of revenue. My version is that 'Michael Moggs tried to miss his period.' Well, the 'proof' was apparently some quiz Mr. or Miss Anonymous found in the wastebasket. Great fun!"

"I hadn't heard," Henry fibbed and then thought he hadn't technically prevaricated because, well, he had not heard Faye Roberts' version. In fact, he had no idea what had become of the episode he had initiated. He only hoped it would turn out shipwreck for Moggs.

"But what happened exactly?"

"Well, Mr. young Henry, all I know is that somebody turned Moggs in, and the registrar launched an investigation."

"What was the outcome?"

"The outcome? That's the hilarious part. It turns out that Moggs had not missed his period after all. He's not pregnant!! He not only gave all three of his required final exams, but each one of them lasted the full three hours. I heard that in one of them he submitted a passage from Hart Crane they'd never seen before and made them explicate it. Can you imagine? I didn't know we taught hieroglyphics at Illyria College."

"Uh, but what about this, this thing somebody found in the wastebasket?"

"Well, my sources tell *me* that Young Moggs was able to prove that that was a quiz from last month. He even got student documentation."

"Ah, is that so?"

"It is, Henry. It is. And now—again, this is what I heard—a goodly portion of the faculty wants to know who tried to 'frame' Mr. Moggs. Framed? Not only are we teaching hieroglyphics at Illyria; we're also doing a fairly good imitation of Lucky Luciano! I love it. I love it. I love it!"

"It's all very intriguing to you, I'm sure."

"It is. But equally intriguing is this water in front of The Bill of Wrongs' office door. What the hell? Oh, wait, I see. It's a leak."

"Oh, yes: from the ceiling. I see."

"That's it, Henry. It's getting plenty wet. I'll call maintenance. Leaks, as you know, can be dangerous."

Henry could only agree. He had no choice.

Chapter 19: The Menacing Habits of Telephones
(December 30, 1959)

The phone in Winston's office had rung. He knew not to ask for whom it tolled. It tolled for him.

As expected, it was Eve. Now they were in mid-confabulation.

"But Eve, this arrangement is a death knell. It's almost worse than no arrangement at all. I can't possibly proceed with these conditions."

"Your problem, Winston, has always been that your first passions rule over you. It was that way when we were married. You would go to a meeting, come home in a stew (I almost decided to serve it to you so you'd have something to swim in), and then I'd show you how your first reaction was uninformative."

"Yes, yes. Perhaps that's why we're no longer husband and wife."

"Yes, yes, yes, Winston. That *is* why we're no longer husband and wife. You grew weary of my lifelines."

"I wouldn't call them that. I'd call them my inability to resist your overbearing ways. Look, Eve, I know I'm no angel. But this job requires a public confidence, and living with you meant I always had to fake it. I couldn't take it any longer. Meanwhile, Ann...."

"...flattered you. I know. I will say this, however, Winston. You're no different from most men. And at least you've had the self-knowledge to admit your semi-hollowness."

"Very funny, Eve. But if we might get back to the main motion, how can I possibly sell a lease of the Burdette Building—world-class though it may be and lucrative in its location—to any booking company that has to abide by Charles's 'wholesome' clauses?"

"You always find impediments where few exist, Winston, and then you end up marrying a real one."

"You?"

"Wrong, Winston. I'll give you one more guess. But look, Winston, I've found, just using the reference room of the Philadelphia Public Library, at least five impresarios who specialize in meetings and lectures of moral uplift. The great U.S. of A. is full of these God-bothering types. Many of them are in the South, yes, but they would love to get out of the heat there in June and further on. Vermont summers are cool. Boston is easy to fly to nowadays, and bus service to Illyria is but a little over two hours from the plane. I predict you'd have at least twelve meetings a month in Charles's handsome building in the summer alone. The National League for the Furtherance of the Public Good—yes, I just made this up—will likely be knocking on your door in the fall and spring. Charles is a prig, morally self-righteous, but he'll fall for anything that sounds principled. He's an old man, semi-addled. He'll go for anything from the American Society of Holy Rollers to the International Consortium of Anti-Vivisectionists."

"Well, all right, Eve. If you're right, you're right. But I wish you'd not sneaked in this 'Charles must approve' clause. They were beyond my instructions."

"Well, Winston. You weren't there. Let me say that again: You. Weren't. There. I could see Charles was skeptical and wavering. He thought your plan meant he was losing control. It was a further weakening of an old man, once powerful. I gave him the chance to regain control. It worked. That's the end of the story. Pretend this is an Italian movie, and 'finis' has just flashed on the screen. Say it aloud, Winston. It will make you smile, that word. And don't tell me about 'your instructions.' I'm not secretary of state, and you're not the damned president of the U.S. Not that the one we have is much better."

"All right, all right, all right, Eve." Winston was furious: with himself for letting things go, with Charles for being an old hard sofa, and above all for Eve for once more taking over. For good measure, he was mad at Annie for being able to come up with nothing better than a giant mound to impede the spectacular viewing of The Illyrian. He was tired of every phrase that started with 'the': *The* Illyrian, whose sightlines were now threatened by the mischievous marble mound gift of Mo Reaper; *The* Final Exam Period—*the* Period, which sounded as though every December and May Illyria College would have "its" period and bleed students; and finally *The* Deficit, which for all the world seemed to be bidding fair to close the college forever. Winston was in a bad way. He knew others thought he had a stone face of great grandeur. Now he felt as though The Illyrian itself had become the rocket it already looked like and was heading straight towards the once great rock known as Winston Adams. Winston felt a bit like smithereens. Then he recalled that female praying mantises get the males to inseminate them just before killing them. And since the Illyrian was both rocket and mantis, Winston felt that this work of art, once the chief glory of Illyria College, was now an ironically decorous weapon poised to destroy him, though whether by force or toxins he could not rightly say. What *could* he rightly say these days?

Eve was a bit perplexed. Winston hadn't said anything for fifteen seconds. She wondered if the line were dead.

"Winston? Well, it's out of both our hands now. Charles has agreed in spoken words. I suggest you get the lawyers to draw up a concord with him. You know that. Get it in writing—or typing. All right?

Look, I have to go now. I need to think of ways to spend your extra alimony. And OK: here's the deal. If this doesn't work out, you don't have to give it to me. I owe you that much, I suppose. You kept me in profundity for nearly twenty years of wedlock."

* * *

In Burlington another phone rang the same day.

"Reverend Jameson? This is Charles Burdette's household calling. I'm his personal assistant. Charles remembers you and wants to speak with you about this matter of urgency you have. But he isn't up to it now. He's feeling not at all well. He will return your call, or I will, as soon as he's better."

Royce was disappointed in this. But he would return to his sermon preparation. This one was important, so he decided to write down the exact words and read it:

One of the most dispiriting things of modern life is the constant need to turn august things into something like pals or buddies. This can even happen to God, who is all that is holy and good and right and loving, and not some best friend who shares bowel habits or secret crushes with you. God is spirit. God is not a person, though God briefly came as one simply because we couldn't grasp God any other way. God is the embodiment of what has become harmony and compassion and power in the world. ***But God does not have sex habits.***

Royce read it over again, and adjudged that it was right and good. He even thought of quoting "Wet" in utter contempt to his congregation, but decided against it. It would shock them. Besides, how would he explain that it came from the literary journal of his own, once esteemed, alma mater?

He was sorry to hear about Charles Burdette. He caught sight of himself in a side mirror of his study. Such long retained faith, combined with a fast becoming leonine face, would be an excellent tribune for the powerful message Royce intended to give. And it would be no "con job" either.

***

Yet another phone rang, this one in Henry's apartment. He had noticed the burgeoning clutter and wondered if his usual neatness was deserting him along with his equilibrium. He wondered if there was a linkage.

"Yes, Michael. Yes. I see you got my note. Thanks for calling me back. I've heard about your terrible experience with the final exams—the entire imbroglio. I'm wondering if we might meet before the winter term begins. I have something to say to you about it…Good!"

Henry thought it might yet be possible to staunch any bleeding associated with the Period.

Chapter 20: The Likely Shrewdness of Pre-emptions
(January 2, 1960)

Henry was annoyed. He wondered why Michael Moggs would meet him for coffee without wearing his highly academic horn rims. Wouldn't it have made more sense for Moggs to leave his horn rims off when trying to impress gullible Illyrian co-eds and keep them on when trying to impress his learned colleagues? Or was Moggs's game to make these same girls think he was an innocuous intellectual and then sneak up on them?

Of course this was not how Michael saw the matter at all. His view was that Henry looked like an ambitious weasel and that it would do Henry good to see what a real charmer looked like—sans glasses.

Thus the meeting between them began with uneasiness and doubts on both sides. Hostilities, though, were veiled. Henry had a job to do, and Michael had a curiosity to be assuaged.

"Well, Michael, I thought we could visit because, well, I heard about that whole Final Examination mess, and how you had to go to the Registrar and explain yourself. Well, let me just say that I totally disapprove of this sort of thing. It's an outrage. It's an insult to academic freedom. And as a member of the Curriculum Committee, well, I've got your back!"

"Wow! Thanks so much, Henry. I know you're the youngest member of that group. They listen to you. Yes, you're right. While I've had loads of faculty tell me how upset they were about how I was treated, it's good to know that I've also got a little, shall we say, 'official' backing. I mean, you know, it was just a trip to the Registrar. It never went as high as Dean Portly. But one never knows (Michael felt himself returning to the more formal and dignified "one"): one can always find one's reputation being harmed a little. Anyhow, I'm grateful, Henry, very much so."

"What were you told about how this began?"

"I was told that someone had found one of my old tests in the wastepaper basket!"

"No!"

"Yes, and the hilarious thing—or could have been hilarious—was that it was an old pop test that went back to November. No snow had flown. It wasn't even near 'the Period' as we younger faculty are calling the new regulations."

"Ah. Did anyone tell you how this, this quiz or test got to the Registrar?"

"No one told me, and I decided not to ask."

"Oh, right. Well, if I were you I'd just forget the whole thing. Ask no further questions. I can't imagine what ass would do such a thing. But there's no need for you to get involved. I think it's over, and I will certainly stick up for you, if need arises, in the Curriculum Committee. By the way...."

"Yes?"

"I note you aren't wearing your glasses. Has your vision improved?"

"Not at all. But you see they're mostly for reading. Yes, I do wear them a lot on campus, and I've wondered about that. But I think I wear them for a couple of reasons. Otherwise, I'd lose them; and I never know when I'm going to be asked to read something."

Henry doubted this, every syllable. He was sure Moggs was an actor. But then, Henry thought, with a ruefulness that was rare for him, and in a sudden eruption of intellectual objectivity, that he himself was not beyond a certain thespian dimension.

Anyhow, Henry had done what he came to do. The whole business was fading. The long vacation had disrupted continuity. Everyone would soon go on to other things, if they hadn't already. Even the gossip Faye Roberts would move along. She was already peddling that rumor that the president's former wife had returned to campus. And of course he would never bring up Moggs in the Curriculum Committee. But he had scant intention of dropping his occasional attention to wastebaskets. Call it Machiavellian Archeology.

With that witticism having been self-congratulated, Henry bid a grateful and rather surprised Michael Moggs adieu. A snowstorm was coming. They both needed shelter, and warmth also seemed required.

Chapter 21: The Irritating Surprises of Unexpected Visitors
(January 14, 1960)

Winston had known for a day now that he would be receiving visitors, but he could not fathom why a trustee and classics professor would be teaming up to call upon him. He knew of course that Jonathan Upton and Horace Fuller had been roommates years ago at Illyria and were now both men of about sixty. Had it really been nearly forty years since they were roomies? And Winston knew that they had remained friends. He knew that Jonathan, living near Burlington, was easily able to get to campus—with greater facility than those who lived in Boston or Harford, for example. All of that was clear.

But what did they want?

They might have been Lewis Carroll's Walrus and Carpenter, since Upton was celebrated for his mustache, which was so pronounced that it seemed almost indecorous for him not to be near a large body of salt water, and since Horace, though a Tacitus scholar, might have been passed somehow for an aging fixer of rotten porches. Professor Fuller was barefaced, balding, and stooped. His posture and lack of hirsute traits belied his overwrought delivery. Campus whisperers said that only Winston could out-declaim Hortatory Horace in normal conversation. Most people spoke in sentences or phrases. Horace and Winston spoke in forgettable paragraphs.

"Well, what a treasure to see you two!" Winston lied.

"Yes, well, we stay in touch often. We roomed together, you know."

Winston did know, yet Upton and Fuller always told everyone, as though the news were roughly equivalent to the sinking of the Titanic on the day it happened in 1912. Winston wondered if, after this meeting was done, he would wish that Jonathan and Horace had themselves perished with the Titanic.

"Not only did Jonathan and I room together," added Horace, "we were also boon companions, intellectual collaborators, fellow adventurers, and enduring friends."

Winston realized he'd just heard his first Hortatory Horace coordinate construction of the visit. He hoped there wouldn't be more. He thought of his own homilies as more spontaneous and fluid.

Both Jonathan and Horace were gleeful with the spirit of early old age men, eager to demonstrate what a great feat it had been that they had lasted, and flourished, as long as they had. The young could not be blamed for seeing smugness: "We've done ours. Now let's see if you can do yours." Winston, who was a decade younger, felt as though he were a callow youth who'd done nothing yet. And he fretted that there was something terrible portended in their presence. These were grim and tense times both in Winston's career and Illyria's history. He invited them to sit, and they did. There was something, he thought, comically ordinary, yet eerie, in their pulling up their trousers so as to measure some precisely polite distance between the pants bottoms and the tops of their laced-up Oxfords. Winston remembered the old line about rearranging chairs on the decks of the Titanic—that catastrophic reference again.

"Well, gentlemen, you're not only distinguished but industrious and hence busy. What brings you to my office on this bitter winter's morn?"

"Oh, well, Winston! We bring good tidings of great joy!"

"Well, that's a relief, Jonathan. One never knows these days."

"Oh, you don't need to pretend with us, Winston," said Jonathan Upton. "You've always gone on about your business as though only the Oracle at Delphi—right, Horace—knew what was about. Have you forgotten already that I was in the emergency session of the Finance Committee? We're aware of the college's troubles. Nearly everybody is—well, not perhaps the younger faculty and the students of course. But we who are long-timers have our sources. The point

178

is, we have some good news for you. Yes, *we* have some good news!"

"Who'd have thought it?" asked Horace. "We who studied Plutarch and physics, Aristotle and astronomy, Wordsworth and world history together—of all the duos on the planet, it is we who bring you some relief, Winston."

Winston heaved. For all Horace's voluble fustian, he might say something welcome after all.

"Well, my good friends. What is this blessing you bear?"

"It's a bit complex, Winston. You know that we're also friends with Charles Burdette. We were once Burdette scholars, you know. And we've always been grateful to Charles. And well...."

"Well? Yes?"

Yes. Well. Anyhow we've gotten a phone call from Matilda, who's to be sure not indubitably reliable sometimes. She told us you'd had the lawyers draft an agreement for Charles to sign—something about leasing the building to outsiders to organize moral uplift conferences that we could all attend."

"And that we all need to attend, I might add," and so Horace proceeded to add and add: "spiritual elevation, philosophic enhancement, classical improvement."

Yes. I'll tell you both right now that we got that document off several days ago. I expect to hear from Charles any day now."

"That's what we wanted to tell you: that you may not be hearing from Charles as soon as you thought. You see, he's had a setback. Well, he's only three years shy of ninety. My goodness, it's no wonder."

"What are you trying to say?"

"That Charles has had something or other. It might be a mild stroke. It might be exhaustion. It could also be just a bad case of pneumonia, for he's had sniffles. But whatever it is, he's been bed-ridden now for well over a week. He's rather halting and delirious. He's not up to signing anything now."

"And *this* is your good news, Jonathan?" The college president who posed this exasperated question was now struggling to find funds for the continuance of monthly operations. Illyria was not living hand to mouth. It was living mouth to ground. A hand would have been nice, a luxury. Winston lived in barely contained panic. But a document signed by Charles could be shown to lenders as collateral for future income and payback.

Winston imagined professors lecturing on, as Hortatory Horace might say, "Plutarch and physics" being knocked off their lecterns by a wrecking ball, come to raze the campus for real estate developers.

"Well, yes, Winston. It is good news. Hear me out. Charles is getting better. He sat up for an hour in bed yesterday, had a sandwich, and said he was glad, now that the end could be near, that he could do some final good act for Illyria College. Of course he soon collapsed and is faint now, sleeping a lot (but not in a coma, mind you). Don't you see, Winston? He's recovering. It's only a matter of time until he does. He'll sign. Matilda will get one of the servants to do the mailing. Our troubles, yours included, are soon over."

"Yes," added Horace. "Finis; the end; the last days of darkness."

Winston thought it might be *Charles* who would see last days, and Illyria College with him. He decided he must pretend to be gratified by news that was ambiguous at best.

"Ah, so you and Jonathan presume that Matilda thinks this most recent rally is a sign of better things to come."

"Oh, yes, Winston. We most certainly do. We could hardly wait to tell you. Jonathan got the call night before last and asked me, petitioned me, his lifelong co-conspirator in knowledge (giggle), to accompany him to let you know."

Winston suddenly realized the truth: These two wanted to feel important. They came with pseudo-good news, but mostly they just wanted to be in on the drama. Besides, their good news was hardly free if ambivalence. The fact is, Winston had no idea that Charles Burdette had taken ill. He could die at any time. He could die sans signature. Matilda was hardly a clear channel for news of any kind.

Winston saw the Dynamic Duo out with thanks as prodigious as it was spurious. There was a near senility in their proclamations of self-importance. He watched them from the window as they trudged through the snow. He saw the head-bobbing animation coursing through their furry hats as they conversed about their earth-shattering revelations. You'd think they'd just announced that a meteor had missed, if barely, the planet Earth.

Winston was disgusted. But six hours later, in the late afternoon, he got an unwelcome surprise call from Hortatory Horace. Matilda Burdette had just called Jonathan. Charles had sat up again, this time for two hours, and once again vowing to sign the agreement as soon as he was able to read it with care.

A blizzard warning was up, and Winston needed to walk two-thirds of an ill-blown mile to the presidential house. He decided he wouldn't mind.

Chapter 22: The Edifying Tales of Tigers and Lambs
(January 15, 1960)

"And so this is why I've chosen this pair of poems for us to examine on the first day. The entire semester we'll be investigating nineteenth century theological doubt. Of course much of that was owing to Darwin, and we certainly won't be reading Darwin, though I'll advert to his ideas from time to time. We'll focus on the poetry for the most part, and how that reflects theological skepticism in the Victorian Era."

"Now Blake's two poems, about the Tiger and the Lamb, are strictly speaking from the Romantic, not the Victorian, period," continued Michael. "But in effect Blake is questioning the idea that there is One God, for how could the same God have created the ferocious tiger and the innocent lamb? And we might extend this in a way to Darwin himself, though Darwin of course was not yet in the picture when Blake wrote these poems around 1800. Darwin posited creatures, such as you and me and worms and alligators and flowers, struggling to survive; and then he posited an environment (let's say dreaded cold like we have today in Illyria) that would make it difficult to survive in. So you might say that Darwin, too, suggests two gods: one to create the struggling creatures and another to create the challenging environment. So both Blake and Darwin in their ways are questioning One God. Yes, Elise?"

Elise Morgan! She *would* have to take another of his courses. At least he was no longer entangled with Mamie Rogers. He'd heard Mamie had a new boyfriend—a freshman, of all things, from Montpelier. Whew!

"Well, I guess I'd like to say, Professor, that there may be a gap in your logic here."

"How, Elise? Please go on." Michael did not want Elise to go on. He wanted Elise to go away. He wished she never were, and while he was at it he might pray that one or two or a dozen gods might wipe out Currie's Drug and the Burlington Free Library at the same time. His memories of those places were hardly to be borne.

"Yes, well, thanks. I will go on. You see, Darwin also posited that among the other challenges to struggling creatures are other *struggling* creatures. So it isn't just, say, the grizzly bear against the cold; it's also the grizzly bear against the antelope, who may eat some of the grizzly bear's food, or against us, Man, who will hunt the grizzly. Your idea of two gods works fine as long as you confine environmental challenges to the category of non-living things. But these challenges include living things, so unless you're ready to say that there was a different god that created worms and buffalo and so forth—a worm god, buffalo god, etc.—then your evidence of multiple gods is rather suspect, Professor."

Michael was perplexed. He was amazed. He had to admit that Elise Morgan was precocious. She was light years beyond other Illyrian students. She also had a way of showing up unwanted, and showing him up, too. He stared hard at her drawn pale visage as though in earnest search for signs of some wasting disease that might put an end to her.

Then he spoke.

"Elise, what you say is insightful of course." This was standard issue, Michael knew, but it would give him a few more seconds to think of what he did want to say. "But I must add, Elise, that Blake does raise the question: did the same God who made the tiger make the lamb? I mean, that is in the poem. So I hardly think my musings about theological doubts are made of whole cloth." Michael liked this last flourish. When academics denied that they were not making things up "of whole cloth," it was nearly always an impressive counter. "Yes? Yes, yes…all right, please go on, Elise." Michael wondered if she had paid all her tuition and if not whether he had the authority to forbid her interrogatives.

"I'm not doubting Blake, Professor Moggs, but rather doubting *you*. I'm in doubt about your explanation of Darwin and the idea that his theory suggests more than one god. Darwin presents one integrated system of challenges, traits, and survival. It's a single network called "natural selection." It's perfectly consistent with One God, as long as you can accept that this One God works through natural causes. Blake suggests many gods; Darwin suggests just one, operating through natural selection. You've tried to compare apples and oranges, Professor."

"Well, perhaps, Elise. Perhaps. But I'd still put all of this under the general heading of theological skepticism!"

"So would I, Professor. But I think your comparison is, well, a little wet!"

Wet! Why did she use that word and why was it teamed with a smile at once sympathetic and oleaginous?

The bell rang. Michael thanked however many gods there were for that. For some reason the loud jingle sounded a bit like his telephone on the day that Henry Taylor had rung him up with that odd suggestion for coffee.

Chapter 23: The Objectionable Stupidity of Questions About the Devil

(January 15, 1960)

"And so in this course we'll focus on a wide range of themes, because nineteenth century German literature expresses a number of very different ideas. My personal favorite is Goethe's depiction of the Devil in *Faust*. The background of this portrayal is fascinating, at least to me."

Henry's diving slender face and slightly scaly skin could hardly mask an intensity of thought. Every student knew he was in his element. Blunt of nose, a bit short of limbs, especially for someone so lingering of face, he had worn his best brown dress coat on this opening day, the start of a fledgling decade as well as a new semester.

"The Devil was not originally linked to the serpent who tempted Eve in the garden, or even to the fallen angels mentioned in the later books of the New Testament. It was only later that the serpent and the disgraced angels came together in this figure known as the Devil. Of course Milton combined both the exiled angel and the snake in *Paradise Lost*, but he wasn't original in this. It had been done centuries before. Unlike God, who can be everywhere, the Devil appears unable to be omnipresent, so the Devil has to come to the tempted one, although we know from Marlowe's *Dr. Faustus* that if you give off certain evil signs the Devil will hear them and make his way to you. But the Devil is a labile figure, easily changeable, and this is not only a theological feature but also a literary one—because different writers can depict the Devil in different ways. Above all, in this course we'll see how Goethe treats the Devil as a sort of liberating figure—one by which complacent characters can get shaken up and even made better. The Devil performs a service. Now some would say that this is because the Devil is working for God all along, but I'd put it differently: I'd say in *Faust* the Devil is a sort of positive good irrespective of God. Yes, Miss (Henry had to look at his class roll) Miss Rogers. Mamie Rogers."

A full-cheeked black-haired co-ed had had her hand up for nearly a minute. It annoyed Henry when this sort of thing happened. Why couldn't students see he was in a train of thought that neither wanted nor required any sudden stoppage?

"Well, this may be an obvious question, but what sorts of things does the Devil cause people to do?"

"Oh, well, yes, that is rather obvious, but just so that everyone is clear. The Devil tempts people to lie, cheat, steal—that sort of thing. But we shall have no interest in this course in the Devil's moral aspects—only in his literary traits. The sorts of temptations presented by the Devil will not be our concern at all here. OK?"

"Yes," said Mamie Rogers, "thank you, Professor Taylor."

Imagine a student of literature being interested in Sunday school morality. Henry wondered if this moon-faced Mamie Rogers had the pre-requisites for this course.

He would check. He hoped she hadn't lied about her qualifications. That would be unforgivable. Henry abhorred liars.

Chapter 24: The Turgid Confusions of Registrars
(January 17, 1960)

"Hey, Mike. This Mamie Rogers thing, OK?"

Thus began five minutes of terror for Professor Michael Moggs.

Waldo Vole, Illyria's registrar, had uttered this inchoate sentence on the telephone. It was typical of the goofy and officious Waldo, who seemed unable to begin a conversation properly. Michael would generally have paid it no mind, putting it down to the vagaries of dealing with a semi-lovable space cadet. In fact, when Michael learned that "the registrar" had been appointed to investigate the final exam allegations he wondered how Waldo Vole could research anything properly. Thoughts of Sherlock Holmes's bumbling Inspector Lestrade immediately presented themselves.

But now Waldo had mentioned Mamie Rogers, and had added that it was all much too complex to discuss on the phone. So Waldo would drop over, *OK*, and they could have a little chat about it, *OK*. This was also Waldo's wont. He would call a faculty member, say something chaotic, and then announce that he'd just stop by in five minutes.

Michael waited. If someone had said he had once "seen" Mamie Rogers, why would Waldo Vole be asked to confront him? This made no sense. Yet perhaps other, more shadowy figures were using the unwitting Waldo as a first step of incremental terror. Michael had only seen Mamie once, hanging on the arm of her handsome freshman, who looked for all the world like a youngish Cornel Wilde. She had proffered a full-faced smile as though to indicate there was neither acid nor regret, as if their little (Platonic, mind you) fling had vanished as surely as a well-consumed Coke float at Currie's Drug.

Yet having escaped the Winds of Waldo in the final exam fracas, where he was totally innocent, would he now run head first into them regarding Mamie Rogers, where he was mildly guilty? The irony was almost Sophoclean in its acidity. Michael decided it did not bear thinking of as he awaited the hapless recorder of student achievement or lack thereof. The knock seemed unpromising indeed. Would he open the door and find that Waldo had become a raven announcing that "nevermore" would Michael have a career at Illyria College?

No, it was just Waldo, disheveled, stricken, jittery Waldo, wire rims glued to his face, as though a large and sun drenched raisin not only had spectacles but even seemed to feature them as a natural and recurring trait. Michael invited him to sit.

"So, well, OK, Michael. Sorry to be bothering you like this, OK? You're Mamie Rogers' advisor, right, or you were last year?

(Michael shuddered.) Well, she's got this problem with some transfer credits from…oh, no, that's another girl. OK, let's see. Oh, yeah, now I recall. I just want to make sure that this other girl, Jennifer Madole, is majoring in English, right? I know she's indicated that she is, but we have to double-check everything. So did you sign her Declaration of Major card? Do you recall?"

"Oh, yes, Waldo. I signed it; here—just a minute—I can find it in my file cabinet. I always keep a record, you see….right here: I signed it in May of 1959. The 3rd to be specific about it."

"Great. This is just great, Michael. We've had some incidents where these students say they've declared a major but haven't got the faculty co-signature. That's why I have to monitor these things."

Michael didn't know why Waldo couldn't have done all this on the phone, and Michael said so. He added:

"But no great matter, Waldo. As long as you're here in the clutches of my office, I wanted to tell you something." Michael sensed that he should leave the quiz biz alone, but Waldo had irritated him with this little Mamie scare. Those leaving the isle of great fear oft find an anger zone.

"I've had one of the more influential members of the Curriculum Committee tell me that he's supporting me in this whole final exam mess. Now I'm not blaming you, Waldo. I know you were assigned the job of checking, just as you're checking on this, this Rogers or Madole or whatever her name is. But perhaps I should tell you that Henry Taylor has informed me that he has my back. I do think this absurd charge against me goes to the heart of faculty rights."

"Yeah, well, OK, Michael. I just had to call you up and ask you and then stop by and make sure the charge was groundless. OK? But hey, one thing I'm a bit perplexed about."

Michael thought that if there were only one thing Waldo was perplexed about it would be a far better than average day for him.

"What's that, Waldo?"

"Well, OK. You said that *Henry Taylor* is supporting you?"

"Yes. So?"

"Yeah, OK. Well, I think I'd better leave now. I've got to stop by Les Cole's office, too."

Michael could not understand why Waldo had left his office so briskly. Such determined gait seemed at odds with the usual shuffle with which Waldo shambled through life and files alike. You'd almost think the guy had a *purpose*, Michael thought, and then returned to marking quizzes on imagery in the verse of Arthur Hugh Clough.

This time, however, he'd made sure not to toss any master copies in the wastebasket. He had made a New Year's vow: all such masters were to be metamorphosed, after use, into not fewer than 32 pieces. Michael thought it was a transformation as useful as any found in Ovid.

He chuckled to himself at this joke. Life was good after all. Any day now he should surely be hearing from the poet Mr. Rayster, expressing gratitude to Michael for having published the magnificent "Wet." (Michael wondered why Rayster had not yet written.) Even Elise Morgan seemed no longer a threat--a stream, misleadingly deep to be sure, which Michael had forded at last, emerging upon a dry land where no drowning was even remotely possible.

Chapter 25: The Uncanny Events of Committee Rooms
(January 25, 1960)

Henry decided to get to the committee room ten minutes early, but he still could not fathom why. Was it because he still had cunning left in him and wanted to soak up the atmosphere in which he would have to exercise it? Or had he given up and chosen to come to the execution chamber early just in order to punish himself even more?

The wait reminded him of a time more than twenty years before, when he had sat with his cocker spaniel waiting for his parents to return from a base cocktail party, for Henry's father had been "military," as it is called in the United States, and had led Henry and his family from place to place, town to town to city, and from base to base. Henry's father was never the thundering colonel type, like Lester Cole. He was a taciturn supply sergeant, saying nothing unless he had something to say and even then with minimal audial oomph. But as a child Henry had rarely been able to settle anywhere, and his newness, combined with his incessant stoop and elongated facial resemblance to an aquatic mammal, made him the immediate butt of both childhood and pubescent jokes. If only, Henry still thought, he could have settled down somewhere. The kids would have gotten used to him, grown accustomed to his face and his posture, seen in him an intelligence and perhaps even a warm loyalty that a shallow acquaintance would never reveal (for Henry was always guarded). He might have been—oh, the ache of that high school word—*accepted*, even if never popular.

His two older sisters had no doubt suffered from the same feelings of being temporary, but they had been more mainstream, more outgoing, and more attractive. They had taken almost no interest in the little brother five and six years their junior. They were close to each other. Henry had come along as an afterthought, as, he once thought, a musical coda that few think is really necessary, optional at best. His parents had been kind, if distant.

On that day about which he reminisced he sat watching out the window for the return of his parents and feeling sorry for himself, the little dog napping at his feet. Henry had always been a smart and informed child. He was already in possession of sentimental impulses, even at age ten, and so he was able to envision quite easily that the dog was his only friend, a fact about which he had mixed emotions, as the dog was loyal and yet just a dog and thus not overly discriminating. Henry's gratitude at the existence of the dog blended with a self-disgust that only a dog would find him worthy.

He had learned about antibiotics by then and imagined on that day that in an earlier time, if the dog nipped him, he might die of blood poisoning with no penicillin to bail him out. He even wondered if he wouldn't have been better off—the self-pity was truly working up lather by then.

Now of course Henry had grown up; gotten his doctorate from Rutgers; and he had learned that syrupy emotions are regarded as third-rate in the literary pantheon of taste. And yet, sitting in this committee room without even the pup to comfort him, if that's what the pup did then, he could not rid himself of this schmaltz, which made him feel even worse about himself.

For not only had Henry been caught out; he had also now regressed into the very emotions that the Goethes and Schillers and Machiavellis thought of as lacking restraint and rigor. Henry had become a character in Mary Shelley's *Frankenstein*, a novel he loathed for its phony, in his view, big bow-wow incantations about the grandeur of mountains and its melodramatic invocations of monsters as victims. Henry had once laughed at the idea of a monster as cruelly put upon, and yet he could not resist thinking of himself as…a monster cruelly put upon.

In sum, Henry felt sorry for himself, and felt doubly sorry for himself because he had *allowed himself* to feel sorry for himself. It was though he were depressed not just because he was facing censure but also depressed at the brute fact of depression itself.

What an awful spiral he had descended into. He, Henry Taylor, who had become a man of fierce calculation and scheming because he knew that the world was an indifferent and sadistic place, had now morphed into the cheap vicissitudes of a sad little tyke with a soporific cocker spaniel as his only friend.

He rallied. He would explain that he had been placed in an impossible position: having to represent his own younger generation while at the same time supporting a desperate need for higher standards and regulations within the college they all loved. It was no wonder that he had prevaricated with one of his younger colleagues in the name of institutionalizing an indispensable final exam system that had met generational resistance. He had been wrong, he would explain, and yet while ends do not always justify means, sometimes they do. He had simply miscalculated the relationship. That was all. It had been an error of judgment, for which he was sorry. Yet—he would go on to say—he remained a vital liaison between the young and restless and the older and wiser. He and he alone could supply this otherwise missing link.

As his seniors filed in, Henry's self-pity seemed to file out. He would see this through. He would not permit a mean world to make him, of all people, feel guilty. He would yet avenge himself upon all those who had taunted him, in public schools from Fort Benning, Georgia to Fort Monmouth, New Jersey to Fort Sheridan, Illinois— all those adolescents who had, in a perversely beneficial way, opened his eyes to the perfidy of the planet.

Soon they were all seated round the old oaken table, the usual suspects of martial Lester Cole, fuss budgeting Harry Finch, voluble Horace Fuller, along with a few of the committee's non-entities like Wilbur Moffit of Spanish with his perpetually earnest smile and Jeremiah King of Sociology/Anthropology with his leathered skin (too much summer field work?) and bowed head, as though asking everyone to guess whether he was in deep thought or fervent prayer or if there were any difference. Moffit and King never said anything. With the former one was doing well to get a nod of assent. With the latter a victory was mere eye contact.

By then Henry had decided to squeeze both hands, and tightly, around the nest of burs that stood invisibly in the room. He would astonish them with his frankness—they can call it aggressive confession if they like, he thought, or if they are clever enough to label it so.

"Let's please get to it. I shall be apologizing to Michael Moggs. I rifled through a wastebasket and found the quiz." This was true, but so far little attention seemed to have been paid to the fact that the quiz was given as far back as November. Henry hoped there for the status quo.

"The quiz was labeled EXAM, so naturally I thought Moggs had violated policy. I was wrong. But I was trying to help this committee, and all of you, bring some redemption to what has been allowed to degenerate at this college we all love. Now I should never have gone to Michael and offer to support him against charges that I myself had made. That was deceitful, I'll admit. But it was my way of getting us past the incident. *Of course* I could have gone to Michael Moggs and confessed my role, but he would have held it against me, thus resulting inevitably in negative emotions. Or he might have found out on his own, again with a vengeful outcome. So I tried to settle the matter with, yes, lack of candor. I am sorry. I tried to apply, in my own way, a palliative to the wound that I myself first inflicted with my, uh, understandable error about the original quiz. I hope you gentlemen will see that my intentions were honorable, if not my outcome, and that this was more a matter of miscalculation than of outright dishonesty."

It was a good speech, Henry thought, even better for its having been mostly spontaneous. Where now is the sad little boy with the cocker spaniel? He has become a man, a shrewd prince in the Machiavellian mode, and one with yet a career of power and prestige at Illyria College. He had seen the other committee members as he made his case but had not dared to look closely. He was too busy propounding what he had to say to them.

Yet now why was Lester Cole rising to his feet, as though to pronounce judgment? People on this committee did not stand in the committee room. It was not done. Henry suddenly thought that, despite his grand if slippery disquisition, he was about to become beheaded by a senior faculty member—that Lester was about to do to Henry's noggin what some barber had done to Lester's own hair. He could easily imagine Lester's volunteering to commandeer the firing squad.

Henry's frame was in full tremolo as Lester spoke to say:

"You're a dishonest young man, Professor Taylor. Don't try to squeeze out of the box your own mendacity has put you in. But you don't have to apologize to your fellow young bastard, Michael Moggs. You don't need to apologize to him. In fact, if I ever find out you did, I'll be after you with my old Army-issue Luger."

The other members of the committee growled, not in pristine concord but in full approbation.

"But why?"

"You younger faculty are the last to know," said Lester. "It was always so, I suppose. Anyhow, I'll give it to you straight, Slick Henry. You don't need to kowtow to Michael Moggs because he has undertaken the audacious task of closing down this college for good."

"He what? What are you talking about Les? How?"

"How? Because he published a goddamned poem saying that God is a goddamned sex fiend. Is that a good enough reason for you, Henry?"

So far the meeting had not gone as Henry had contemplated.

Chapter 26: The Unpleasant Shocks of Presidential Trash Cans
(January 26, 1960)

The day after Henry learned from Les both the good news—that no one would blame him for trying to ruin Michael Moggs—and the bad news—that he would need to find a new college anyhow, Mrs. Wendell McCrory—Eloise--used her building and office keys to return, at 7 PM, to President Adams' office.

There were several inches of snow, so despite the relative lateness of the hour—for by 7 in the winter a vast darkness reigned—the half moon on white ice lit her way down the sidewalk to the administration building. The half-light made her feel ever more at sea about what she was planning to do. Mrs. McCrory was astonished at herself. But she was not ashamed. Her own peace of mind demanded action, and action is what her mental tranquility would get. She could stand it no longer.

She did not wish to switch on the hall and stair lights—it occurred to her that someone might see them and investigate what should have been a darkened building—but she had forgotten her flashlight. There was no choice. The stairs had an odd configuration, an extreme spiral to a lower landing, followed by straight-on steps to the second floor. Like all of Illyria's buildings, the administration building—Brannon Hall, built 1855—was fairly old. Its facade had endured many phases—Italianate, Second Empire, Attic—before setting on its current bland Modernism. Mrs. McCrory, who would have completed her degree at Illyria had the Depression not come, enjoyed reading about architecture. She thought of Brannon Hall having suffered through architectural insults of various kinds. On occasion she imagined the building, where she had worked for twenty years, had had to undergo the agonies of her own marriage, though fortunately Wendell had done her the favor of crashing into a giant chestnut some eight Octobers before. It had been one of those tricky twilight evenings of the mid-autumn. After Wendell's demise, Mrs. McCrory thought that she, unlike Brannon, could determine her own façade, though she never did. She remained the same dependable mélange of distinguished gray hair, discretely powdered face, and honeydew smile.

Why break up a winning team, for Mrs. McCrory was now an institution in the president's office. Winston was her second chief exec.

But her very assumption of fixity had undergone tremors. The last several days had been one of self-evident panic. Phones rang, calls not going through her but directly to Winston's line. Trustees and town officials came without appointments and were admitted by Winston over her mild objections. Winston himself looked as though he were an eight year-old boy whose birthday cake had been stolen and spinach offered—on the floor—instead. At one point Mrs.

McCrory thought Winston might vomit. At another she thought he might faint. It was though President Adams were, more than ever, the gigantic rock about which people had joked, but that this time the great boulder's very integrity, the togetherness that gave it life and being, was being pulverized, not at once but in unbearable and drawn out stages. Winston was being worn to pebbles in her own plainest and helpless sight.

She must, Mrs. McCrory thought, get to the bottom of this matter. And so it was with a fury that she turned the key to her and Winston's office. She switched on the lights. She knew that her door key would also open Winston's inner office. That was an unwise policy, but Winston could never keep up with two separate keys, so Buildings and Grounds had agreed, grudgingly, to give him one-key-fits-all.

She entered. At this point she knew she was going to turn back. There was simply no way that she would rifle through Winston's files, his desk, or his shelves. Perhaps there was no document that would explain all the near panic of the past few days, no key to all destructive mythologies. There would be no single piece of paper that would account for the pale green in Winston's visage, the dyspepsia in visiting trustees, or the incredulous looks on the oblong face of Kerry Cookson, the town mayor. In any case she would not be looking. What had she been thinking?

And then she saw it. Winston was no ordinary man, or so he thought, and therefore he would not have a naked trashcan upon his well-carpeted floor. Instead he had ordered a spiral shaped green holder in order to give some majesty to the quotidian, prosaic fact of discarded pulp, on which perishable black type had been inscribed. Mrs. McCrory always thought it had been Winston's way of holding off the dreadful reality of transience. She so admired him.

At the top of the can she saw what must have been a Photostat copy of a letter, with *Charles Burdette Candy Smooches* letterhead, that began, perhaps with a threatening stiffness, "Dear President Winston Adams of Illyria College." It went on:

I have been seriously ill and am therefore asking Reverend Royce Rex Jameson to assist me in the drafting of this letter. I am also making copies for my attorneys, although I do not consider this a strict necessity because I have made no commitments in writing. It is true, however, that I did informally promise the former Mrs. Winston Adams (Eve) to allow the Burdette Auditorium at Illyria College to become leased to an outside organization. This promise, if fulfilled, would have contravened my previous agreement with Illyria that the building is to be used exclusively for Illyria College purposes and only for the betterment of human morality both in the United States and around the world.

This contravention was an idea proposed by the previous Mrs. Adams, and it seemed a good one at the time since the outside organization itself was mandated to agree to similar such goals. In exchange of course Illyria, my beloved alma mater, would have been able to raise needed monies from such a contract. However, Reverend Jameson '26, one of my first beloved Burdette Scholars, has brought to my attention a poem recently printed in the Illyria Iamb. *It is called "Wet" and is said to have been written by one Philip Rayster. I do not know Mr. Rayster and have no notions of his linkage or lack of same to Illyria College. I am quite certain, however, that he is morally and ethically demented. Anyone who would state that our Supreme Being has nocturnal emissions is full of mockery and rage. He is also a sign of our times, of hirsute Communists just off our shores, of godless dictators pounding their shoes at international meetings, television game shows riddled by cheats, and perhaps worst of all surgery by which males may become females. A young* Catholic *prepares to run for the presidency, while his prospective chief opponent, ten years ago, called his Senatorial opponent, with monumental lack of gallantry, "The Pink Lady."*

I am aware, somewhat at least, of the financial ramifications for Illyria. I am an old and sick man. What do I know, as the noble Montaigne once asked—I read him in the original French under the tutelage of the divine Professor Leandri during my Illyrian student days. And so I ask, with the immortal essayist from his tower in

Bordeaux, what do I know? I know only enough to know what I want and what God—a Disembodied Being—wants me to want. God wants me to want Illyria to close rather than become a haven of demons who would taunt us with disrespect for the One without Whom, as President Eisenhower has said, the American way of life makes no sense whatsoever.

Charles J. Burdette, Illyria '94

Mrs. McCrory gasped. This was shocking but no surprise. Something wicked had come to the office to which she was devoted. This had been apparent for forty-eight hours. One who got implications quickly, she thought she might have to spend the latter days of her working life with her daughter, helping her mind her Middlebury gift shop, after all. That would do. She loved her daughter and found this affection reciprocal. She only wished her name wasn't Muriel. That had been Mr. McCrory's idea, and by the time he left, forever, it was far too late to modify a birth certificate to read "Janet."

This was the saddest letter, and perhaps the most melancholy event, of Mrs. McCrory's lifetime, exceeded only by the passing of her parakeet Crackle, whom she found one day standing not on his perch but on the bottom of his cage. The next day he was flat on his feathers.

Chapter 27: The Tragic Poignancy of Collective Closure
(February 10, 1960-May 25, 1981)

With an anvil heart Winston announced the closing of Illyria College at a noon meeting in the pristine and cavernous auditorium of the Burdette Building. This was an imprecation by Winston. The large room would not only hold virtually the entire campus. It was also fitting, Winston thought, that the man who turned his back on Illyria should also have given the venue in which its demise was announced. He hoped Charles would learn this fact and that it would hurt him.

Winston's own thoughts about the imbroglio were varied. He did blame himself for some mismanagement and for what he called "development deficiencies." But he also blamed the world for not supporting, unasked, what was self-evidently a *magnificently* noble endeavor. Nor was he amused when, on the late afternoon of his fateful announcement, he found a sign on the door of the president's house that read, "Get your adverbs here." Someone had been amused, or not amused, by Winston's excess application of such words as "magnificently" in order to modify superlative adjectives in no need of further adornment.

As for the poem, "Wet," Winston had surprisingly few thoughts. He was himself a man of grandiloquent prose but not of eccentric verse.

Still, he hardly imagined that the poet had meant literally that God had wet dreams, but even if he did that was no reason to shut down one of New England's greatest hallmarks of liberal education. He did not blame the poet nor did he find particular fault with Michael Moggs. It was Charles Burdette whom Winston blamed—him and a Board of Trustees whose own "niggardliness" (Winston's harsh word but used only in private) had led to "implacably unfixable financial disrepair" (the phrase he used during his disconsolate but (he hoped) eloquent proclamation of the end.

In the event people limped through the final term. Faculty taught classes. Staff nudged paper along. The various parties made their future plans, and several of the younger faculty received encouraging letters from other small New England colleges, inviting them to apply but with of course no guarantees.

It was an early spring. No snow fell after March 11. Robins returned early, though a sudden dry cold spell froze a few of them as dead as Mrs. McCrory's much loved Crackle. Their thin-feathered reunion with Vermont had proven somewhat premature. Mamie and her strapping young boyfriend found one of them on a walk and bought some dirt from a local florist, at Mamie's tender insistence, in order to bury it. Even Mamie's new squeeze was not strong enough to pierce the still frozen ground. His spade would have been futile in the cemented earth, which was as illiquid as Illyria College's assets. They were both planning to transfer to a state college in New York.

The older faculty, such as Lester Cole and Harry Finch, decided to retire. They would soon have Social Security, and their houses were paid for. Horace Fuller often volunteered to address the local Illyria Lions club, where he could always be depended upon for orations about classical values and the American way of life. A judge was assigned to administer whatever assets could be gleaned from sales of college property. All former faculty received compensation checks from time to time. But they were slow and uncanny in their monthly appearances. The last was mailed out on November 1, 1967.

Younger faculty mostly found jobs elsewhere, the majority of them at other schools, but a few had to settle for high school teaching and one went into real estate and another into TV repair, though in time he opened his own store. This was Arnold Ruger, a psychologist who learned his trade quickly by associating various tubes behind the set with types of behavioral complexes. For some reason he linked the tube for horizontal reception with the persecution complex and the one for picture sharpness with the inferiority complex. He once related this little tidbit at a dinner party and when asked to explain his system he declined but added, in a show of wit never exhibited at morose Illyria, "it's complex."

The flora and fauna surrounding the campus seemed little interested in the passing of the college into oblivion. The sap ran in the maples as though by instinct, indifferent to the day, in late fall, when it would no longer run, as though the sap knew it was on a cycle of renewal that had eluded Illyria College, which seemed more like the subversive poet's God, capable of but a finite number of emissions. Holly ferns had as many flowers as ever (none) but found a way to force themselves above the ground, a victory over circumstance that Illyria had also failed to achieve. Illyria would no doubt have been happy to live on, even without flowers, but it would not live on at all. The deer were glad of the warmer air, and the sheep, cooped up for much of the long cold season, gamboled on the Green Mountain sides as if assured that the most they would lose, now that the year was getting on, were the three bags full of wool cited in the children's rhyme. At any rate they would not be providing any more sheepskins for the graduates of tiny Illyria College.

In time the campus was sorted out. The town of Illyria, it turns out, needed both a new city hall and a new public library but had few enough funds to build either from scratch. Illyria's buildings were easily adapted. The arrival of a new plant for manufacture of sodium borate (used mostly as a fire retardant) created a demand for affordable housing. The residence halls once adorned by Elise and Mamie fit this need nicely.

Charles Burdette died the year after the Great Shuttering (as Faye Roberts dubbed it). He said his conscience was not fogged in the slightest. But he must have had some small pang of remorse, for he did leave monies to begin an Illyria College Memorial Fund. It took over Bolt Hall and kept memorabilia of the college's history in a museum. Alums passing from Burlington to Boston or from Burlington to Bangor would sometimes stop by and survey the ruins of their collapsed degrees. Hundreds wept openly or slightly the day Winston announced the college's closing, and in order to remember that day properly the sidewalk to the Bolt Hall museum was officially named the Walk of Woe. The snarky Paul Hamlin, who had long been suspicious of Winston's management, wanted it named "Hamlin's Way: A Walk of Woe, and I Told You So." This was offered in jest, but the appropriate committee overruled it anyhow, just for the sake of thoroughness.

In an irony Charles did not live to see, his own behemoth, the Burdette Building, was taken by the New England Christian Fellowship, which used it for various events year round. Charles had his promotion of moral fervor after all, though most of the preachers were against urban poverty more than they opposed Fidel Castro. Charles had he lived might have thought some of them "pink," and would have said so, for it was not ungentlemanly on his planet to call *men* pink, only to assign that color to ladies and their under combinations.

Winston landed on his feet. Malcolm Mole helped him get a job at a small foundation, where he could give away money instead of having to raise it. This suited Winston's proclivities much better. He lived on until 1975, when he passed away of bowel cancer at the fairly young age of seventy-two. Both Little Annie and Coercive Eve were at his bedside. They bonded over the occasion. Annie had found in Winston's effects a printed poem, a page torn from a book. It read:

I wish I was an ice cream man,
I know just what I'd do.
I'd eat up all the profits
And have some chocolate too.

On this page was scrawled, in Winston's mother's delicate hand, "Memorized by Winston and recited by him to great applause at expression school, Marblehead, Massachusetts, 1908." Over coffee in the hospital cafeteria, as Winston lay dying upstairs, Annie and Eve agreed that this discovery revealed for him what the sled "Rosebud" had been to Charles Foster Kane in *Citizen Kane*. Inside all Winston's bluster was the scared little boy whose best defense had been the successful offering of a poem. Thus had Winston come to depend on eloquence, more than deeds, for the rest of his days. Kane in the movie had never again enjoyed the sheer pleasure of a childhood snow sled and spent his lifetime in a futile attempt, via overbearing power, to get it back. Winston longed for constant redundancies of that first, stirring oratorical feat.

So Eve and Annie concluded about the man they had both loved, sort of, though each confided to the other that perhaps they admired the monument more than they had loved the man behind the marble. Their positing of Winston's inner terror supplied a gilded grandeur to his lifetime habit of bull. It also suggested that Winston had a complicated relationship with poems. He died the next morning at exactly 6 AM. The Illyria College Chapel Bell, had it still existed, might have tolled meekly, as was its wont, for Winston.

Faye Roberts had been several years older than Winston, but she outlived him by ten. She died at 89, on a May late afternoon, handing a gin fizz to William Montague, the Bill of Wrongs, who had taken his act in American constitutional history to Keene State in New Hampshire and had come for a visit back to dear old Illyria. By then he was himself retired, never married, and never regretful. He drank Faye's tart Kool-Aid to her very end.

Michael Moggs at Illyria had been a conventional young scholar with slightly unusual modernist interests. Round Dean Richards, whose career also ended with Illyria's demise, had told Michael that no one really blamed him for "Wet," that it was just the final straw and that other elements had really caused the death of the college. There would be no retaliation, and the dean would gladly write him a strong letter relative to other employment. But it was though a switch had been pulled in Michael. Soon enough he drifted west, living on odd jobs, reading more Hart Crane but also the syncopated and oft rude verse of Ginsburg and Ferlinghetti and Bukowski, and becoming more and more certain that a new poetics, and hence a revolution, was airborne, and waterborne too. He settled in San Francisco. He became an unrecognizable version of his Illyrian self. His beard and long hair turned him into what Faye Roberts, had she seen him, would have called an armpit with eyes. He snorkeled the deep and surfed the waves, but found that peyote ill mixed with either or both. His body washed ashore in June 1967. He was wet until the end. His hippie girlfriend, who looked nothing like Mamie Rogers, found a check from Illyria College in his mailbox. She forged his signature and spent it all at a Happening in Haight-Ashbury.

On February 10, 1960, in the Burdette Building, in its splendid acoustically perfect and spacious auditorium, Winston had called the perishing of Illyria a "an immeasurably profound tragedy." Yet within an hour, lightly bundled against unseasonably moderate elements for February, seated on a bench by The Illyrian, were Elise Morgan and Faye Roberts, over four decades apart. They chatted with glee. Elise had already decided to transfer to Smith, Faye's alma mater, where her precocity would be better appreciated and challenged; while Faye would stay in Illyria and write a delicious book about the Great Illyrian Shuttering. They laughed and laughed that day. In 1971 Professor Elise Morgan would publish a prize-winning tome on Darwin and Blake, but Faye never finished her book. Still, the notes became one basis for the present volume. They laughed some more that day. The waning cold had no discernible effect upon their mutual hilarity.

Epilogue

(November 14, 1989)

"I think we've done about as much as we can for you for now, Dean Taylor. There are more questions than answers about the future."

This was about as good a statement as Dean Henry Taylor could have hoped for. He'd tried to ignore symptoms—the occasional bleeding and incessant weariness—but finally his wife had insisted, so off the clinic he went, in fear and trembling but with a relief that at last he would find out.

"I'd say stop the chemo and radiation for at least six months. Come back; let's run the tests, and who knows, we just might have some good news here," said Dr. Edwin Poynter.

Poynter was on the young side of middle age, with sandy hair thick enough to be a fortress and perfect incisors that almost seemed to applaud when he talked. He had a better bedside manner than most of his fellow technicians did. He was like a sympathetic car mechanic who tells a customer he'll need a brand new transmission but they hardly make them any longer for that model. Henry Taylor was lucky to have Dr. Poynter—oh, how well he knew that! He thought, "I am not an ungrateful man, whatever else you might say of me."

But Henry was not grateful for a superfluity of bad cells in his bladder.

"By the way, Dean, I never asked you: why did you ever leave German? That was my favorite language when I was an undergrad. In fact, I was getting close to fluent and if I'd spent a term in Berlin as I'd planned, I'd have gone all the way with it. But of course I decided against Berlin in the end; had to study for the MCATs."

"Well, that was one of those decisions we all make from time to time; forks in the path, Robert Frost, road not taken, and all that. What was it that baseball player said? 'If there's a fork in the road, take it?' I always get a laugh from that one. But you asked about my own decision to leave the *teaching* of German. Well, you see, I'd always wanted to be a dean. That's rare for a professor, I guess, but that was just I."

"I was never so well-aimed," said Thomas Poynter. "I wanted, ironically, to be a German teacher but then got into medicine. And then I wondered if I could become a doctor in Munich or something—but that was a fantasy. No, I had to decide. And I chose oncology, so I could give some hope to deans!"

"Ha! Well, you've given some hope to me, or should I say, *some hope*?"

"But seriously, Dean Taylor, why did you want to become a dean?"

"An excellent question, Dr Poynter, and probably an accursed one, too." If Poynter had once not been "well-aimed," as he called it, by now Henry was "well-zapped." He wore a baseball cap to hide his total loss of follicles (chemo), and his legs, never thick, had become what felt like chalky matchsticks (radiation). "Well, the answer, I think, is that I was always drawn to rules."

"Rules?"

"Rules. Oh, I'm almost ashamed to admit it now, but what do I have to lose at this point, right? Your prognosis isn't awful but it's short of great. I'm a bit guilty about it, but I, once a scholar who should have reveled in the shades of ambiguity found in Rilke or Thomas Mann, was almost addicted to rules. I always had the idea that if we just had a rule for this or that, all could be well—or at least better. My idea was that rules could head off bad things. And who better to propound and enforce rules in the academy than a dean, right? Thus you see sitting before you—clad in a Reds cap (I love baseball rules)—Dean Henry L. Taylor."

"So, Dean Henry L. Taylor—quite an august title—how did you first learn that you were in love with rules?"

"This is just between us, all right, Dr Poynter. Well, it was in about 1959. I was a faculty member, a young man, the junior member of an important faculty committee that was supposed to represent the rights and privileges of my colleagues. It was at this little school in Vermont—it closed, and you'll have never heard of it. The group was a sort of labor union committee, though of course we professors are too elitist to think of ourselves as unionizing. And so I began to think somewhat administratively. We had to meet with the dean at the time—quite a lot, actually. And I saw that rules could be written or changed to favor the faculty or the administration, and we had some struggles over that, though now I forget most of them. And then one late autumn day I happened by a wastebasket near my office. That changed everything."

"A wastebasket? You know, Dean Taylor, I have a new patient to see, but I think I can be late. I think, now that you've mentioned a *wastebasket*, that I *should* be late!"

"Well, Doctor. I don't want you to cheat your next victim. But if you have a few moments…"

"I do."

"Well, all right. This story does me no credit, understand, but you see, we had just put in this new rule. We used to have final exams during the last week of the regular teaching term, but this had proved unworkable and chaotic so we put in a special exam period. *And profs were not supposed to give any final exam except during this new period. That was the rule.* Well, one early December day I was passing down the hall when my eye spotted this half-sheet of paper with the word "Exam" at the top. So I picked it out of the basket and read it and discovered that there was a series of questions on the poet Hart Crane. I became a bit maniacal and realized that this 'exam' had been written by this colleague of mine in English, who specialized in the modernist poets. I really despised this guy for his flamboyance and, admittedly, his popularity with students, and I was sure he had flouted the new exam rule. So I gathered up the evidence and marched the next morning into the curriculum committee meeting and then into the dean's office and then into the registrar's office and I said, 'Look. Look. Look what I've found. And look, are we going to let people do whatever they want around here? Isn't that why we put in this new rule?'"

"And what did they do?"

"They did precisely what I had forced them to do. They took up the matter with this man Moggs, who was as slippery as ever in getting out of it. He said, 'Why, this is just a quiz. This isn't a final exam at all.' So I had no case; the dean, the registrar had no case. End of story. Or so I thought...."

"Ah, I sense, Dean Taylor, that there may be some sort of reckoning for somebody here."

"Yes, yes, yes. Indeed. A reckoning for someone! Well, Moggs immediately told as many colleagues as he could about this summons from the dean and the registrar, and of course there was an uprising about how bureaucratic we've become and how the administration doesn't trust us and is trying to oppress us, and so forth. And then someone asked: 'Well, how would they have known about this little quiz in the first place?' And before I knew it the very committee I was on was charged with carrying on an investigation; you see, despite our name as the Curriculum Committee, we were also the group charged with protecting the status and rights of the faculty. Dr. Poynter, you now look not only at a man who had a few too many cells in his bladder; you're also looking a man who, in his younger and healthier days, was in a very tough spot."

"So what happened, Dean Taylor?"

"What happened is that I suffered a first-rate invasion of panic. But first, I admit, I virtually wished Moggs were dead, or would die. I always thought Moggs full of constant self-congratulation about how free he was and how uptight he *wasn't*. It never occurred to the liberated Moggs that the world needs rules and that someone has to enforce them. He was in a sort of permanently suspended adulthood if you ask me—I know you didn't ask me, Doctor. I was in such a state that I would be found out—and the whole faculty would despise me—that I realized for the first time that when one's own survival is at stake you'd wish death on the whole planet if that's what it took for yourself to last and prosper. And then, perhaps suffused with this grim awareness, I did something monumentally, colossally dumb. *I went myself to Moggs and told him that my committee—and I personally—would get to the bottom (no pun intended, since we're talking about a wastebasket) of the whole sorry mess. I told him I myself was personally on the case."*

"Wow! In other words you tried to take charge of the case in order to make sure the truth was never found."

"Precisely. Sounds corrupt, doesn't it? Well, I guess it was a tad corrupt. But you see, I'd forgotten something in my machinations: The dean and registrar knew who had reported Moggs. So when the two of them started complimenting me to their colleagues, it got back to the registrar and dean, who then proceeded—they thought they had no choice—*to tell Moggs that it was I who had reported him in the first place."*

"Gracious, as my old gram used to say. Were you ruined, Dean Taylor? Evidently not, since you are *Dean* Taylor."

"No, not at all. You see, while I might have been wrong about Moggs and the final exam, I wasn't entirely wrong about Moggs himself. He edited a poetry journal on campus that printed an obscene poem that offended the school's leading donor. The whole place shut down as a result. The school lost its angel. I don't know what happened to Moggs, but I managed to get another job—the wastebasket scandal was nothing compared to the poetry scandal—and eventually went from teaching German to becoming a dean, for in truth I liked governance a lot more than liked Goethe. As I said before, I just wanted to be a dean. I liked rules. If you have strong rules that every faculty member is supposed to erase her or his own blackboard, then other faculty members who inherit the room wouldn't have to do it and we could avoid the inevitable grumbling that occurs when Professor X complains that she has to erase Professor Y's board. Rules are just underrated. We can all pretend to be hippie profs and disdain them. But they protect us; they save us time. They give us predictability. Thus saith Dean Taylor."

"And now? Now what do you think—I mean, Dean, that, just as you say, my prognosis is iffy."

"Well, now I don't really know for sure. I've managed to keep up with the job somehow, even through all this chemo. But as you know, I'm thinking about retiring early. My wife wants me to. We have no children, you know, so it's just her to advise me. Can Goethe teach me how to die? Should I go back to him? Can Rilke instruct me in Mortality 101? Now I'm, I'm struck by the fact that dying is also a rule, one we all must obey. This has lessened my love of rules a bit. And if I recall correctly, Goethe himself once said—I'll give you the English version—'A useless life is an early death.' Am I dead already? I've a feeling, Doctor, that it's too late for the scholarship to save me now."

"But didn't you accomplish things as dean of Bricker?"

"Oh, yes, I did. And one of them was to install a set-aside final exam period. Isn't that a kicker?"

"Well, I'm late for the next victim, as you call him. But...so right now what do you think is the meaning of your life?"

"I can't even start to answer that, Dr. Poynter. But, well, maybe you can ask me that again in six months."

"During what might be your final exam period, you mean."

Dean Henry Taylor did not reply. He stirred the toothpicks that were his limbs. His face had been ravaged, he knew, by the alien cells, which had turned his mug into a softened walnut trampled by an elephant. He tightened his Reds cap. He managed himself off the examination table and hobbled out of the examination room. It hadn't been a full confession—he was still prevaricating about some elements—but it was as much of an admission as the world deserved. There was something badly wrong with his bladder, but in his pride he would never permit any malfunction of his determination. He had nothing more to say.

Dr. Poynter never spoke to Henry again, but he was intrigued by his odd confession and so, three months later, attended Henry's memorial service, where the new dean (who owed his job to Henry's fatal illness) praised Henry as an able man who had brought uniform policies to Bricker College. He included in the list the official final examination period. No one said that Henry had taught Bricker to "have its period." Everyone knew that would have been impolite.

Yet they little knew that Henry had been one of the better things to emerge from the long ago imbroglio of Illyria College.

The day after the memorial service, after Henry had presumably faced his ultimate final exam in Ohio, back in Vermont the New England Christian Fellowship finally raised enough money to purchase The Illyrian. Still a stone mélange of propulsion rocket and praying mantis, it was renamed "The Miracle."

The End

The Second Novella:

What Happened to Professor Elves?

Whoever fights monsters should see to it that in the process he does not become a monster. And if you gaze long enough into an abyss, the abyss will gaze back into you. –Friedrich Nietzsche

Whenever I climb I am followed by a dog named Ego. --Friedrich Nietzsche

In memory of Professor Theodore Elves (August 7, 1859-October 2, 1926). Life flees. Art endures. –From a plaque on the Elves Art Hall, Belton College

TABLE OF CONTENTS

MAJOR DRAMATIS PERSONAE

I: EARLY SEPTEMBER 1926

II: LATER SEPTEMBER 1926

III: OCTOBER 1926

IV: 1936-2006

Major Dramatis Personae

Theodore Elves: Professor of Classics, Belton College—a devotee of ancient Greek beauty and bilious enemy of Professor David Grendel

David Grendel: Professor of Philosophy, Belton College—an adamant skeptic and foe of Professor Elves

Irving Muldrow: President of Belton College—self-blaming and tormented, with an unwanted fetish for cobras

Gwenela Sulloway: Assistant Professor of English (Victorian Literature) and matron of McGregor Hall—nearly fanatical protector of well-clothed virtue

Harold Barker: Member of the Belton College Class of 1930—bright, mischievous, and (according to his girlfriend Gladys Sockwell) very cute, but afflicted with a tea party crisis.

Ronald Barker: Belton '26—the troubled, flailing older brother of Harold

Scott and Hansen: surnames of the Belton *Bullhorn* editors—too clever by three quarters and prone to create further difficulties where they already exist

***Editors of the Belton* Daily News:** unnamed and anonymous, they have a spiteful relationship with Belton College even as they pretend to boost it

I: EARLY SEPTEMBER 1926

Letter to Professor Theodore Elves
September 1, 1926

Dear Theodore:

I quite agree with your suggestion that we not meet directly for some time. Our most recent conversation fell into such strife that future face-to-face encounters are ill advised. It is possible, if barely, that our communicating by letter will improve civility.

This seems in one sense a silly move to make. After all, Belton College is a small place, and it is almost impossible for us to go even a week without spying one another. In that likely event I propose that we acknowledge one another but then move on. The less said in that forum, the better.

Here I can only restate, if briefly, what I have said before: that the role I assumed in bringing you to Belton was meant as an act of good will and charity. I was aware of your unhappiness at Illyria, and in Vermont, and was both eager and glad to bring you to Belton, and Wisconsin. Our Rose River valley is small but happy. Our institutional identity is modest in size but proud in achievement and potential. We have aspirations here.

That you would believe my role was somehow conniving and self-serving is poignant to me. But I must accept that that is your view after all.

We are both civilized men—gentlemen, I hope, of learning, I know. We were affable graduate mates at Columbia. Let us both endeavor to behave accordingly. You with your vast knowledge of classical languages and learning, and I with my interests in philosophical questions of knowledge, might make for a fruitful collaboration. But if it is not to be so, so be it.

Please respond to me in any way you wish, as long as it is in writing.

I remain your faithful servant and colleague,

David Grendel

Diary Entry by Professor Theodore Eleves
September 2, 1926

It is with some anguish that I got the latest letter from Grendel. He continues to pretend that he had no ulterior motives in smoothing my way to Belton. I shall be the first to confess its late summer beauty. The sunshine seems quite mellow this time of year. It has a thick and slow beam, a generous portion almost of joy, as though it is lolling about for as long as possible before being kidnapped by clouds. I find that the older I get, the more romantic balderdash of this sort I write. Meanwhile, I sometimes suspect, in much more pedestrian terms, that I am being lambasted behind my back because my gray flannels do not match my blue coat and tie. Thus do I venture back and forth between insecurity and cheer.

I am confessing to you today that I find myself unhappy. My suspicions of Grendel make me miserable, and yet I am sure they are true, and I must not abandon truth just because it is inconvenient for my soul. Above all, I miss my Diometa, who left me in Vermont, due to no fault of her own but entirely to the horrible pangs and complications of childbirth. With her has gone—you already know this, Diary, but I need to tell you again—our stillborn child, to whom it seems even now futile to attach a name. Especially of chagrin to me is that I was in Greece, conducting a tour, when this alarmingly premature birth, and subsequent tragedy, occurred. I should have been in Vermont. I was not.

Diometa and I were fifteen years apart in age. She did me the favor of loving me, an old sofa. She could have gotten someone younger and more vigorous. She chose me. I let her down. I shall endeavor to speak more of her later, Diary, during this coming autumn. It helps me negotiate the melancholy of the approaching season, which teems each year with memories of the lost Diometa.

I fear my prose is melodramatic. This also condemns me, for I can find no words commensurate with the tragedy and loss. And I must deal with Grendel's machinations on top of all else. I do, at least, have my classes and my scholarship—a pursuit of classical beauty is not ample recompense but far better than the void of which the Dionysians spoke.

My ultimate thought today is that because I have been inarticulate in so addressing you, Diary, that I might find greater consolation in my lectures. If I do not speak with you again for a spell, be offended not. There are enough already of those being offended here, such as Grendel. I promise, dear Diary, that this will not be the last visitation I make with you.

From the Belton College Catalogue (1926-27 Academic Year)

Belton was founded in the mid-1840s by pious men of Congregationalist and Presbyterian stock who left the confines of Yale University to bring both salvation and education to the wilderness of the West. Belton itself was located near two bodies of water, a river and a creek, there with the prospect perhaps of a water wheel and hence of some commercial manufacturing establishment. The trees cleared, these men immediately set forth a village green, a Congregational Church, and a college (Belton), which was originally a single building and seminary for the study of Latin, Greek, and higher theology. Among the first to matriculate was a young man who walked over seventy miles to enroll. The campus is situated on a high bluff near the Rose River. The mounds of ancient Indians irregularly but pleasingly roll across the lawn. The architecture is varied, ranging from Romanesque to Attic. The buildings tend to be small to moderate in size. The spirit of the landscape, both built and natural, is one of modesty and calm, as free as possible of various wild diversions that might afflict the life of the mind.

Notes From Professor Gwenelda Sulloway's Opening Lecture in Victorian Literature, September 3, 1926

I am taking the full class period today because, although it is the first class and you've yet to get a reading assignment, I don't want you to miss a single urgent moment of what I regard as an urgent course. This is why I just read to you Tennyson's great poem about Ulysses.

It is a poem above all about the denial of the flesh. Ulysses never says much of anything about his body in this poem. He never says anything of great import about whether his muscles have atrophied or his vision has faded. We can always presume that he is, though an old man, still hale and hearty, and of course here at Belton we want you to swim and run and play sport because we believe in healthy bodies. We might wish to think that Ulysses has lived a clean life, free of the mockery of wine, and that as a result he is still full of vigor.

But that is not the point, which is that he rarely thinks about his body. He only thinks of his resolve, which is a matter of attitude and will, and not of flesh. This is the great lesson of the poem. He is, as he says, "part of all that he has met," but for him these people whom he has met, and been instructed by, are not laurels to be rested upon. They are only preparations for the future—a future that, for Ulysses, he is still resolute to pursue. It is a matter of mental and spiritual attitude, not one of bodily health. The poem is a triumph of mind over matter, of virtue over flesh, whether decaying or fresh.

In your life--even, I regret to say, at Belton--you will find false prophets, those who will tell you that the only real thing worth following is beauty and that its ideal is in the human body. This is a dangerous idea. The body is vastly overrated. It is not a source of beauty. It is something to be done virtually without, if necessary, if we are to pursue the great goals of work and progress and resolution.

Beware of false prophets who would tell you to the contrary.

From the Diary of Belton President Irving Muldrow, September 3, 1926

Dastardly weather. Nothing but rain all day. Talk of the Rose flooding. The roof on Stratham Hall was supposed to have been repaired over the summer, but it's leaking again. I'm hopeless about these things. What do I, a minister (albeit a "presidential" one) know about roofs and rain. If the rain is hard enough will it puncture the shingles? I have no idea. I can only call the roofers and get their best advice, but they cannot get up there until these storms abate. When I took this position I imagined my life as one of great ideals and enchanting spirit. It's turned out to be buildings and dollars.

Did I mention people as well? The feud between David Grendel and Ted Eaves has apparently boiled over. I am told on good authority that they are down to letter exchanges now. They cannot be permitted in the same room, lest there be a clash between the idealistic widower and the skeptical bachelor. I am concerned about Teddy. He was chased here by the Vermont tragedy of a decade past. Pursued by lingering trauma, he trusts almost no one and has decided that Grendel has all sorts of ulterior motives arrayed against him. The thing is, Teddy is a pain. He is difficult. He is easily offended. I can see that David Grendel has a point of view.

Elves is also something of a genius. He has taken classics here in directions hitherto never thought of. But Grendel is not his only foe. Others, I fear, are perhaps jealous of him. The new Professor Sulloway is the sort who would be scandalized by Theodore's emphasis on the idealized human form. I should not wish the prim Gwenelda rooting against me. Besides all that, Theodore is now in his sixties. He is said to have epilepsy. Someone said he fainted last year, but I was not there to see him do so. I cannot say.

And about that roof, likewise: I cannot say. Where is presidential certainty anyhow? I never expected to find it so fleeting.

From The Belton Daily News, September 3, 1926 (An Editorial)

A recent article in *Harper's* Magazine concludes that in Florida, when men smell money, it is like the smell of blood for a wild animal. This is a pithy summary of the current Florida land boom, or land rush. We think it highly regrettable.

There are two reasons. One is that the desire for such a commodity is likely out of proportion to its long-term value. Bubbles burst. The second reason is that any inordinate desires for material gain are likely to be full of vice.

Here we are in the upper portions of the Middle West, just north of Illinois, in an early September where already are signs of approaching winter. In Florida of course palm trees sway in temperate breezes. But this is precisely the sort of thing that can deceive men.

There is a stern reality in our northern, cold clime. We understand that summer is fleeting and winters long. The recent heavy rains have presaged as much. This has a tempering effect on our own desires. The coming autumn and January give us perspective.

Here in Belton, Wisconsin, voluptuous desire for anything is likely to be slaked by common sense, even on the campus of Belton College, which we admire but sometimes worry about, as a few of its faculty sometimes get funny ideas about this and that. But a certain wintry realism seems always, thank goodness, to put paid to that sort of thing.

A Letter from Professor or Theodore Elves to Professor David Grendel on September 4, 1926

Dear Professor Grendel,

It is with a certain heaviness of heart that I respond to your most recent missive at all, and also I am distressed that I once called you David. I had thought, and perhaps you had thought as well, that we should not communicate any further.

I cannot, nevertheless, allow your previous communiqué to go unanswered. I cannot help but notice the blasé way in which you dismiss my own grievances and the casual manner in which you insist that they are chimeras of my own imaginings.

It is quite true that you were instrumental in "rescuing" me from my unhappy memories in Illyria, ones created not only by Diometa's death but also by the departmental infighting. But I suggested not long ago, and I suggest again now, that your motives were not altruistic but were prompted largely by an attempt to create difficulty for your own faculty rival here at Belton, the recently late Professor Nelson Wheeler, and by your perceived desire to appear great-hearted to an internal audience that had come to suspect you as entirely self-interested.

My own philosophy, as well you know, is one of idealized form. A world in which Plato's Ideals came to earth and devoured their lesser copies—their cheap imitations in the parlance of the day—would not be one of which I would be fearful and in fact should be one that I would cheer. Fortunately this devotion to idealized form in the Greek presentation of the human body has sustained me in my hours of need. It has caused me to become unsurprised that your own apparent idealisms are likewise "cheap imitations," unfortunate deviations from the real thing.

Only my love of the (sadly broken) Venus de Milo sustains me as I think of your own deviations from high ideals. Should the Platonic Forms come to earth, you should be among the first to be absorbed and reduced to atoms, but then as a strict materialist perhaps you would not mind.

Professor Theodore Elves

A Letter from Professor Gwenelda Sulloway to Her Older Sister Jeanine (September 4, 1926)

Dear Big Sister,

I can only hope that the Twin Cities have been spared the torrential downpour that we have suffered here in Belton. You know my views about lives built on incessant humor, but even I found myself telling the lame old joke about needing to build an ark. This may have been a Biblical desecration. May our Lord forgive me?

It has not, however, been only the wetness but also the gloom that has been a trifle overwhelming. I have tried to keep a ray of light in my soul, but it has been complicated. It is not the rain, however, but fretting over my mission here that has most distressed me. This is no doubt partly because I am new: in my first year. It also stems from my wishing to do my best in what I, an admittedly large-boned woman from the Plains, consider a task of monumental importance—if only my possibly imposing frame were all that is required.

I am not only an instructor of English, especially Victorian, literature. I am also a residence hall matron and as such am responsible for the vale in which the souls of fifty women will be made for good or ill. Of course I wish to protect them as much as possible, but in general our hours policy (all must be in and accounted for by 8 PM) enables such security quite adequately. Their bodies are safe. I worry over their souls.

It is imperative that they grow to maturity with a sense of both restraint and virtue. They must be free of impulse, but that is only the negative side. On the positive they must also be practitioners of a virtue that is imbued with charity and discipline alike. A disciplined charity may seem old-fashioned in these decadent, modern times, of speakeasies and bobbed hair. To me, it is the key to a good womanly life. For me, this involves, and shall always involve, putting the material body in its place well on the back shelf, where it is reached for only as often as absolutely necessary.

I have recently begun my major class with the Tennyson poem "Ulysses," about striving in a kind of cultivated ignorance of bodily infirmity. Most of my class (about three-fifths) consists of young women. I hope the point found its way home. I fear that there are other voices here at Belton that would dispute with my own perspectives. I have mentioned these voices but only in a general way to President Muldrow, and I have but the vaguest inklings of them now. But they are the subjects of another letter at another time. I shall thus finish this one, as I am tired, and shall post it in the morning. Good night, my dear sister.

Your faithful Gwenelda

A Letter from Professor Theodore Elves to Harold Barker, a Belton College Student (September 4, 1926)

Dear Young Harold,

I am delighted that you have joined my class in Homeric Heroism (Studies in Classical Civilization). Since you have come to Belton well versed in classical Greek from your training at the Parker School (to which I understand your parents sacrificed to send you and your older brother) I have no qualms whatever about admitting you as a freshman. One can only hope that you will not be disappointed with the relative lack of philology and translation in the course. I was myself trained in that tradition and have never departed from it.

Still, I have come to believe that the greatest spirit of the classical tradition is not to be found in its language but in its art; not in its words but in its form. You asked after class if I had ever seen Michelangelo's David in Florence. I am pleased to say to you again what I said this morning: that I have seen it many times. And yes of course it derives significantly from the tradition of Greek statuary. I can think of no better example of what we call now the Renaissance—the rebirth of classical ideals and forms.

The Florentine David sustains me in troubled times.

I should encourage you to study the David from your perspective here in the Middle West, though of course you shall have to be contented with photographic images of the very same. I have a number of these, taken with my own camera in Italy. Please come to tea at some point in my dwelling on Steeple Street. There I will show you my slides of the David.

We must always remember that the beauty of this statue, and of Greek statues in general, stems from the overall form and not the specific details. With that proviso in mind, you may join me for tea at any point of your choosing, and I would enjoy hearing from you.

My best wishes always,

Professor Elves

Notes From a Lecture by Professor David Grendel in Survey of Philosophy (September 5, 1926)

One of the greatest philosophical disputes has been over the issue of form versus matter. "Form" is not just to be viewed as the shape of something, as in the form of a triangle. Rather, it has also come to mean something beyond material things—an ideal, a vision, invisible except to something called "the mind's eye." This is why philosophers sometimes call Plato's "ideals" or "ideas" "forms." Another way to look at it is this: Meaning and significance are not to be found in the material details of something but in its overall arrangement of these details. This arrangement cannot be reduced to matter. It is some sort of ineffable form.

I feel I am losing you, so let me try some more. Take a human being. We know that each of us humans is made of matter—hearts and lungs and blood vessels and the like. That is why we die. But we are not humans because we have these material features. We are humans because these material things are arranged in a certain way. We are "formally" human beings, not "materially" human beings. Perhaps this will make this business more clear.

Now in my view, students, this is fine as far as it goes. We know, for example, that words and letters set in just any old way have no meaning. They have to be set in a certain way before they make sense. But there are still two huge problems in the entire matter.

First, we can never get away from matter. Yes, in order to see and read, our material elements must be in a certain form; but without these material elements there will be nothing to form. You can't sit in the form *of a chair. You can only sit in a* chair, *and for that we need matter: wood or iron.*

Second, those who think "formally" all the time—who insist on ignoring material facts—will often see visions where there is nothing at all. Common sense realism is abandoned. We know there are those who think they have seen God on a Thursday afternoon at the top of the church, looking down at them. There are those who see shadows in the forest and think they are beasts out to gobble them up. These are the sorts of people who might think they can eat off the abstract form of a table.

These people also get funny ideas about other people: imagining slights where there is no material evidence whatever that such insults have actually occurred. This is what comes of exclusively "formal" thinking. But I feel I am getting somewhat off track. So let us return to Plato's view....

From the Diary of President Irving Muldrow (September 5, 1926)

My days as Belton president grow ever more distressing, I fear. Costs to repair the roof—again—will be nearly four hundred dollars at a time when our fall enrollments have declined three or four percent. I am under growing pressure to do something called "de-accessioning," which means selling outright some of the artifacts that Belton professors and students gathered earlier this decade in Egypt. One of these is apparently the gold-inlaid cobra—called, I am told, an uraeus—which once coiled at the top of an ancient crown worn by a pharaoh. This artifact has yet to be assessed in value, and the museum people are outraged at the very thought of our doing so. Yet with roofs in need of repair and new students in sudden paucity, it may be necessary.

After all—this is my reasoning—the cobra will always be for gazing at only. It does not materially improve the education of any Belton student. It gives us prestige, I suppose, in that we actually have it. Yet it is detached from the crown, and was discovered only by happenstance on one of our Egyptian "digs," as these people like to call them. I think the term undignified.

I consulted a book in the library yesterday to learn that the cobra sat atop the pharaoh's crown in order to warn his enemies that he might strike with his venom at any time. This too seems to me a somewhat undignified thing for a fine college to be showing off. While I am aware of the various arguments against "forbidden" knowledge, I do not see that that is the issue here. I am not forbidding the display of the uraeus—only stating that in difficult times we must not confuse a valuable freak for the mainstream education of our students. And if a sale can enhance that education, then we ought to be willing to think about such a move.

Diary, I say this only to you: I sometimes wish I could be more like a pharaoh myself. This is a disgraceful thing to say, and I should never say it in public or act upon it in any way. But one cannot always help how one feels. There are moments when I wish I could unleash my own venomous cobra in order to solve Belton problems. And between the Grendel-Elves feud, and the embittered insecurities of our new English professor, Miss Sullway, I am ready to unleash the uraeus!

This is to my shame.

A Letter from Professor David Grendel to Professor Theodore Elves, September 5, 1926

Dear Theodore Elves,

I was both angered and heart sick to receive your accusatory letter. I should like to respond by engaging with your logic. Apparently your adoration of the Venus de Milo and other ancient statuary forms has lessened your linguistic investigations, which may in turn diminish that part of the mind that best forms logical inquiry and conclusion.

I am only guessing about this point. I have no evidence, and unlike you, I am not in the habit of proceeding in the dearth of proof.

Still, there is the matter of logic even in the absence of evidence. Logic, as you once knew back in our Columbia days, can help guide us to considerations of evidence even when there is none.

I am especially taken (aback) by your insistence that my motives in assisting you were self-interested. I do not know how you can possibly know such a thing. What proof do you have? However, let us proceed on the assumption that you are right. What great difference should that necessarily make?

A fact in clear evidence is that I did work assiduously to get you away from Illyria and off to Belton, where you dwell among us today. Suppose that I wished to curry here the favor of being a good fellow, or even conjecture, if you wish, that I wished to harm the interests and viewpoint of Professor Wheeler. Even so, did I not secure for you a position here—something that you stated you very much wanted and needed?

The world works frequently on the basis of mutual interests. That I was able to get my own interests taken care of, while also helping assure the servicing of yours, should hardly be surprising. You seem to want a purity of motive. which likely does not exist in the world, before you are willing to be grateful or trusting. This is, I submit, an unsustainable approach to the world, and to the affairs of men, which will only make you unhappy and bring misery to those about you.

Having said all this, I also deny that I had any such self-interested motives. Thus I feel that I helped you and have in return been abused. I remain

David Grendel

From An Editorial in the Belton Daily News *(September 6, 1926)*

This small editorial board never ceases to find amazement in false promises. Thus it was with a sense of wonder that we learned recently of a new product, deemed European, called Flo-Ra-Zo-Na. The product is advertised as melting excess fat away through the skin if the overweight user will only soak in it for a quarter of an hour.

Members of our board are generally on the trim side, so we have no need of Flo-Ra-Zo-Na for our personal use. If any readers of the *Daily News* do attempt the procedure we should be glad to hear of a report. Discretion is ours.

Meanwhile, we remain happy in these early autumn days, when weather begins to give us an admonishment about reality, to be dwelling in a land of harsh winters, where the rapid fixes of Flo-Ra-Zo-Na will be inefficacious and incapable of temptation. It is quite difficult to maintain belief in spurious paradises like Flo-Ra What's Its Name when we are contemplating thirty inches of snow in but a few months. We are also contented to recall the little college on the hill above our offices, where professors insist that there is no royal road to learning. May Belton College never be tempted to offer a Flo-Ra degree to its dedicated and hard-working student body!

A Letter from Professor Gwenelda Sulloway to Her Older Sister Jeanine (September 6, 1926)

Dear Big Sister,

I am more than aware, please be assured, that you have not had time to reply to my most recent. I write you again so soon only because I have become quite disturbed by an incident in my residence hall, where I am to watch over the safety and virtue of myriad Belton girls.

I am convinced that one of them, Gladys Sockwell, sneaked into the hall after hours last night. As you might know, at precisely one moment after 8 PM I have the girls gather into the small commons room of the hall so that they may be accounted for. Though these are early days this has gone well until last night, when the Sockwell girl failed to appear.

Her absence was quite notorious, and of course I immediately asked the balance of the girls where she might be. Please do not believe that my motives here are vengeful. I was concerned over all for the girl's safety in this woeful world. None of the other girls knew, or if they did, they did not say. I was quite perplexed and showed myself in this state. The girls looked at the floor, whether on account of my upset or in guilty knowledge about the Sockwell girl, I cannot say.

Within five minutes she appeared, stating that she had lost track of time and had been somewhat queasy in the washroom. There was no material evidence left over that would confirm this latter claim, and of course if the former claim is so, then this does not speak well of her. Promptness is a virtue, too—not as much as a conquest of the body, to be sure, but a virtue nonetheless.

I became rather short with the Sockwell girl, whom I sense may be a bit too trim and lovely for her own good—just the sort to overestimate the value of the body. I wonder what she might have been up to. My small fit, I fear, has upset her a great deal, though, and I have reason to think that she may be taking up the matter with the higher administration.

I myself advocate locking all doors at 8 PM on the dot as a way to insure the compliance with our hours policy. But I have been told that this might be perilous. What if a girl is locked out and in some straits? I suppose it is a dilemma. At any rate, my adored Big Sister, if you have advice, please do not fail to deliver it as soon as possible. Punctuality, as I said, is no vice. I will keep you posted on whether or not anything further comes of this matter. I am told the Sockwell girl's father is a donor to Belton.

Your affectionate Gwendela

From the Diary of President Irving Muldrow (September 7, 1926)

The hiring of Professor Sulloway may have been an error. She came to us renowned by her sponsors at Northwestern. They told us she was a precise and able scholar of nineteenth century English literature, an energetic lecturer, and of course a most proper woman and thus highly decorous to double as the mentor and monitor of McGregor Hall.

Here at Belton we very much wish to have, as models, women of both chastity and learning. Miss Sulloway fits the bill. But the devil—and I fear the Devil is lurking about Belton these days—is in detail. It is a matter of discretion. The Sockwell girl may very well have come in late and fibbed about it. This seems impossible to know. I myself would have given her a gentle reprimand but taken no further action unless she made a custom of such tardiness. Miss Sulloway preferred a somewhat more drastic approach, though I still cannot get the straight of whether she did so as a matter of policy or emotion.

Miss Sulloway may be deeply unhappy. I applaud her view that the body is greatly overrated in the path to educational virtue (though we do have extensive physical education at Belton). Yesterday I read a rather amusing editorial in the *Daily News* about a new product designed to melt away excess poundage. Is it unkind of me to say that Miss Sulloway's own ample girth, rather than her love of

Tennyson, has led her to this devotion to the idea that the body must be kept in its place? This is a question, Dear Diary, which comes to your discrete ears alone.

At any rate the Sockwell girl has complained to her father, who has called me long distance from Lincoln Park, where he has a rather impressive domicile. We do not wish under any circumstances to see him withdraw his daughter from our premises. The loss of funds would be rather discernible. We should miss it glaringly. Yet it is with reluctance, extreme, that I would fail to back Miss Sulloway. So I told Walter Sockwell that I was sure there was a misunderstanding, and I gave undertakings to warrant that it would not happen again.

This is of course a rather soft and cowardly way to proceed on my part. But I have found that a college president cannot always be forthright. I have asked Miss Sulloway to have a visit with me. I have no idea how that will proceed. I shall feel my way.

What else can I do? Now where is that poisonous cobra when I especially need it? Perhaps I should apply it to myself, Cleopatra style.

A Letter from Harold Barker to His Older Brother, Ronald (September 7, 1926)

Dear Ron,

I hope and trust that all is well for you in Chicago. So far my Belton education seems to be going well, but I know it's early yet. It seems that the Belton experience has prepared you reasonably well for a financial position on LaSalle Street. Who cares if it's low level, right?

Just as these are early days for my adventures at Belton, they're also early days for your investment career. But it's a terrific line to go into. I truly believe that in ten years we'll have abolished poverty here in the good old US of A.

You asked about my classes. I have Professor David Grendel in the philosophy survey course. He's a fine lecturer, and if he senses the class doesn't quite get something, he explains it in some other way. He's pretty good at making these big ideas plain and small enough for even a dummy like me. The thing is, though, it's almost as though he's allergic to big ideas if they're really abstract. He's sort of a factual guy, which seems unusual for a philosopher. But what do I know? How many philosophers have I known in my life? Well, he's the first.

And then there's this Miss Sulloway in the literature survey. She's my least favorite. She's got this crabby way of talking and wants to turn every poem into a sermon. She seems mostly speaking to the girls in the class. There are only four of us guys.

My favorite class is Professor Elves's. It's the only advanced course I have, but good old Parker courses in Latin and Greek have prepared me for it. Even better, though, is that he's light on the language and grammar and heavy on the art of ancient Greece. It seems like every class we spend at least half the time looking at the human form, ancient Greek style. I must say, these old Greeks were never shy about showing off "beauty in the buff" (if that's what it is). Anyhow, it's clear that Professor Elves thinks so. This seems to be a mental vacation for him every time he shows us one of his lantern slides of ancient statuary. He's on the oceans of thought alone, as Dad might say.

But I like him and am getting converted to his idea of bare beauty, I guess. He's even invited me for tea. I'm flattered. Should I accept? I'm just an eighteen year-old idiot, right? Do advise.

Oh, by the way, I've got this girlfriend of sorts. Gladys Sockwell: her father's a big banker in Chicago. Maybe he can help you get ahead?

Hope this finds you well. Wait. I think I already said that.

Your loyal brother, Harold

Letter from Gladys Sockwell, Belton Class of '30, to Her Friend Edith Hessell (September 7, 1926)

Dear Edie,

Well, there are times when I wish I'd gone east to school, just as you did. How's life in New England and at Illyria? Staying here in the middle of the country has opened me to all sorts of restrictions. I don't know: maybe they're out there, too. I've heard Vermont can be strait-laced. After all, it's the home state of our beloved prim president Cal!

I had a bad nasty with the residence hall matron, Miss Sulloway. I was saying goodbye to Harold Barker, who's sort of my new boyfriend, and lost track of time. So I was about three minutes late getting into the hall for hours check. Old Miss Sulloway—who has an ample girth along with ample self-righteousness—said I was five minutes late. I wasn't. So I told a little fib; said I was sick in the washroom.

I wasn't, but I decided to tell Daddy about this whole thing anyhow. I just think that being three minutes late isn't a mortal sin. I thought I should warn people about how unreasonable Old Sulloway is.

Well, that's my story. How about yours? Before you ask, yes, Harold is really cute. I think he's smart, too. He knows Latin and Greek already—not that that's the main reason I like him.

Always, dear friend, I am your

Gladys

From a Wire Service Story in the Belton Daily News (September 8, 1926)

Chicago—Over a thousand rounds of bullets were aimed at the Cicero, Illinois headquarters of reputed gangster Alphonse Capone on yesterday.

The Capone group reported no fatalities, although injuries were not a subject on which anyone would comment.

"It'll take a lot more than a thousand rounds to stop us," said one Capone spokesman.

It was widely assumed, according to police sources, that a rival North Side gang was responsible for the melee. Gangland feuding and gunfire have become almost daily staples of Chicago life for the past several years.

(In an editorial on the shooting published the next day the *Daily News* proclaimed that, "once more we have reason to rejoice in where we live, where perhaps a squirrel accidentally trapped in a domicile or a sparrow flying into a church window is the extent of ruckus in this town, secured by, among other things, the quiet groves of academe at Belton College.")

From Lecture Notes by Professor Theodore Elves in His Greek Antiquities Course (September 8, 1926)

Here we see my lantern slide of the Venus de Milo, a statue of the goddess Venus, or Aphrodite, discovered on the isle of Milo and likely done by the sculptor Alexandros of Antioch about one hundred years before the birth of Christ. I will show you in a moment several views of the work, which is now in the Louvre in Paris.

The most singular popular feature are the missing arms, as well as the plinth on which the statue was originally set. It is likely that the left arm was holding an apple, consistent with the myth of Paris, of which I spoke in the last class, and resting on the plinth, which was a column with a small platform atop it. It is not clear how the arms were lost, though the most popular explanation is that they were broken off when the statue was removed in 1820 from a narrow cave to which for some reason it had been consigned.

I shall now leave any further discussion, for now, of the historical Venus de Milo and shift my attention to a few remarks about the good life. It seems clear, at least to me, that there are two great traps in life. One is a life of pure abstraction, a retreat into pleasant daydreams, however shifting and transitory and vague, that remove us from the far more realistic mess of human existence: its dirt, its blood, its errors, its terrible coincidences. The other trap is to revel in this dirt and blood, to allow oneself, as some of our so-called "realistic" writers (like the regrettable Stephen Crane) do, to wade knee and neck deep in the unpleasant muck and mire of daily life. I call the first of these traps the Daydreamer's Trap; the other one I call the Al Capone Trap, in honor of the hoodlum who seems obsessed with poisonous beer to be drunk and endless blood to be spilled.

Between these two traps is a third way: To find the truly beautiful in a concrete vision. This is where, if I may now turn back, the Venus de Milo comes in. It is why we are spending so much time on statuary in this course and so relatively little time on verbs and nouns and syntax. It is because ancient Greek art gives us a vision of ordered loveliness that is not the stuff of abstract dreams but the inspiration of actual marble shape. This is not some misty, opaque idea of form but real, perceptible form. It is as though some beautiful ideal has come to Earth and, like magic, taken on something we can really see, as if some great oneness of beauty has inhabited marble. We can meditate on this form: on the lovely, perfectly poised sweep of Venus' back and the sheer grace of her flowing robe. We can find in this third way an escape from the gobbledygook of opaque thought and the disgust of Mr. Capone's noxious bullets and beer.

Please believe me when I say that the disappointing demeanor of my fellow men prompts me to find, in such beauty as this, the only true salvation for a spirit otherwise dreary. You may ask, of the Venus de Milo, where are the details—where are the colors of hair and flesh and eyes? Well, the details *of life are the devil's own work. The details of life only reveal its myriad misfortunes. The beauty—in outline form—of the Venus ignores such details and thus supplies a spirit far better than the realistic "facts" of this distressing thing we sometimes call "life."*

Letter from Ronald Barker to His Younger Brother Harold (September 9, 1926)
[Edited to correct spelling errors]

Dear Young Harold!

I'd like to call you "Child Harold" after Byron, but the spelling and terminology would be wrong (not that my own spelling is good), and besides, you're no longer a child. It was grand to hear from you. I have never met Gladys, though I believe her father is, as you say, a fairly prominent banker here. Professor Sulloway is new, so I can't comment about her attributes. I did have a course from Professor

Grendel, though, and concur with what you say. He is a model of clarity. He really believes that if you can't explain it in plain language, it really doesn't exist. Mind him well. He'll teach you to think with admirable lucidity. He did so for me.

Of course Teddy Elves is comparatively new at Belton, though he has been around for about nine years by now. I never took a course from him, but I did learn indirectly that he's a bit of a controversy on campus. For one thing, the tradition at Belton has always been to study the language of Greek and Latin, whereas "Teddy" is almost turning the classics department into a branch of the art department with all that stress on David and Venus and so on. And another thing is that he tends to proclaim his love of these statues in pretty wispy language. I would imagine that Professor Grendel would find him both opaque and confused, though I hear Old Teddy can certainly turn on the rhetoric.

I'm always amused when I think of Elves and Grendel together, since Elves is a string bean so thin you could blow him down while Grendel is so short you could almost step on him! He is, however, though diminished in height, quite a muscular fellow.

Anyhow, if you go to tea at Professor Elves's place, do so with the awareness that he's regarded as a little off. But as I say, you're not a child. You can use your own judgment.

Keep me informed, dear brother.

Ronald

A Letter from Professor Gwenlda Sulloway to Her Older Sister Jeanine (September 10, 1926)

Dear Big Sister,

Thank you for your recent words of comfort, and I shall try to take your advice and cease to worry about what will probably turn out to be a comparatively minor incident.

But Miss Sockwell did indeed go to the president about the matter, or should I say, she had her wealthy father do so. And this means that I shall have to have a little chat with President Muldrow. I don't expect to be terminated. In fact, I received a note from the president stating that he fully understood my need to enforce rules strictly in order to protect the discipline and virtue of the girls. "A little repression never hurt anyone." He actually used those very words!

Yet he did say he wanted us to chat, not only so that he could get to know me better but also so that he could rest doubly assured that I had done the right thing. This is consoling.

I must say, Big Sister, that Belton is not, however, all that I thought it to be. The Sockwell girl has performed an act of rebellion, and among other distressing signs is that the study of Greek and Latin here has become the study of semi-nude statuary. Perhaps I exaggerate. I am told that this Theodore Elves does teach the languages, but his heart, I have heard, is in the visual, not the philological. This seems to me inconsistent with the president's view that "a little repression never hurt anyone." I am glad to see the president objecting to the odious theories of Herr Freud. But I fear that there are other malign influences still lurking about Belton College.

I shall post this in the morning but must now get my rest. Thank you again for all your comforts.

Your devoted sister,

Gwenelda

A Letter from Professor Theodore Elves to Professor David Grendel (September 10, 1926)

Dear David Grendel:

It is with bitter regret that I respond to yours of September 5, and in fact I have waited for nearly a week before offering my riposte in the not altogether vain hope that my reply will be temperate.

And so it shall be. You have distorted my views in your last missive. I fully understand that favors done may also benefit him who does the favor as well as him who shall receive it. But when favors are significantly self-interested on the part of him who offers it, then the recipient, though grateful, is also right to be wary. And so I have become with you.

You are known on campus for your pristine lucidity. I trust that the paragraph above is lucid enough for you to grasp. If not, I shall restate it here: I do not regard your assistance to me in my coming to Belton to have been disinterested. And I must take note of this. If the roles were reversed, you would do the same.

What you regard as simple ingratitude on my part is in actuality a certain caution. And it is my bluntness about this caution that has apparently so offended *you*. And yet you continue to insist—to others (I have my sources)—that it is I who is the chronically offended one.

This is unfair, but it is also what I have come to expect from your quarter of the campus.

I am equally aware of the criticisms that have come my way due to my concentration on the ancient visual arts. This is neither the time nor place for me to defend such focus, such scholarly interests. They have to do with my understanding of classical contribution to civilization, and to my own philosophical and aesthetic attitudes, which need no more defending than do yours. But I am in possession of some knowledge that it has been you, among others, but especially you, who has spread allegations that my love of Venus, etc., is a form of pathology, and that it harms the purity of the young.

You should be aware that I am not without weapons of my own in such a contest.

Theodore Elves

From the Diary of President Irving Muldrow (September 11, 1926)

Dearest Diary: I don't know whether or not I am more pusillanimous or psychological. I should not wish to have to talk with Mr. Sockwell and Miss Sulloway at the same time. I should be caught out dreadfully.

I have assured Mr. Sockwell that I will caution Miss Sulloway about becoming overzealous. But I did no such thing, or if I did, I did so quite mildly and tacitly. I feel that with a potentially overwrought woman like Miss Sulloway it is vital to reassure her, above all, that the college supports her in her main mission, which is also our mission. Thus I told her that indeed she was correct that various and sundry temptations did lurk about campus here and there, and that she is quite correct in taking an adamant arms against such a sea of troubles.

As the fight over "de-accessioning" our Egyptian collections heats up, I almost suggested to her that these divers evils about campus might take the form of gold-inlaid cobras! But I refrained from any such jest. It would have gone eminently unappreciated.

I did suggest to her, though, that perhaps a two-minute grace period might be in order, not in order to be permissive with the girls but only to allow for mistimed watches and clocks. She agreed but then added that the Sockwell girl was five minutes late, so it could not have been the result of a slow watch.

I think it still could have been but did not demur. I can only hope that she has somehow "gotten the message" about allowing her zealotry to go beyond bounds.

I am a coward, Dear Diary. I feel wretched at times. And then there is still the matter of that cobra, which I am told will fetch the college eight thousand dollars or more. The cobra continues to coil, Diary. Who knows where it will display itself next? And whom will it bite?

Letter from Harold Barker to His Older Brother Ronald (September 11, 1926)

Dear Ron,

It was grand to hear from you. I hope your career gets started in earnest right away and that you do the Belton class of '26 proud!

Yes, Miss Gladys Sockwell and I continue to "see" one another. Not long ago, as we paused by the door of the residence hall for a brief "good night peck" I wondered if she weren't going to be late getting into the building on time.

Classes continue to go well. You know, I have a confession to make. I really do enjoy Professor Elves's class. I was expecting to brush up on my translation skills, but he's really breathing a lot of life into what the Greeks contributed. He shows a ton of lantern slides, and while I've got to admit a lot of them are of nude or semi-nude gods and goddesses and heroes he always discusses them in terms of their overall form. It's like they have this mystical shape that you can see in one way but have to "feel" (though the mind) in another way. This must be a bit of how a séance goes!

I've still not decided whether or not to take him up on his tea offer. He hinted at it again yesterday, but I said nothing. I'm a little nervous about encountering so great an intellect, what with the distance between me and my relative ignorance and him and his vast learning. I'm inclined to get out of it instead and waver between my gratitude at being flattered and my anxiety about showing up.

I've heard rumors that he and Professor Grendel used to be great friends and went to school together but have had a major falling out. But, Ron, you hear all sorts of things on this postage stamp sized campus. Meanwhile, this Miss Sulloway has become a real harpy in class. I feel like every class is a church service—really just the sermon.

Well, keep me posted on life in the big city. Break a leg, brother, or at least a balance sheet!

Yours always,

Little Harold

Letter from Professor Gwenelda Sulloway to Her Older Sister Jeanine (September 13, 1926)

Dear Big Sister,

Well, I've had my discussion with President Muldrow, and it went well. So as a result I've found myself with much confidence and have felt that I have sufficient institutional support for my mission here. I suppose that in this day and age, when you hear about all sorts of louche behavior in some of the cities, moral earnestness seems to be old-fashioned. But just as I am ill suited by body to wear a short skirt, so am I not suited—and this is even more important— by temperament and soul to be anything other than a person of moral fervor.

And this is who I am, and who I shall continue to be. I think President Muldrow understands that.

Still, I have had yet another minor upset. I think it's minor, but the more I think of it, the less minor it seems. I shall explain.

There is a young man in my class on the Victorians—his name is Harold Barker. I have been teaching a great deal of Tennyson (*In Memoriam*, heavily). I also read to them, the other day, a passage from the divine Carlyle on how one should eschew the verse of the rebellious libertine Byron, with his quips and irreverence, and turn instead to the morally transporting Goethe. You recall the famous passage: "Close Thy Byron; Open Thy Goethe." Well, after this class, which I thought had gone quite well, this young Barker appeared at my desk with what I consider to be a mischievous smile lurking beneath his well-parted brown hair (I would say "curls" but it would be wicked of me to do so). He had an anthology of Robert Browning's poetry and directed me to one of Browning's monologues (dramatic soliloquys, to be more precise) called "My Last Duchess."

He asked me if I had read it.

The answer is yes, I have. Of course I studied Browning at Northwestern and am generally familiar with this poem, which is spoken by a corrupt Italian duke or count about the painting of his late wife, the Duchess, whom he had murdered because she equated his kindness and love with everyone else's. The wicked Duke insisted on being loved alone. Before she died he had her portrait painted—the portrait is called "My Last Duchess," as is the poem. I am convinced that this young Barker showed me this poem as a provocation.

He knows, I firmly believe, that it is not the sort of Victorian poem I would be caught teaching. It is a truly sinful sort of poem—the sort of thing Browning was easily tempted to write—about not only the murderous tendencies of a duke but also the glorification of woman's flesh (via the portrait). It is a poem steeped—I wish I could say "drowned" and be done with it—in the permissive culture of the Italian Renaissance. This is the same culture that produced Michelangelo's David and other fleshly and misleading monstrosities.

Young Barker asked if I might not read the poem to the next class. Of course he pretended to be earnest and sincere. He was neither. He was provoking me. He was resisting the very ministrations of my pedagogy.

I should like to say, "I won't have it." But I put him off rather mildly, replying only that I might be prepared to think about it. This young Barker bears watching. I sense that he may be future trouble.

This is naturally too minor for me to be bothering President Muldrow about it. But I am sure that he would lay all his sympathies on my side. One wonders what gets into these young people.

I feel better now that I have written this small tale of woe and hope and trust that you continue to flourish in your marriage and homemaking. Thank you for reading my narrative of occasional troubles. I remain

Your Loving Sister,

Gwenelda

From a Belton Bullhorn Editorial (The Belton College Student Newspaper) on September 13, 1926

Well, wouldn't you know it? The hot new gadget in the good old Land of the Free (not to forget Home of the Brave) is…the zipper. Just when you thought they couldn't possibly outdo themselves with the radio and movie, they've come up with something even more revolutionary. And you don't even need a doctorate in engineering or physics to understand it.

Having trouble dialing the radio when the static's up? Ever seen a film projector break down? Of course you have. But the zipper is simple and easy to use. They've just "come out," but we have yet to see one break.

Now we won't even get into the vexed question of what good the zipper might do. It certainly makes it easier to "button up." The question is whether it's also easier, too, to "button down." Will it become just *too* easy to button down? Zippers will get us into things. Can they get us *out* of things, too? And in getting us out of things will it also get us *into* them?

We'd better stop this prepositional editorial right now before the faculty and administration get too upset!

Editorial in the Belton Daily News (September 13, 1926)

The public prints these days bring news not only of plastic surgery being performed—this is hardly new—but even of professorships in the subject. This is novel.

It seems now that plastic surgery has become so advanced that it is a science rather than, as in times of yore, a hit and miss art.

We have mixed feelings.

The small editorial board here may have need of plastic surgery, but we cannot afford it and it would do us little good in the larger world. We look as we look, and it is unlikely that a couple of quintagenerian males could profit from even a dramatic improvement in the visage department. We suppose, however, that for those who have suffered facial damage through no fault of their own, the new developments are a charitable boon.

We are confident that our local Belton College will not be installing any professorships in plastic surgery. It is a small liberal arts college, where Plato on the subject of beauty is preferred to enhancements of physical beauty via the beneficent cuttings of a surgeon's knife. Indeed, Belton, we hope and trust, will ever instruct its students in the wisdom of mind over body—the wise transcendence of the human soul over the fleeting goods of the physical.

We have as yet no reason to doubt that this is the college's very own mission, to which we trust it will be dedicated now and forever.

From the Diary of President Irving Muldrow (September 14, 1926)

This early autumn is already shaping up as the late start of an *annus horribilis* for me. Will this be the worst year of my presidency? There is not only the vexed question of de-accessioning the golden cobra—a poisonous issue, if I may be permitted, Dear Diary, a small quibble. There is also the restlessness of Miss Sulloway, though that seems for now to have subsided. And I am given to understand that the conflict between Elves and Grendel continues apace—just what I need!

But the latest is the louche editorial published in yesterday's *Bullhorn*. There can be no doubt as to its intended meaning, although late this morning the two editors, Scott and Hansen, appeared in my office, smirking, I thought, to assure me otherwise. They insisted that they were referring to no more than the unintended consequences of any new invention, whether radio or zippers. But I pointed out to them that radio might inspire sins of the spirit—the use of vile propaganda, for instance—but that their reference was to sins of the body, and that *Belton College was dedicated to the proposition that the body was vastly overrated as a key to any viable proposition about the good life.*

I almost felt as though I were as homiletic as Miss Sulloway might have been, but I feel the point went home to the lads. They seemed a bit on the back foot and promised to be more careful with future editorials. I hope so. I had them in not because I necessarily desired to do so but because faculty members were calling the office insisting *that* I do so.

Diary, please forgive me when I say that I should like to send the quirky and rebellious Scott and Hansen into a small room with a live cobra or subject them to a lifetime of listening to Miss Sulloway. Or perhaps I could terminate both Grendel and Elves and appoint Scott and Hansen in their places. At least the two of them get along well, for now.

Dear Diary, May I be pardoned for such thoughts as these.

A Letter from Professor David Grendel to Professor Theodore Elves (September 14, 1926)

Dear Elves:

The intemperance of your previous missive seemed to me almost minatory. I can only hope and trust that this is not the case. But if you are threatening legal or other sorts of harm, then to me this lessens even further the justification of all your words.

I can only appeal to you: If you are seriously preparing to inflict damage of some sort (you mentioned "weapons"), does this not suggest that your case, unless backed by the most solid empirical evidence, is perilously flimsy, even self-destructively so?

You are a man of aesthetic ideals—even spiritual ones, I dare say, as derived from your perceptions of beauty and its sources. To me, this is a mistaken reliance upon subjective appraisals as a method of seeing things. I, as you know, am an empiricist. I take my cue from another David, Mr. Hume, who said he could not perceive any concept of self that did not depend upon what he heard, smelled, saw, touched, and tasted. I am a man of the five senses. No doubt your views of the Venus and the David and all the rest of classical art likewise depends upon sensory data.

But you wish to go further and rely upon something not seen but—how should I put it—felt or intuited or (that old standby word) perceived. That is your privilege—an error, I think, but also your right.

When, however, your "intuitions" about art and beauty creep into your social life—when you "perceive" my wishing you harm and actively seeking it to bring it about—without any empirical evidence whatever, then I must object. I do object. I even ask you to reconsider.

If you have any proof whatever—based on what I have said or written—that I wish to do you ill, then please proceed as you will. But in the absence of such proof—have you spoken to anyone who has heard me say x or y or z, or have you access to anything I have penned—please, I beg you, desist from using such inflammatory terms as "weapons" in future correspondence with me.

These things have a way of becoming an arms race. If you do not believe me, I can supply you with a Mount Everest of empirical evidence, starting perhaps with our recent Great War. Facts: I refer to facts, Professor Elves.

David Grendel

From a Story Carried in the Belton Daily News (September 14, 1926)

Washington—Secretary of State Frank Kellogg announced today that he and French Foreign Minister Aristide Briand would aim to establish a multi-nation peace pact within two years.

As described by Kellogg, the pact would involve as many nations as possible and would require them, as signatories, to agree to disavow declared wars as an instrument of foreign policy and to cede their disagreements to arbitration, as yet undefined as to location and source.

Kellogg denied that such a treaty, in discouraging only declared wars, might actually lead to a rise in undeclared wars, or that a treaty outlawing the use of weaponry might also lead indirectly to a clandestine stockpiling of arms.

"If Minister Briand and I can successfully culminate the treaty we have in mind, world war will be averted for the balance of the twentieth century," said Kellogg.

From Lecture Notes for Professor David Grendel's Philosophy Survey Class (September 15, 1926)

Today I wish to make clear, as I abidingly try to do, what is at stake if one is rooting his philosophy in the primacy of sensory experience. This is called empiricism, as you well know by now, and it really means that when one gathers evidence about the world and how it works and even what it means, he should rely on what he can detect readily and directly through sound, taste, touch, vision, and smell.

Now it is crucial to understand what this does not mean. It does not mean that we are not sometimes mistaken about what we detect via our senses. Someone can disguise poison to taste like nectar. Nor does it mean that we can live our lives only on the basis of what we find out immediately through the nose or eyes, etc. If you are asked whether or not a rock dropped from a cliff will fall, then you would be silly to say, "I do not know unless I see it first-hand." We make assumptions all the time on the basis of what has happened in the past. We think it likely to happen in the future. We may, again, be wrong sometimes, but we really have no choices. We have to make guesses in life. We cannot wait on evidence all the time before deciding something.

You had no direct evidence this morning that Belton College even existed, but you came to class anyhow.

But while an empirical perspective is limited—careful in its sifting of evidence and yet prone to errors and mistaken assumptions—that is also one of its glories. For consider this: Knowing these limits, and being careful to look at data directly and factually—keeps us skeptical and such skepticism then keeps us out of trouble.

It keeps us from jumping in where empirically minded angels—this is a joke—fear to tread. It keeps us from assumptions about other people—good or bad—without a careful weighing of direct evidence. Curiously enough, empiricism can help us bring peace, for it warns us against presuming bad motives in the absence of direct proof.

II: LATER SEPTEMBER 1926

A Letter from Professor Theodore Elves to Mr. Harold Barker (September 16, 1926)

Dear Master Harold,

It has been with difficulty that I have managed to get your attention after class. You seem in some haste to get somewhere once you have completed inspecting, along with others in the course, my sundry lantern slides.

I write you now, partly as a substitute for speaking with you after class and partly in order to reaffirm my previous invitation that you join me for tea, either some Sunday afternoon or perhaps some weekday evening. I should be profoundly remiss if I were to impose upon your Saturdays—surely, the *student* day of rest!

Let me also take this opportunity to raise hopes that you are enjoying my course. I deeply believe that once a young person has grasped the visual joys and abstract inspirations of Greek statuary, he shall find in it a well of refreshment that dries not until death. And when I say that such inspiring is "abstract" I do not, in stating it to be so, intend to diminish it in any way. As a theologian once said of God, he is nowhere so that he may be everywhere. And so is the ineffable beauty of what our ancient Greek forebears have proffered to us over these past twenty-five centuries.

Regardless, to be perhaps overly terse, or to *risk* being so, I ask once more--how about that tea?

Yours faithfully,

Professor Elves

A Letter from Professor Gwenelda Sulloway to Her Older Sister Jeanine (September 16, 1926)

Dearest Big Sister,

Thank you for yours of a few days ago. I am glad to hear that you and Frederick are faring well and that he is fond of his new position. You asked after my current feelings. I am happy to say that they have stabilized and that the earlier jitters that afflicted me seem to have subsided, perhaps with an enhancement in overall conditions or maybe as a result, simply, of my becoming accustomed to my new milieu.

The Sockwell girl has been on time, and the Barker boy has not mentioned any further adventures in the rather outré poems of Robert Browning. My classes continue to go with ostensible lack of rough waters. I have recently advocated the Arnoldian dictum that we must all dedicate ourselves to reading "the best that has been thought and said" and gave the Barker boy an icy stare as though to say that Browning verse about louche dukes is excluded. This is not to say that other Browning works would not present themselves plausibly within Arnold's ambit, but "My Last Duchess" is not one of them. This is not the Browning of which we wish to hear, or desire to read.

There has been one rather disturbing incident, but I am happy to report that it has little to do with me. Two of the boys who write for the school newspaper—unhappily called "The Bullhorn"—recently published a rather sassy editorial about the zipper. While I have heard that they pleaded a generalized defense—that in suggesting the zipper might have unfortunate and unintended consequences they were simply illustrating how this may become true of any new gadget—I firmly believe that they were indicating a point—dare I even say it—about easier access to the bare body. This is rather shocking. I have always believed, as you know, that one must not judge what one has not inspected. Hence I forced myself to read their fatuous words. I am fully persuaded that their import was not generalized and philosophical but specific and scandalous.

But I have also heard that President Muldrow put paid to their daring and that it shall not recur. I should not even have to mention such matters as this, especially now that my own affairs go well, or seemingly so, but I cannot entirely shake, my dear one, a certain vague feeling that there are snakes in this garden that may yet slither into some form of mischief.

I must retire. I close now but remain your loyal and devoted

Sister, Gwenelda

An Editorial in the Belton Daily News, September 17, 1926

We readily confess that from time to time we question the value of new inventions, the latest of which is the automatic potato peeling machine, a labor saving device that, in our view, also has the side effect (a medical term) of diminishing the sort of family unity that can only come from a communal hand-peeling of spuds.

We think of various other family activities, such as shucking corn, or pea bladders, that lead to the joy of group efforts. The family that shucks together perhaps stays together. We are less certain about the family that owns an automatic potato peeler.

Thus the general idea that fresh gadgets are not always good is one that meets with some approval in these quarters.

Recently, however, it has come to our attention that the young men editing the Belton *Bullhorn* campus newspaper have also attempted a version of this proposition but chose a new article of clothing as their example. Under the guise of arguing for traditional values, it seems to us, they made rather sinister suggestions about the erotic implications of this new article. Here was a case of a dog pretending to wag its tail while all the while the reverse was actually going on. The young men did not fool us, and (we are dependably told) did not fool President Irving Muldrow either.

We trust this will be the end of such editorial shenanigans at our beloved Belton.

Not long ago we offered a small lament about the rise of another novelty: plastic surgery. While we do not wish to say much more now, it has come to our attention that some form of plastic may be in the *happy* future of Belton College. When we know more details we will offer them in our news section.

From the Diary of President Irving Muldrow (September 18, 1926)

Last night at dinner a sweet faculty wife, brimming with plain living and high thinking, asked me to explain the origins of the Grendel-Elves feud. I found to my astonishment that I could not—not quite at any rate. They were once friends, I know, going as far back as their graduate student days at Columbia. David brought Teddy here after the twin blows of his wife's and child's death and nasty faculty contretemps drove him from Vermont and Illyria College. All seemed well until about four years ago, when Teddy began to accuse David, or so it appears, of having all sorts of ulterior motives for bringing him here—both to curry a reputation as a good person and to make life more miserable for Nelson Wheeler, whom David had never liked. Now Nelson has died and has not been replaced, leaving Teddy as the main classicist. But it is difficult to put one's precise finger on what is driving poor Teddy.

Perhaps it is something to do with his brain, as I understand, though have never verified, that he suffers from occasional seizures. Or perhaps it is that Teddy has been affected all too profoundly by the death of his wife and daughter in childbirth. Teddy is also an aesthetic idealist, while David is a cynical materialist. Teddy needs demonstrations of purity such as that found in his beloved Greek statuary, while David finds such ideals as mere persiflage, since he believes that reality is a matter of, well, matter alone. Behind everything, David believes, is a rather unglamorous concatenation of particles. This rubs Teddy wrongly, while for David Teddy's lust for abstractions seems ridiculous.

Well, that is as well as I can do with analysis of the affair. Meanwhile, Diary, the ever reliable and troubling Belton *Daily News* has now picked up on the mischief of the *Bullhorn* column about zippers. I suppose I should have expected it, as the student paper is printed at the *Daily News* offices. The editorial, however, was fairly benign. It was just the editors telling me that they keep tabs on what happens here on "Holy Hill." And speaking of keeping tabs, they also revealed advance knowledge of what I regarded as a most private secret: The announcement, coming soon, that we have acquired the Greek casts from the Columbian Exposition of some thirty years past.

Whatever else one can say of Teddy's abrasions, he has excellent contact with the Greek government and has managed to secure this gift. They are plaster casts—hence, the *Daily News* word play on "plastic"—and include all sorts of grave monuments, friezes, statues, and balustrades. This will be a monumental collection (though I am told the plaster is fragile) and may well justify the sale of the golden cobra. Perhaps I should say that Teddy's "gift" (arranged by him) will become a diversion from the sale of the snake.

Yet I cannot, Diary, become overly confident on this latter point. The anthropologists and "Egyptologists" are batting heavily against me, while the financial committee of the Board is trying to back me. I am caught in the middle, or shall I say, muddle. A ten thousand dollar sale could do wonders for Belton at a time when we suffer from a slight but discernible diminution in the numbers of the Class of 1930.

Can a plaster Medusa be ample recompense for a lost cobra? We shall see, Dear Diary, we shall see.

That is what I am afraid of.

A Letter from Ronald Barker to His Younger Brother Harold (September 19,1926)

[Edited to correct spelling errors]

Dear Harold,

I was glad to get yours of the 12th. Thank you. I wish I had better news for you here, but I fear that my financial clerkship isn't gong well. I made what might have seemed a minor subtraction error in my reporting of an asset fund, but minor distortions in math, as you must know, can lead to serious distortions of results. And so my error turned out to be one hundred thousand dollars off. This in turn led to the bank's investing in an overvalued asset. I have been told in no uncertain terms that this must never happen again. My arithmetical skills seem to be no better in the pinch than are my defective propensities for correct spelling.

I fear I have lost some confidence here. I am shaken. Enjoy your Belton days, for they are rather privileged ones, where an error can lead perhaps at worst to a C or D and not to overbearing shame and threat of termination.

Meanwhile, I am pleased to get these good reports about your relationship with Miss Gladys, who must be a charming girl whom I am anxious to meet at some point, if I can ever get out of Chicago and auditing in order to travel to Holy Hill. It's with more trepidation that I hear about the persistent invitations of old Teddy Elves.

I have heard that he came to Belton from some sort of unspecified tragedy in New England. I have no details. He is certainly a bit controversial on campus, ridiculed by some for his eccentricity but admired by others for his rapturous visions of Attic beauty. I really don't know the old gent very well.

But I don't think he should be bothering you with invitations to tea. It puts you, a freshman, on the spot. I'd not myself want to chat with Old Teddy—his blend of weird learning would be hard to take—and I can surely see why you would not wish to do so either. On the other hand, for you to tell him point blank that the answer is no, no, no, is to put your own final mark in potential peril. So you seem to be in a bind. This angers me.

In fact, Harold, I find myself in quite a bit of anger these days, including animosity towards myself for my boneheaded miscue. Perhaps I am not the best person to advise you. Let me think for a few days and I shall write you again. Meanwhile, the world seems to me a most mixed-up place, between my poor subtraction and the indecorum of Professor Theodore Elves.

290

At least you and Gladys are getting on! Right?

I remain your devoted older brother,

Ronald

A Letter from Miss Gladys Sockwell to Mr. Harold Barker (September 19, 1926)

Dear Harry,

This is just a short note via campus mail to say how much I enjoyed going to Billy's Orient with you Sunday afternoon. It was good to get off campus and especially for a while away from the dormitory, where old Miss Sulloway sermonizes each night about the need to begin arriving for hours check-in a full five minutes before 8. And each gathering is now accompanied by inspirational readings about the value of wholesome living. I think the translation is, "No flappers and gin for *you*."

It's all rather tiring, to say the least. Since you have her for one of your classes, would you do me a favor? Ask her why the class isn't reading Oscar Wilde! Maybe that will put her so on edge she'll forget her "powerful message" next time. Mr. Wilde, as I understand it, was one of those perverted men who are normally obliged to shoot themselves.

Meanwhile, I'd like to risk all by saying that it's good to date you. Maybe someday it will be good to mate you, too. Ha! I'd better stop at this point. Mating is years away. And whatever Professor Sulloway may think, I'm a very decent girl and aim to stay that way.

Hugs.....

Gladys

From Lecture Notes for Professor Theodore Elves's Classical Civilization Class (September 21, 1926)

I begin this class with something unusual: an announcement. There is a joint statement appearing today in the public prints. It will come from both President Muldrow and the Belton Board of Trustees, so there is no hazard in my presenting it to you, now. I can think of no more proper group to learn of this news in some advance.

Working with the Greek government—whose policy I support against the Turks—I have secured for Belton a large collection of plaster statuary. To be sure, there is no marble here, nor is there bronze either. But these constitute a portion of a rather famed collection, which was shown at the Columbian Exposition in Chicago a mere thirty-three years before.

The balance of the collection will remain in Athens. We have a good part of it, however.

Among the plaster artifacts are the following: several temple balustrades; statues (both facial alone as well as fuller bodied) of Hera, Athena, and the Medusa; a relief from the Acropolis; a headless (admittedly) torso of the winged goddess Nike; and a full statue of Poseidon. These are but the highlights of the collection.

So far in this course of study I have had to rely upon my lantern slides, though these were all procured with my own box camera on site in southern Europe. Now we shall be able to see these gracious models up close. They are slightly fragile, so we shall have to handle them with greatest care. I have not yet thought through all the policies, which may be necessary in order to warrant their survival and flourishing at Belton. These will no doubt come to me.

The full collection shall first be put on display, behind a rope, at the Belton College Museum. The exhibition shall open on November 1 of this year. (A special showing for faculty and trustees only shall occur on October 1.)

I can virtually assure you that once you have entered this world you will leave your other one behind, and gladly so. You shall be treated to, and uplifted by, a world of graceful form and elegant design, a universe of aspiring heroism and beauty as abstract as it is concrete and as concrete as it is abstract—a most dazzling paradox, and yet there it will be, before your eyes.

All that I have tried to convey in this course will be open to you.

I know you join me in rejoicing. This will permit us to leave behind a woeful world with its deceits and suspicions. Beauty of the right sort—this beauty—is ample remedy for a world that is wrong.

From an Editorial in the Belton Daily News, September 22, 1926

As we suggested in a previous editorial, Belton College has now acquired some plaster!

This is not just any old plaster, but the brilliantly formatted plaster of Greek statuary and artifacts given to the college by the present government of Greece. The materials were first exhibited at the Columbian Exposition at the Greek Pavilion in order to display Greek contribution to Western culture, and what better portion of their influence to lay bare for all to see than Greek art?

This is surely the view of Professor Theodore Elves, who is to be congratulated for arranging for the gift, and of the college board, and of its faculty.

We editors are hardly qualified to pass detailed and specific judgment on Greek art, ancient or modern, or even on the Greek chapter in Western civilization. But it is certainly obvious that the Greek expression of beauty, both unashamed and yet mostly demure and tasteful, was a significant chapter in what makes Western man differently aspiring: a love of beauty, of truth, and of good in all its manifestations. This collection will not only uplift generations of Belton students. It will also offer important instructional supplements for studies in the classics. It is perhaps as though the department of mathematics had secured Euclid's blackboard, if indeed he had one.

Kudos to Belton College!

From Lecture Notes for Professor David Grendel's Philosophy Survey Course (September 23, 1926)

The recent arrival on our campus of Greek plaster statuary, to which we shall all be exposed in approximately six weeks, shall supply an excellent lesson in what we have been pondering: the linkages between empirical experience and notions of the self.

While it is of course glorious, I am sure, to have a portion of the Acropolis and a bit of Athena in our midst, or it shall be so, there is in another sense nothing special about them. The idea that they somehow bring some external *force to the self—to your self and mine—is patently false. Our "selfhood" shall be altered by our experience of them, of course, but that is only because we shall perceive them, through our eyes, and (perhaps) shall touch them, with our fingers. What shall occur is not that we shall be having, for instance, some sort of séance with Greek sculptors of twenty-five hundred years ago, or that these models shall inform the very air we breathe with some ghosts of perpetual beauty. No. What happens shall occur within us—through the enigma of brains becoming minds—and whatever changes in our understanding of self shall function precisely through this empirical inspection.*

I cannot say of course how brain waves become mind thoughts. Nor can anyone else. But at least I know that I do not know, which marks me rather different from those who are certain of all, including their own hooey ideas of beauty. In any event, what shall happen to you in the museum on November 1st might be salutary, but your sensory experience of an unsanitary alley on the west side of Belton will be no different, in fundamental process, from whatever you get from a plastic Aphrodite. So, students, please retain your perspective.

A Letter from Professor Gwenelda Sulloway to Her Older Sister Jeanine (September 23, 1926)

Dearest Big Sister,

I write to you once more in something less than full tranquility. It is hardly my aim to worry you, you who must certainly be weary of my plaints. The truth is, some days I feel I belong here and am performing my tasks as corresponding to the sacred mission of Belton; while on other days—and this is one—I believe I am not only unequal to the project at hand but even being conspired against.

I have now spied the Sockwell girl and the Barker boy together. It seems they are in some situation of amour, though they never touch (strictly forbidden) but only smile one at another. They are at least friends. It was Gladys Sockwell, you shall recall, who tested my will and severity when she appeared late for hours earlier this month. Being late is one thing, but declaring that one was not really late but fiddling in the washroom is another. I think she was not only lying, but also knew that I knew she was lying and in effect was raising the question, "What shall you do about it? What *can* you do? Nothing."

This was as disheartening as it was enraging. I can readily inform you, now, that it shook my confidence mightily, but although I am now confessing this to you, no doubt you drew the inference of it earlier. Then the Barker boy, her ostensible partner in crime, suggested we read the embarrassingly candid poem by Browning about the murderous Duke of Ferrara and his fetish for portraits of his duchesses and victims. Today, after class—we were pursuing the verse of Arthur Hugh Clough—he appeared again with his smirk (although I must confess that it was a cherubic smirk) and wondered if we might also read something by Oscar Wilde.

Since, dear sister, you are not in academics, you will not be overly familiar with how impudent this very request is in actuality. Let us leave aside the odious and unspeakable Wilde. Even if the Barker boy had suggested we read Shakespeare or Dante, he would have been drastically out of line. Once a professor has set a syllabus it is not to be altered. Even to hint that it should be is a direct challenge to professorial authority.

But now the Barker boy is volunteering his interrogation (and by implication his opinion) about the advisability of including Oscar Wilde. He knows full well that Oscar Wilde is a ghastly blemish upon the ideals of civilization, of nature and discipline and restraint and sacred love. How much else he knows, I do not know. But let me add to you, dear one, that Wilde was also guilty of many irreverent sayings, of a self-important rebellion that in some benighted quarters goes by the name of wit.

I sense a certain ganging up. The Sockwell girl is barely civil to me, and now the Barker boy is inserting Wilde into my discourse with him.

You will be pleased to know that I kept the even tenor of my ways, though inside my very coherent integrity felt under terrific assault and I sensed myself as a broken mirror whose silvered pieces were falling slowly, one by one, over an agonizing several hours.

I told the Barker boy that there would be no Wilde and added that he was not really a Victorian, whereupon Barker rejoined that he had been given to understand that he was late Victorian.

I said Wilde was a modern and then had the cleverness—though I don't like to think of myself as clever, as it breeds bad habits—to say that I had an immediate appointment with President Muldrow. Mr. Barker would have to excuse me. This took him aback. Did he think I would go directly to the president and report him?

He might well have done, for I must tell you, Jeanine, that I was sorely tempted to do precisely that. Only a sense that President Muldrow would not wish to hear anguish from me again so soon kept me from entering his outer office. In the event I repaired to my apartment in the dormitory, there to rest and, let me concede, weep, both with tremors and with fury.

I am not well. I feel that my competence and self-assurance, not to mention my supervisory powers, are being questioned at all times. I welcome sleep as a respite, but then sleep itself is reluctant to arrive, I am sorry to report.

Please, dear sister, if you have counsel, let it come now. I need it.

Your devoted sister, Gwenelda

A Letter from Professor Theodore Elves to Professor David Grendel (September 25, 1926)

It was of some astonishment to me that your previous letter was sent on September 14, some eleven days earlier. I was surprised, but not ungrateful, that such a relatively long time had passed. It told me that I had largely been free of your zealous self-interest and self-absorption for over a week, and that I had barely thought of it, or of you.

I did review briefly the contents of yours of September 14. They were to the effect that I had not "empirical" evidence of your treachery. Leaving aside the question of whether I did or did not on September 14, I certainly have some now, for your most recent remarks about what is the capstone of my academic career—the Columbian Models—have now reached my ears. Because you made them publicly, in class, or semi-publicly, to other faculty, they are now a matter of some solid record.

They drip of course with bile and envy in equally noxious portions. Your view—that the perceptible experience of the Models will be no different from that of dirtiest alley in Belton, Wisconsin, is not only pernicious but also false. In some ways I feel pity for you, for in your world it all comes down to the dreary concatenations of cells and meat and molecules. There is no larger vision. There is only inordinate pride in skepticism. There is only the hubris of not being fooled.

But the greatest foolery of all is to disbelieve in the purity and transcendence of beauty.

I shall once more warn you about attacks upon my adequacy and reputation. They shall not be tolerated. Ye, who is so assured of the material basis of reality, shall perhaps, and sooner than you think, discover the fragility, not only of this improvident world view but of the material itself on which it is based. He who lives by corpuscles may also die of them.

I hence admonish you.

Theodore Elves

Letter from Theodore Elves to Harold Barker (September 26, 1926)

Dear Harold,

It is with utter certitude that I inform you this shall be my last letter. I have received no reply to my earlier invitation to tea, and your eagerness to leave class on the dot of its ending prevents my speaking with you directly.

I can only add that the invitation is still open, and that in addition to Earl Grey I shall also be able to share with you, in advance, certain of the Columbian Exposition Models. They are somewhat sensitive to eager and aggressive touching. I have no doubt that this will present no hazard to thee or me.

Do please let me know your pleasure. It would give an aging man, now rather at the top of his academic game, immense satisfaction simply to hear from you. Having tea would be even more joyful.

I remain ever devoted to the moral and aesthetic instruction of those who come after me.

Yours very truly,

Professor Elves

From the Belton Bullhorn (September 27, 1926)

A Dialogue

Only in the Greeks, said Professor Elves,
Can we ever find our selves.

Replied Professor Grendel,
"It all comes down to Mendel."

Said Professor Elves:
Put empiricism on your back shelves!

Replied Professor Grendel:
I'd love to crash a Columbian Model!

Letter from Ronald Elves to His Younger Brother Harold (September 28, 1926)
[Edited to correct spelling errors]

Dear Harold,

I'm pretty outraged that Old Elves keeps putting pressure on you about this tea thing. I suppose the old Papa Stringbean must think he's the cock of the campus walk with this Greek models thing. Ha! But that's no excuse whatever for putting the vice on you. I'm starting to think that maybe his intentions are not altogether sincere or admirable either.

Don't get the wrong. I do not like to think ill of people, although it's pretty clear that both my bosses are thinking pretty ill of me. I have got to tell you, Ron, that so far my career has been a bust. I guess I should never have tried this investing thing. I really never had any economics courses at Belton—just a smattering or two—and I just do not seem to have the head necessary for canny asset assessment. You know how our parents pushed me into something practical when I would just have soon stayed with French and gotten really good at it. I could even spell well in French!

In sum, old pal, I think I'm about to get fired. I do not know how I will ever tell the folks about it. They aren't rich and have sacrificed to send you and me to Parker and then to Belton. Confessing failure—well, I don't see how I can do it. But what else I can do? I cannot live in the streets, and without a salary....

It's ironic, you know, that Elves is pressing you. I think if my bosses invited me for tea or a speakeasy beer they'd put cyanide in it. I just wonder if there's anything I could do to help you out. I sense that the Elves thing is weighing on you, getting in the way of life with Gladys Sockwell and your studies. I did enjoy the Oscar Wilde joke on Miss Sulloway.

Still, brother Harry, I sense that you are fretting behind all the bonhomie. Can I help? Can I at least help somebody these days, even if I cannot help myself? Can I do something right for a change?

Your discouraged but increasingly furious brother,

Ron

From the Diary of President Irving Muldrow (September 29, 1926)

This has been my worst week since taking on the travails of becoming Belton's fourth president. At least the golden cobra matter is settled. We have sold it to a museum in Cleveland for twelve thousand dollars. The Egyptologists are furious that I overruled them. But we need the money, and there was obviously no way they were going to incorporate the cobra into their instructional patterns. It would have been for show alone. Belton at this point cannot afford show unless it comes free.

And this is where I could hug Theodore Elves, for his long support of the Greeks against Turkey and his ties to the Greek Orthodox Church (not a member but a supporter) has paid handsomely. The Columbian Models are ours, and I freely and confidently predict that on November 1st or thereabouts thousands will come hundreds of miles to wonder at them. I have only seen Theodore's slides. They promise to dazzle when they manifest themselves at the art hall. I myself expect a similar pleasure and sensation on October 1st when I, along with the board and the faculty, receive a special preview showing.

Ergo, Diary, one might think this has been a good week, with the cobra profitably gone and Aphrodite profitably on her way. But no:

this has been a horrific week. And it all goes back to the unending and ulcerative conflict between Teddy and David Grendel, which the former has made worse by his obviously burgeoning hubris, and the latter by his envy and trenchant criticism, and then the *Bullhorn* has made its own contribution with a couple of little ditties about the fight between their two eminences.

I am ready to throttle them both, the editors Scott and Hansen, and before the cobra left for Cleveland I wish I could have turned it, magi style, into real snakes to set upon the two editors of the paper, who have struck again. I can hardly wait for the nosey bodies down at the *Daily News* to get hold of this chaos that hath come again.

The *Daily News*: it doth love—and hate—Belton College.

I have had all of them in my office—not at the same time of course. The visit by David Grendel was the worst. He came bearing a letter sent to him by Teddy that, circumlocutions and all, came near to threatening bodily harm. I cannot take this with much earnestness, however, as Teddy is a tall wisp at best, while David, five years younger, is a muscular, stocky man, albeit short. Theodore's missive was, though, intemperate. It is clear that he is feeling his oats with these models, and wants very much to be allowed to have his head go where e'er it wishes. Grendel is in an absolute snit about the letter and reports, in a certain menacing style of his own, that he has grown hyper exasperated with Teddy's accusations and demands.

As for Elves, he thoroughly expected, before getting down to the Grendel business, yet another round of encomiums for his having escorted the models to our little campus. Of course I had to show my appreciation for the nth time. He is sure that David put Scott and Hansen up to the ditty in order to embarrass him and filch from him his reputation in his time of greatest glory. I tried to explain that Scott and Hansen are a couple of clever nobodies who, someday if we are lucky, will have bratty children of their own. Meanwhile, the distribution numbers of the *Bullhorn* are hardly plentiful enough to injure any repute that Teddy has built up over thirty or more years of teaching and scholarship in the area of his beloved Greek art. However, apparently now that Teddy has gained his greatest accolade he is extremely jealous of his academic pearls and fears that even losing a piece of just one will be a strategic disaster. This is a lesson, I suppose, in human nature: when once we have suddenly accumulated great fame, it makes us fret and strut our hour upon the stage in fear that we shall lose even a second of it untowardly.

Grendel was angry, but the irritation almost seemed to agree with him and make him more robust. As for Teddy, I fear this whole business is taking a toll on what has always been a highly-strung and almost emaciated frame.

I wonder where all this will lead, but I believe I can contain it if only the *Daily News* does not publish anything about it. The editors have always pretended to love the college when in fact they dislike it, I think, because both of them went to regional public universities and lack the prestige of Belton. And they are both senior versions of Scott and Hansen in a way: more responsible, yes (though that is saying but little) but still rather sophomoric in their essays in editorial humor. They would love to stir up more trouble on what they sardonically label "Holy Hill." What can I do to prevent this?

As for Scott and Hansen, I was contented, when they were visitors in my realm, to state that they knew almost nothing of the real issues between Teddy's aestheticism and Grendel's skepticism: that these were crucial issues of which they had made light, and that they would have terrible lives if their present course persisted. I dismissed them. I do not quite believe what I told them, but I am glad to have done so anyhow.

Perhaps one of the Greek models will fall on them—a frieze from the Parthenon perhaps. But as they are only plaster, these models, the damage will be to the frieze and not to Scott and Hansen. Again here is evidence, if more proof were required, of the injustices of life.

At least may the cobra be happy, in its new abode!

From a Wire Report in The Belton Daily News, September 29, 1926

The Hague, Netherlands—The War of the Stray Dog is officially over, according to a statement by the League of Nations today.

The conflict between Greece and Bulgaria, possibly started when a Greek soldier sought his stray dog over the tense border between the two countries, led to hundreds of casualties and League of Nations intervention.

The Greek government was ordered to pay Bulgarian civilians 45,000 pounds sterling, a directive the government resisted but has now complied with.

The military head of the Greek government, Theodoros Pangalos, was deposed for pursuing the conflict.

Greek's King Constantine was deposed three years earlier. Pangalos is the latest in a string of leaders in the Second Hellenic Republic.

A Letter to Professor Theodore Elves from Harold Barker, September 30, 1926

Dear Professor Elves,

I write this letter with some hesitancy. I will also say that I have asked friends to help me with its composition.

I appreciate the invitation to tea and am sorry to have been standoffish about it. Yet I feel that because I am only a freshman, and in awe of your learning, I would be poor company. I therefore ask you to forgive me when I say I decline your invitation, and I ask also that you will please be assured how flattered I have been to receive it.

Yours truly,

Harold Barker '30

III: OCTOBER 1926

From an Editorial in the Belton Daily News, October 1, 1926

Today is a special day at Belton College, for this very afternoon, or by the time you read our words, the faculty and trustees will have seen a preview of the Columbian Exposition Greek Models recently procured by the college. This lavish display (or so we are told) of friezes, heads, and torsos (among other things) will surely enlarge the imagination.

Your humble scribblers here at the *Daily News* will have to wait, however, to see if our certitude is well placed. We are not invited to the special showing.

Even aside from the artifacts, though, Belton has been a special place indeed of late, notably because of the upstart editors of the Belton *Bullhorn*—a term we have often worried about, for we have long thought the Belton *Bugle* would have been more decorous. Our suspicions about the name have been rather confirmed lately. The student editors recently published an ostensible lament about the unexpected and deleterious effects of new inventions but conveniently used the louche zipper as its example. For that, we are told, President Muldrow chastised them in no ambivalent terms.

But now they have struck again, this time publicizing in the most inappropriate way a dispute between two of the college's most erudite professors, whose names we should never reveal here. Any such controversy should never be treated lightly, yet that is what our youthful editors have done. And while, as graduates of the lowly state universities, we do not pretend to understand the nature of the conflict, we are certain that it must be one of high seriousness. Even we who have gotten but a "public" education can believe that!

We trust that the argument between Professor Y and Professor Z will be kept within bounds, however, and will have no effect on the college's celebratory mood as it contemplates the acquisition of plastered Heras and Zeuses.

A Letter from Professor Theodore Elves to Harold Barker (October 1, 1926)

Dear Young Harold,

I am dashing off this note quickly, as today, as you would imagine, will be a hectic one for me. I must work with the museum staff to assure that all is prepared for this afternoon's faculty-trustee showing of the models.

I did receive your note and was disappointed to get it. I shall make one final endeavor to get you to change your mind. Please refrain from being offended if I manage, even at my age, to "chase you down" for one final plea!

My very best wishes to you from

Theodore Elves

A Telegram Sent by Ronald Barker to His Younger Brother Harold, October 1, 1926

AM TERMINATED STOP IN DESPAIR STOP HEADING TO BELTON STOP WILL STAY AT PHI PSI STOP AM FURIOUS WITH THE WORLD STOP SEE YOU SOON STOP RONALD

A Letter from Professor Gwenelda Sulloway to Her Older Sister Jeanine, October 1, 1926

Most Dear One,

It is near midnight here, with autumn asserting itself outside in the persona of a cold wind. If I look with care out my darkened window I can see a leaf fluttering downward here and there.

This might seem to you a normal fall night. To me it presages an inexplicable fatality. I shall be the first to concede that some of what occurs is to be found within my own spirit. I sense that I should have never taken this position at Belton. My constitution is possibly not up to it.

If my next letter asks you to meet me at the train station in Minneapolis, do not be surprised. I am quite uncertain of how long I can hold on here. I write in despair and from an inability to sleep.

While my own structure is perhaps deficient for the challenges of this milieu, I must also insist that the milieu itself is lacking in restraint and overly long on a subtle decadence. I have told you already about the Sockwell girl, the Barker boy, and now must add a general inattention in my Victorian literature course, as though the energetic high principles of that noble generation were some sort of bore, or perhaps that I myself am only a servant of ennui. But now something else has happened, which has wrenched my spirit or perhaps stretched it to the point of remorseless fracture.

I myself was an innocent bystander. Like other members of the faculty I attended a preview of a recent Belton acquisition, the Columbian Exposition Models of Ancient Greek Art, a gift to the college from the current Hellenic Republic. I thought, without thinking very much, I admit, that the display would be inspiring and anything but enervating or unnerving, although I have had some concerns, if fuzzy, about the overall matter of bodily display even in the name of high art. But as I came ever closer to the exhibition room, I saw none other than the sponsor and curator of the event,

Professor Theodore Elves, speaking with some agitation to the Barker boy, who seemed transfixed if slightly uneasy in the line of the professor's entreaties and discourse. I must tell you, dearest Jeanine, that it occurred to me, even then, that it was not the Sockwell girl who had induced the Barker boy to bedevil with talk of Browning and Wilde, but Professor Elves himself who had done so—albeit in a sneaky way and with subversive and seemingly guiltless methods.

This may seem to be you quite absurd. Why would Elves be disposed to sic the Barker boy on the likes of me? Theodore Elves is above sixty-five, tall and still erect though razor thin, with a gray mustache seemingly added as an afterthought. He came to Belton from a school in Vermont, Illyria, some ten years before. He is an acclaimed expert on ancient Greek art. He has conducted tours in Asia Minor. He is a friend of the Greek government.

That such a being would be in the business of creating havoc for me, and through one as seemingly lowly as the Barker boy, would seem not overly creditable. But I saw what I saw, and my intuitions remain competent even if my nerves are in tatters.

It was when I actually entered the exhibit that I came to the truth in all its full furor and malevolence, for in that exhibit hall was a veritable riot of human torsos, bare for all to see. There were plaster statues of Greek goddesses in various states of disrobing, and Greek gods and heroes in the most ghastly states of shameless, total exposure. You know, dear one, that I long regarded the human body as overrated, mostly a means to get us here on earth so that we might then go from strength to strength in decorum and temperance. Here, however, was a gauche celebration of the body itself. The only consolation I managed to have was that at least it was an exhibition of plaster casts. Had I only had a hammer....

I did not. Philosophically the whole business seemed to me a grand huzzah for the *means* of life as though it were the *end* of life. This struck me as a great mistake, but such a consideration does not convey to you the overwhelming sense I had of being in the presence a great evil, about which other faculty and dignitaries seemed happy and of which they actually seemed proud. My head spun. My intestines seized up. I had to get away and did so at once. I doubt if my stay consisted of even three minutes. I would have nothing to do with *that*.

It was then that the full realization and I had our fateful collision. Yes, indeed, it *had* been Elves who had colluded with Barker against me. At Belton College is a cult (of this I am convinced), working contrary to all that I had been told was the moral signature of the institution. Because I, for one, had come to burnish that signature more gloriously than even before, it was I whom they must rid themselves of. I have been the victim of a conspiracy of great treachery and viciousness, of temptation and malignancy.

The question now is what I am to do about it. I do not feel up to the sort of combat against Elves and his fellows that would be necessary for me to prevail. Even President Muldrow may yet not be trustworthy or blameless. I do not ask that you reply to this letter, Big Sister. There are two reasons. One is that by the time I received your response the matter will have already gone beyond control, so any advice of yours will be futile. The other is that I fear no counsel of yours could possibly be adequate to the grand evil that I have encountered. I hope you and Frederick might allow me to find refuge among you. I long to be in a place where the likes of Old Elves and Young Barker cannot discover me.

As I look back on this letter I am surprised at how self-controlled it is. This is proof, I think, that a proper Victorian discipline can even manifest itself in moments of greatest panic. My soul seems rather calmed by the writing of this missive. Nonetheless I am your *frantic* sister

Gwenelda

From Lecture Notes for Professor David Grendel's Philosophy Survey Course, October 2, 1926

Dear students, there may come a time your lives when you will be accused of envy. I hope that such accusations will be false, as they

have been of late against me. Let me say at once, however, that I do not envy those who may believe that there is no linkage between mind and brain. We are used to thinking that "mind" is some sort of disembodied ghost, which is why our current word for "mind" was once referred, in less scientific ages, as "soul" or "spirit." You and I can tap our skulls and feel, in a matter of speaking, our brains, but it is very difficult to touch our "minds." Thus mind would seem to be some sort of abstraction (like God, everywhere but nowhere) while brain would seem to be as palpable as a combustion engine.

But as I say, I would never envy those who believe that mind is one thing and brain entirely another thing. There have been too many instances of how brain damage has led to serious difficulties with the functioning of the mind. So those unenviable persons who see no connection between the two are denying hard facts. This is why they are not to be envied. We are not jealous of those who will not face the truth.

I did not attend yesterday's grand preview of the Columbian Models, but doubtless some who were present felt that "the mind of ancient Greece" was paying a ghostly visitation in the room. No such thing was happening. Instead, as many as attended—let us say seventy-five—had brains that were firing. This was no séance with the "mind" of ancient Greece. This was a case of seventy-five cranial instances--of electrochemical charges--in the present tense (and not in 500 B.C.). Those who think otherwise deserve our pity, not our

318

envy. I feel rather strongly about this point. While I cannot advocate
any pity for such individuals, I would be less than candid in finding
fault with you should you choose to dislike them.

From The Belton Daily News, October 4, 1926

Belton—Professor Theodore W. Elves passed away late on October
2.

Elves, a well-known professor of classics who recently was
instrumental in securing important plaster statuary models for Belton
College, was found deceased on the morning of October 3 in his
classroom.

Early indications are that he died of natural causes, quite possibly a
stroke or heart attack.

Students found him in his classroom in West Hall when they
appeared for his course. It is speculated that he died gathering
lantern slides for that class in classical civilization, language, and art.

"The entire campus and Belton family are in a state of at least mild
shock," said President Irving Muldrow.

Elves came to Belton ten years ago from Illyria College, Vermont.

As the *Daily News* goes to press, it has learned that in two days there will be a funeral in the college chapel followed by an entourage of the community, which will escort Professor Elves's bier to Oakwood Cemetery near campus.

Future editions will include updates.

From the Diary of President Irving Muldrow, October 4, 1926

Belton College cannot afford the publicity of racy stories or sordid deeds. Thus was I happy to see the *Daily News* coverage (so far) of Teddy's death. The BDN is our first line of defense. If it learns nothing amiss, then it is unlikely that the press in general will do so.

The paper reports Teddy's passing as entirely natural and the result of a stroke or heart attack.

The actual scene tells a much more problematical tale. I have seen it and hope never to see the like again. Teddy's room was the outcome of what can only be called a violent mess: a carnage of someone's vilest tantrums. The desks were overturned. Teddy's own desk was missing all its papers, strewn near and far on the maple flooring. The lantern slides were also floored, two of them split. An inkbottle was overturned, its black flow a splotch upon the light green carpet near the front of the room. There were detectable wisps of blood on the white walls. A framed map of Greece and Asia Minor was on the floor, the glass shattered and the document curled up out of its frame as though in abject terror. From what was it hiding? Can a map be traumatized?

The man himself lay on the landing of the stairs. He was naked. His clothes, including spats and cravat, were left behind dolefully and scarily in the classroom. Teddy's head was a red pulp. I swore I saw a sliver of gray brain tissue on the landing, although one of the janitors has insisted that it was only the mortal remains of a decaying insect. Upon Teddy's visage was a look of horror. His mouth was twisted almost cyclonically, his eyes in a protuberance of the most disquieting dread. I could swear I heard his roaring scream even in the shocked silence of those of us tardily attending him.

I think Teddy was murdered. Board members have called and visited, all of them with the same advice: Put this down to natural causes and say that Teddy may have fallen from an epileptic seizure. They do not wish to know any details. I have consulted his medical records from Vermont, and true enough his doctor indicated some suspicion of epilepsy. But Teddy has never had a fit here, or not one that I have seen.

In time, we decided that even attributing his death to epilepsy might be rather scandalous; after all, epileptics are not allowed driver's licenses and are viewed as a sub-class in some quarters. We put it down as natural causes due to something more mainstream. The coroner has gone along. The birth certificate is now official. No suspicious contemporary journalist or future archivist will ever find anything amiss there.

The students who found Teddy naked have been sworn to secrecy. I doubt if they will take this information to their graves, but I believe they will at least be slow to pass it on. Fortunately it was only the two who arrived early, and they then broadcast an alarm that brought Janitor Curry and myself along soon after. Thus only a few of us have seen Teddy's utter state of undress. Let us hope indeed that those rapscallions Scott and Hansen do not discover any facts of this horrid business.

What happened in that room? That Teddy died, or even that his room was in a condition of chaos might be explicable by the course of natural events. His nakedness is not. I can think of no way to explain it except with reference to a foul play that I myself do not wish to fancy or fathom.

I think it was homicide. I shall keep my eyes and ears open. And yet to find the culprit is to expose the public airs to reprehensible facts which Belton College can ill afford to reveal. We must ergo hush up this matter forever.

My timorous ways as Belton's fifth president shall continue. I am shocked and rattled, Diary, and feel that the description for my position should include, "Successful candidate must vow always to do the disingenuous thing."

Poor Teddy, alas. He did not deserve this, difficult as he was, and regardless of what role he himself might have played in the tragedy. I cannot contemplate that role. I do not want to.

From the Diary of President Irving Muldrow, October 5, 1926

The latest is this: Gwendela Sulloway has left campus abruptly, though I now have a telegram from her sister in Minnesota which says that Miss Sulloway is ill and resting and staying with the sister and her husband. I am wondering what to do if she does not return, which intuition tells me is likely. I have gotten assurances from Professor Nollton that he can take over her Victorian Literature class, and my own dear wife Ruth has agreed to become dormitory matron for the balance of this autumn term.

All this in addition to the horrible enigma and loss of Teddy: I sometimes wonder in these early days of the catastrophe—Diary, please forgive me—if none other than David Grendel had anything to do with the bloody and ignominious passing of Teddy. Theirs was a bitter enmity indeed. Meanwhile—and now, I know, I am on the verge of raving—could Miss Sulloway have been responsible? At times I have thought her near the fatal cliff of insanity, an obsessive woman with hives even to the slightest breach of self-professed principle and certainly big enough to do in even me, much less Teddy Elves. The dean tells me of a rumor, unconfirmed (and I shall *not* be about the task of confirming it) that Teddy pestered a young male student with invitations. This was innocent but on Teddy's part unwise. He was lonely. Could any of this have had anything to do with anything incorrigible and amiss?

And where were Scott and Hansen?

Dear Diary, I pray to get through these coming days and nights with a body intact and a soul yet fit for eternity.

From The Belton Daily News, October 6, 1926

Belton—In a somber ceremony in the Belton College chapel yesterday, the campus remembered Professor Theodore Elves, who died on October 2.

President Irving Muldrow recalled Elves's "contributions to campus and community alike, his capacity for being an inspiring teacher, his devotion to all things Greek, and his impeccable scholarship."

The city of Belton sent a large floral wreath of the Parthenon in Elves's honor. An entourage of hundreds accompanied the wreath and Elves's coffined body for burial at Maplewood Cemetery.

Before that, students had stood as honor guards around the coffin, which lay for twenty-four hours in the chapel.

These students included Timothy White, president of the student body, and Thomas Scott and Sloane Hansen, editors of the Belton *Bullhorn*.

President Muldrow said that discussions would soon ensue about a proper memorial to Elves on campus. The *Daily News* learns that the construction of a new art hall, to be named after Professor Elves, has not been ruled out and is under active consideration..

Editorial from The Belton **Daily News,** *October 6, 1926*

We should last say a word about Professor Theodore Wesley Elves. Although he was not a long-timer in our community he was a civic one. He wrote the script for our Pageant of Progress and directed Greek plays, in the original language, upon the steps of the college library. It was, not to put too fine a point, Greek to us, but we enjoyed the emotions and the togas.

He died at the dawn of his greatest academic triumph, the acquisition of the Columbian Greek Models, of which much has already been said and written. Though he seemed an energetic man of sixty-seven, he was self-evidently not a healthy one. We are sorry about his sudden misfortune, which is in good part ours as well.

IV: 1936-2006

Letter to the Belton Bullhorn, November 23, 1936

To the Editor:

Please count me as among those who have now arguably had contact with the late Professor Theodore Elves. On Wednesday night I entered West College near midnight in order to put a paper under the door of Gary Winston, professor of English—I turned the paper in early because I had to be off campus the following day. Professor Winston's office is what used to be the "room" of Teddy Elves.

Because the building is dark at that hour, and it is now one of the darkest periods of the year, with the days drawing in early, I carried a flashlight for navigation. But I found it gave me little solace when, upon bending down to slide my paper on "The Pardoner's Tale" beneath Professor Winton's door, I heard a faint but nonetheless audible low moaning. I could not locate the source of this sound, which seemed everywhere but nowhere. I immediately thought of the wind, but it was a still and starry night. The moan was a sound both human and inhuman.

It did not, however, seem to be a cry for help. Rather—and I can't prove this—the sound seemed to come from some source that felt at home, as though it were not it but I that was the trespasser.

I submit that this was the ghost of Teddy Elves, hovering about the place of his death a decade ago, but that he visits only late at night and found me to be an unexpected interloper. I never felt in any terrible danger but left immediately.

Make of this what you will. I report this as a public service to the campus, even if I have not quite worked out how it might become so.

William Clarity '37

Letter from Mrs. Frances Read (nee Muldrow) to Roderick Rotterdam, Belton College Archivist, October 1, 1965

Dear Mr. Rotterdam:

When my father died in office in 1942 he made no declaration about the final disposal of his papers. I can only assume that he meant for the family, his descendants, to have them all. However, now that I have grown older, myself nearing seventy, I have concluded that the college archives would benefit from the eleven volumes of his diaries. If you will let me know whether or not your archives would desire the receipt of them, please so inform me, and in the event of a positive response I shall ship them to you forthwith for your disposal and study.

I myself have but barely perused their contents.

Yours sincerely,

Francis Read (Mrs.)

Letter from Professor Jonathan Millet to Roderick Rotterdam, Belton College Archivist, February 4, 1966

Dear Mr. Rotterdam:

I have been inordinately slow to respond to your recent inquiry about my late uncle David Grendel. This is not because I find your interrogatives offensive—I do not—but because I have wanted to make as careful a reply as possible.

As you may know, David Grendel was my late mother's brother. He himself never married, and I grew up in far away New York State, so my chances of spending time with him were somewhat limited. I mean by this not only the distance between Hamilton and Belton but also the fact that he never produced any young cousins for me to visit. Thus was the motive for assembly reduced.

Nonetheless, by the time of my twenties I was able to spend time with Uncle David, and he it was who clearly inspired me to become a philosophy professor at Ottowottama. I often think Uncle David would be disappointed in my field of endeavor, for the philosophy of language was not his field or to his liking. He knew little about it, of course, because it has burgeoned only since his death in 1929. But he understood enough of it to say that it did not deal with first-order questions.

As for first-order questions, Uncle David always believed that he was addressing them. He was a short but very strong man, even into his sixties (he died at 65). He was, truth be told, a rather dyspeptic man, a fussbudget rather set in his ways. You have asked the origins of the dispute with Theodore Elves. My answer to this question is based on remembered fragments of conversation in the late 20s but mostly on my own imagination.

He did not like to speak of Elves, only stating that. "What happened was regrettable." But he did allow one summer that he found Elves self-absorbed and philosophically erroneous for believing in what, as I recall, he termed "Elves's absurd aesthetic metaphysics." I have heard that Elves was what today we might call a somewhat paranoid man who was ungrateful for my uncle's earlier ministrations to him. But my guess is also that Uncle David was a fervent believer in his notions of sensory materialism and found Elves's claims about some externally mysterious "spirit of Beauty" to be horrific. Uncle David took ideas quite seriously. For him they were nearly matters of life and death.

I can imagine that in another life he would have wanted to exile Plato.

And this brings me to one of the central questions you asked: Could Uncle David have brought about the death of Elves? I must answer in two ways. First, I cannot possibly say. You might as well ask me how many ants were in Greece in 1950. I was in New York State on the night Teddy Elves died, however he died. But second, while I think it unlikely that Uncle David had any hand at all in what, after all, as I understand, may yet have been a natural death, I could not rule out his participation. He was a muscular man who probably could have overpowered the relatively emaciated Elves. He could be a furious man. The controversy with Elves had reached fevered pitch. He might have confronted Elves in his room that night and decided to "have it out with him." I cannot believe that Uncle David went there to kill him.

As for the nudity in which Professor Elves was left, I can see, barely, how Uncle David might have removed his rival's clothes in order to send a message that in the end it is not the vague and wispy form of "beauty" that count but human, material flesh in all its aging homeliness. This might have been a symbolic expression of David Grendel's convictions.

Having said all this, however, I think it doubtful, probably highly so. But I do not mind facing what might have been the truth, however unlikely, and my own view of human propensity is not sentimental, even when it comes to an uncle with whom I spent, in my lifetime, only about fifty days here and there—but enough to make me a philosopher (of sorts!).

My best wishes in your search for the "true facts,"

Jon Millet

Letter from Mrs. Jeanine Morris to Roderick Rotterdam, Belton College Archivist, February 15, 1966

Dear Roderick Rotterdam:

In your December letter you said you hoped your inquiry was not offensive. Well, you hoped in vain. I have been in a quandary about whether or not even to write you back. But I have decided to do so. I am a seventy-five year old widow, with well-earned master's degree, now retired from teaching and long devoted to my late husband Fred. I was also dedicated to my late sister Gwenelda. Some things a person must stand up for. Gwenelda is among them, but she was never a *thing*. She was a person, something that you, in your eagerness to stir up the past, seem to have forgotten.

You mentioned in your letter—you said you wanted to put the matter gingerly—that my sister was a large framed woman who could have overpowered the aging Theodore Elves. Well, she was a "large framed woman," but you should know that when she died at only forty in the sanitarium up here she had ceased to eat. She had been there off and on for nearly eight years. In the end she never thought she would recover and stopped eating. They didn't put "starvation" on her death certificate but they might as well have. She was skin and bones.

I have never gotten the straight of what was going on when my sister spent those few months at Belton College. With an advanced degree from Northwestern she was eager to take on the task offered to her. I will be the first to admit that she was a somewhat brittle person. She had always suffered from an oversensitivity to life's travails so that what might but bother some of us, she found overwhelming.

Yet I am also convinced that Belton itself was to blame. It was never the serene place of high principles that she had been told about when she was given the position. As she described it to me in increasingly frantic letters in the early fall of 1926 it was a place of bratty students, potentially loose ethics, and a promotion of the nude body that trustees and faculty alike seemed to praise without conscience. I am not a prude, but I must take Gwenelda's side. She was a finely tuned person who had been misled and heard the discord in the official music.

From your letter I have learned the distressing news that Theodore Elves was found both bloody and naked. I never knew my sister to be violent, and while she had placed Elves towards the end of her Belton time under the glare of vociferous suspicion, I cannot imagine that she would ever strike him, or even confront him. That she would disrobe him does not bear thinking of, and it is so fatuously out of my sister's character that I shall not dignify it with further comment.

Once she returned to Fred and me here in Minneapolis, she was extremely reluctant to speak of events in Belton. She did refer on occasion to "that terrible man with the torso," by which I assume she meant Theodore Elves.

I am sorry for what happened to him. My sister had nothing to do with it. I am far sorrier for her.

Please do not correspond with me further.

Jeanine Morris (Mrs.)

Letter from Harold Barker to Roderick Rotterdam, Belton College Archivist, April 2, 1966

Dear Mr. Rotterdam,

I have yours of March 20 and apologize for not responding sooner. I am now a fifty-eight year-old insurance agent (I own my small company) in Green Bay and was away on business. I have never used my degree in government from Belton directly, but I always believe that my Belton education was one of the most magnificent things of my life.

Apparently you just discovered somewhere or other some indication of the letters that Professor Elves wrote to me during my freshman year. Let me say at once that I will always be grateful to "Teddy" for introducing me to ancient Greek art. My education in line and form and angle has helped me in every art museum I have ever visited, including the Payne in nearby Oshkosh. But it's true that his persistent and even annoying letters to me about tea, though flattering, were also scary to me, a mere eighteen year old. By my sophomore year I had broken up with Gladys Sockwell, who died tragically young in a car accident at age thirty-six; but during that early fall I did confide in her about my upset with Teddy's constantly beseeching me.

Please know, however, that I never saw anything morally amiss in his invitations. Looking back, I think Teddy was a solitary old man of over sixty-five. He had lost his wife and child in Vermont. He had only his beloved theories of beauty—he'd lost interest in Greek language—and wanted to share them. He looked for enthusiasm and approval. David Grendel was an imposing campus figure, who had gone after Teddy's ideas as insubstantial. Teddy Elves was not a pervert, but he did lack decorum about those constant invitations. And when the Columbian Models came, I believe he got a little high on his Trojan horse. In my last conversation with him he virtually demanded that I accept his invite. I walked away. I never saw him again.

You asked about my brother Ronald, who committed suicide in the late 1930s. I will tell you now—why should I hide this—that he was going through a very bad patch indeed around the time Teddy died; and since then, I have heard rumors that Teddy was found in a state of bloody undress. I can't verify that. I can only tell you that Ronald was quite angry with Teddy for badgering his little brother. But Ron was *generally* upset during that period. He had lost his job in Chicago, felt he was a failure, had no idea how to tell our parents, and had taken the train to Belton in early October to see me—a familiar and comforting presence—and stay at Phi Psi, his old frat. Reading between the lines, I am wondering if you think Ron had anything to do with Teddy's death. Well, I am still given to understand (rumors notwithstanding) that Teddy died of a stroke. Ron did not cause Professor Elves to have a stroke.

He arrived in Belton at some point during the evening of October 2. I saw him the next morning. We met for breakfast at the Gold Griddle, a few blocks from campus. Is it still there?

Ron was agitated that morning, but I think we can safely put that down to his having been fired. He was never quite able to right himself. He was married and divorced and went through several jobs, from brick salesman to legal assistant, before discovering he was not suited to any. He was a very bright guy who always had trouble with basic things, like sums and spelling. I think he'd have been much happier as a French translator or professor, but our parents would not hear of either of us doing anything they deemed impractical.

My parents meant well, but in the end I believe their strictures may have done Ron and me alike a disservice. I have gotten through this long, though. Ronald did not.

This is about all I can tell you about my brother. How sure am I that he is disconnected to Teddy's passing? I would say 1000%.

Give my best to the old sod.

Best wishes,

Harold Barker

Letter from Christina Royce, M.D. to Belton History Professor Evelyn Boykin, July 29, 1996

Dear Professor Boykin,

I enjoyed our recent chat about the Theodore Elves matter, which you are enviably researching. I wish I had the time for such a fascinating inquiry. Alas, the pursuit of neurological medicine is not as interesting as one might think.

You had asked that I recapitulate in writing, for your purposes, my analysis and our conversation. I should begin by stating, again, that the trail is much too cold for me to say anything definitive about Dr. Elves's death. His corpse was taken away immediately and his death attributed to natural causes, and, as I understand it, the room was restored as soon as possible to its previous condition. This prevented any real autopsy, and though forensic science was in its infancy then, relative to today, if the room were a crime scene, it should never have been touched until the authorities arrived.

Any possible incriminating evidence is lost forever.

This leaves me with only one possibly constructive endeavor: to state an opinion about whether Elves's nudity could be consistent with death by natural causes without human intervention or criminality. I will say that it is possible but not likely.

Professor Oliver Sacks has done an admirable job of popularizing our field in his classic and best-selling book *The Man Who Mistook*

His Wife for a Hat (1985). I know you have read this exciting book and are familiar with the bizarreness of behaviors influenced by neurological disorders, including twins who cannot read or multiply but have a genius for finding prime numbers; victims of aphasia who cannot read the emotions of faces; and even one man who behaves normally except in so far as he thinks it is 1945 and cannot be convinced to the contrary. Therefore, a brain malfunction can lead to uncanny results indeed.

If Dr. Elves were epileptic—for which we have no evidence save the remarks of President Muldrow in his diary—and *if* a seizure caused him to fall on his head with a severe frontal lobe injury, then it is *conceivable* (if barely) that Elves might have become so confused as to trash his room and then disrobe himself before finally dying. I would put the odds of this explanation being true at no better than 5 out of a hundred.

That, I fear, is the best I can do. But I should add one thing: consistent with my opinion is that there exists a better than nine out of ten chance that Dr. Elves met with foul play by person or persons unknown.

This, too, though, is bound to be a trail quite frigid.

Yours truly,

Dr. Christina Royce

From Lecture Notes by Professor Theodore Elves for His Classical Civilization Class for October 6, 1926 (A Class He Never Taught)

Here in this slide we see the figure of the god Dionysus from the east pediment of the Parthenon. You will observe that he is represented here as a reclining figure. He dates from about 435 B.C. He is looking across the pediment at the chariot of Hellos, the sun god, often called Apollo. The chariot carries Apollo, which is being observed with care by Dionysus, the god of wine. I shall not try to characterize with certainty the look on Dionysus' face except to say that he regards Apollo with great eagerness and interest. He does not seem to fear Apollo, sometimes termed Dionysus' antithesis, but neither does he appear to be angry with him. He appears to regard Apollo with serene attention.

A German philosopher has discussed the opposition between the two gods as one between rationality and individuality on one side and ecstasy and abandonment of the individual on the other. When we are analyzing the single parts of a painting or a chemical element we are sons of Apollo. When our individual identity dissolves as we join a chorus of a thousand people in singing Beethoven's "Ode to Joy," we are sons of Dionysus. I draw from this distinction two lessons.

First, the two gods represent different spheres of human activity. They are not necessarily rivals, but rather they complement each other. This is why Dionysus does not look with fear or anger at the arrival of Hellos.

Second, another philosopher, a certain one here at Belton College, has said that those of us who adore ancient Greek art are claiming a will o the wisp form of reality, conveniently detached from material things. But what could be more material than the clay and marble out of which these statues are made? And is not this professor's view that there is nothing individual about any of us, that we all depend on the same material substratum, anticipated in the symbol of Dionysus, who celebrates the moment when our unique selves dissolve into a symphony greater than the "specialness" of any of us?

May each of us caught in conflict come to see, as did Apollo and Dionysus, that the world, in order to exist, requires multiple kinds of viewpoints and ideas.

There are moments when I must confess to feeling misunderstood. But let us hasten on to the next slide, that of Dike, the Greek goddess of justice.

Carving on the Far Lower Corner of a Stairwell, Found by Renovators of the Phi Kappa Psi House, Belton College, July 2, 2006

GOOD NITE TEDDY

The End

I am grateful to Art Robson, Elizabeth Freeman, and Charles Westerberg for their helpful suggestions about this book. Thanks to Amy Sarno for suggesting, in the 1990s, the dramatic possibilities in the mysterious death of Theodore Lyman Wright, Professor of Classics at Beloit College, October 1926.

•••

Tom McBride, the author of this book, taught English at Beloit College for forty-two years. From 1991 to 2014 he was Keefer and Keefer Professor of Humanities there. He has co-authored *The Mindset Lists of American History* (Wiley, 2011) and *The Mindset List of the Obscure* (Sourcebooks, 2014), and authored numerous articles and essays.

32971944R00191

Made in the USA
Middletown, DE
24 June 2016